INVASION

KEN LOZITO

ACOUSTICAL BOOKS LLC

Published by Acoustical Books, LLC

KenLozito.com

Cover design by Jeff Brown

IF YOU WOULD LIKE TO BE NOTIFIED WHEN MY NEXT BOOK IS RELEASED VISIT

WWW.KENLOZITO.COM

ISBN: 978-1-945223-44-0

1

An audible chime drew Connor's attention to a nearby holoscreen, where an amber-colored notification hovered in the upper-right corner of a darkened, semi-transparent box. He hated notifications. They were a distraction but unavoidable sometimes. Lenora had no such reservations about notifications, which was why he usually switched off her workstation when he was in their home office.

Berwolf Pack Tracker.

He pursed his lips as he tapped the notification. A regional map opened, prominently revealing Sanctuary's location. Several trackers flashed northeast of the colonial city. He peered at the cluster of pack designations and frowned. Berwolf packs usually traveled apart, but the tracker data showed that the cluster had banded together a few months earlier and was steadily making its way toward Sanctuary's borders.

Connor selected the largest pack cluster and a data window expanded, showing preliminary reports of the berwolfs' biochips. His lips lifted as he recognized the pack alpha.

"Bull. You've been productive."

He hadn't realized that Lenora still kept track of the berwolf cub she'd rescued all those years ago. Connor leaned back in his chair. That must have been almost ten years ago. He frowned in thought. Had it been ten years? He couldn't remember. He hadn't seen Bull in years.

Berwolfs were giant canine specimens the size of an Old Earth grizzly bear but with the agility of a wolf. They were pack hunters and natural competitors to ryklars, New Earth's other apex predator.

Bull must have absorbed two other packs during his migration and probably collected more than a few battle scars. Connor's eyebrow twitched at the thought.

Another notification appeared, but this one was on Connor's screen.

Nathan Hayes: Connor, this just came to my attention and it's . . .

That's all the message header showed, so Connor acknowledged it. As he read Nathan's words, his brows pushed forward in consternation, and he blinked several times. He shook his head and read the message again.

Samson, why didn't you tell me?

The front door opened, and he heard his daughter run inside.

"*I* want to tell," Lauren said, and then in a much louder voice yelled, "Daddy!"

Connor braced to stand as Lauren raced into the room, leaping up into his arms with all the power and speed her four-year-old body could muster. He grinned and growled playfully as he stood, pulling her into a bearhug.

Lauren squealed in delight amid a peal of laughter. "Daddy! Daddy, I'm getting a baby brother!"

That kicked Connor out of his mental zone. He stopped

spinning his daughter around and tilted his head to the side. "What?"

"A brother! I'm getting a baby brother!"

"From where?" he asked, the words escaping his lips before he could stop them.

Lenora chuckled from the doorway, her eyes gleaming. "Where do you think, soldier?" Her mouth twitched at the corners.

Connor lifted his eyebrows, and Lenora tilted her head to the side. Her long auburn hair cascaded past her shoulders while sparkling sapphire eyes stabbed him. "You sure?" he asked. Blood was rushing to his head, and he felt the heat rise on his cheeks.

"Yes, love. You're going to be a father again."

The dam holding his thoughts hostage burst. He crossed the room, pulled Lenora in, and held both his girls in a family hug.

"We have to name him," Lauren said.

"I think we need to give Daddy a minute or two, dear heart," Lenora said.

Lenora's pregnant.

Lauren peered at him with a pair of sapphire eyes that matched Lenora's.

Connor's eyes darted from his wife to his daughter, and he swallowed hard.

"A son," he said, his voice becoming thick.

Lenora gave him a small nod, both in acknowledgment and in understanding. He'd had a son who was left behind when he'd been shanghaied onto the colony ship. Connor felt a pang seize his chest that was a mix of both sorrow and happiness. He closed his eyes and held on to his girls, an image of their happy faces clear in his mind. The warmth of their bodies made him feel whole, pushing back against the sorrow. His son had died long ago, and while Connor would always regret not being there for him, he had found balance in his life, even though he'd never be at peace with leaving his son behind.

A son.

They left the home office and headed to the kitchen.

"So, can I name him?" Lauren asked.

Connor arched an eyebrow toward her. "It's a big deal, choosing a name."

Lauren's eyes widened. "It is?"

Connor smiled. "Yes, of course it is. Your mother wanted to name you Punky, but I wouldn't let her."

Lauren's mouth opened wide, and she swung her gaze to Lenora.

"Don't tell her that," Lenora said.

"She also wanted to name you Snail because babies crawl on the floor."

"Eww," Lauren said and regarded Connor for a long moment with an expression akin to her mother's. "No, she didn't."

"Lauren, I am your father, and I would never lie to you. You were almost our Punky Snail Gates."

He watched Lauren look at Lenora, and when they both looked back at him, they were united. His four-year-old daughter was a realist.

"I'm going to make a list of names," Lauren said as Connor put her down.

She ran to the table and activated the holoscreen.

Connor looked at Lenora.

"Surprise," she said.

The lump in his throat had gone down, but it was still there. "A good surprise."

Lenora smiled. "I just found out while we were taking a walk," she said and glanced toward Lauren, who was recording a list of names using the speech-to-text application. "She was so excited and couldn't wait to tell you."

"I guess she really wanted a sibling," Connor said.

"She's asked before, and even more often recently," Lenora said softly, her voice sounding a bit distant.

"How do you feel about it?" he asked.

"We're ready, and even if we weren't, he's coming," Lenora said, gently rubbing her stomach.

How could they not be ready? They were already parents, but Connor knew their lives would never be the same when their son was born. Lenora sent him the report from her biochip that confirmed her pregnancy. He was still in shock, and it hit him in waves of realization.

"I almost can't believe it myself," Lenora said.

Connor exhaled. "I'm glad you said it because I was thinking the same thing."

He looked over at Lauren, who glanced at him through the semi-transparent holoscreen and beamed a smile. Then she turned her attention back to the task at hand.

"How do you feel about it?" Lenora asked him.

"I'm sure after the shock wears off, I'll be happy about it, but I might need to stay away for a few days," Connor replied.

Lenora's expression became severe for a moment, and then she punched him in the arm. Connor laughed.

"Jerk," she said. "You—"

"I know. I don't know how you put up with me." He leaned back on the counter and sighed. "A lot of changes."

Lenora frowned. "Why? What happened?"

"Samson is leaving."

"Leaving? For where?"

"He's volunteered to go with the second colony. Nathan just sent me a message about it."

"He didn't tell you himself?"

Connor shrugged one shoulder and shook his head. "He's off-world."

Lenora looked unconvinced. Samson had been part of the original Ghost Platoon with the NA Alliance military. He'd helped Connor create the Colonial Defense Force but left the colony before the Vemus War.

"Still, I think he should have told you something like that himself. It's odd that he didn't. How did Nathan find out?"

"Saul Ashworth, the director of the *Ark II* program, told him," Connor said. "Actually, he was checking to see whether Nathan would okay the transfer, and I don't think Nathan would have okayed it unless Samson had told him his intentions."

"What's Samson going to do with the new colony?"

"He's going to head up security. I think so, anyway."

"And he never said anything to you?" Lenora asked.

He shook his head. Connor was Samson's commanding officer and, more importantly, a friend. Finding out about Samson this way was like a punch in the stomach. It shouldn't feel personal, but it did. Connor could veto the transfer. So could Nathan.

"I'm going to talk to him about it," Connor said.

"Good. You should. I know you two have been at odds, but . . . I guess I'm just surprised."

"He never wanted to be here, which is why he left the colony before. He only came back because I asked him for help," Connor replied.

He'd recruited Samson back into the CDF to help them prepare for the Krake, an interdimensional invader that had conducted terrible experiments on the Ovarrow—New Earth's native inhabitants. The Krake were aware of humans and were undoubtedly trying to find New Earth as diligently as the CDF was hunting for the Krake home world. It was just a matter of who would find the other first.

Lenora regarded him. "Listen to what he has to say."

"I am. I will. Why would you say that?"

"Because I know you. You're taking it personally."

"You just said that he should have told me himself."

"I know, and maybe he *is* planning to tell you but wants to do it in person."

Connor was quiet. He looked at Lauren and then back at Lenora. Over the years, he'd begun to understand why soldiers chose to stay home. Off-world missions were incredibly high risk. Connor had had more than his share of them, but as he looked at his family, it was becoming increasingly difficult to leave. And now that he was going to become a father again, he expected that leaving would become nigh impossible. He'd already begun delegating more dangerous missions to other officers. As a general in the CDF, that's what he should be doing, but sometimes Connor still wanted to be there. It wasn't that he craved life-threatening danger. He didn't. He just believed he was still best suited for the job of protecting the colony. But he couldn't figure out a way to defeat the Krake from the safety of New Earth, and with a growing family, maybe it was time that he let others take the lead.

2

THE CDF AERIAL TRANSPORT VEHICLE, better known as a C-cat, climbed into the sky and headed for Sanctuary's Civilian Recreation Consortium—a wide expanse of both indoor and outdoor activities designed to expand the growing database about New Earth. These events ranged all the way from hands-on laboratory exercises to physical conditioning. There were several campuses throughout the city that were accessible not only by students but by any adult who wanted to participate. With its cyclical curriculum, colonial education was tailored to individual learning styles.

The colony had more than doubled in the last fifteen years of its existence. Three hundred thousand human beings had gone into stasis and traveled for over two hundred years, covering a distance of sixty light-years from Earth. The population of those original colony members represented a unique genetic makeup that hadn't happened in all of human history. For the first time, children ages fourteen and under had been more plentiful than adult colonists. Procreation was one of the prime tenets of the colony and the key to its survival.

For just under a decade, Connor had been preoccupied with establishing the Colonial Defense Force rather than starting a family. He'd convinced himself that he didn't have time for personal attachments, which had nearly cost him everything. After the Vemus War, he'd married Lenora, but many years had passed before they'd had Lauren. Now Lauren was four years old, and he was going to be a father again.

Ever since his daughter had come into his life, he'd begun to pay more attention to how the colonial youth were being educated and prepared for a life on New Earth. Colonial preparation for the Vemus War had been centered on the theory that a catastrophe had affected Old Earth, and that whatever had caused that was coming to New Earth. Preparations had included the formation of the CDF and outposts that monitored the interstellar space-buoy system that went all the way back to Old Earth. Colonial preparation had included education in small civilian arms so colonists could protect themselves. However, with the advent of the Krake—a threat much closer to New Earth—they now required a more aggressive posture for the education of all colonists in the event that the Krake invaded New Earth. The question inevitably came up as to whether or not to include the colonial youth in these training efforts that were undeniably military in nature.

"We'll be landing in just a few minutes, General," the pilot said.

Connor nodded.

The pilot flew them to a landing field near the campus, where the activities were already underway.

"Looks like Governor Mullins's transport has just arrived as well."

"Maybe we should circle around a few times," Connor said.

Surprised, the pilot looked at him for a moment. "Say the word, General Gates."

Connor was a little tempted. Mullins wasn't in favor of the CDF's contribution to the education of colonial youth. "Thanks. As you were, Lieutenant Donovan."

"Yes, General," Donovan said and brought the ship in, setting it down with the precision of the adept pilot he was.

Connor waited on the landing field alongside his military escorts, who occupied a position several meters from his location. He heard the dopplered wail of a C-cat, along with Field Ops and Security Hellcats that landed on two smaller landing pads nearby.

Connor watched as Bob Mullins walked down the stairs, leaving the C-cats behind. Mullins had short-cropped, curly hair that had an oily shine to it, and his face wore its usual piggish gaze. Even though he'd had a rocky start as acting governor of the colony, Mullins had grown into his role. He'd taken over when Dana Wolf had become sick and couldn't serve out her term. Recently, Mullins had been confirmed beyond the position of acting governor, meaning that he would serve out the remainder of Dana Wolf's tenure as governor, at which point another election would be held. He and Connor hadn't always seen eye to eye on more than a few things, but they could work together because they had to. Dana Wolf had advised Connor on more than one occasion to try to work with people like Mullins. They might never be friends, but at least they weren't adversaries. Connor had endured that under a different governor during a time when the colony could least afford it.

Mullins walked over to him and smiled a greeting. "General Gates."

"Governor Mullins."

In a show of solidarity between the colonial government and the CDF, General Nathan Hayes, the leader of the CDF, had put forth the suggestion that they attend these events together. Connor had come to accept that Nathan was, by nature, much more diplomatic than he could ever be.

Mullins traveled with a group of advisors who helped him with his day-to-day tasks. He looked at his entourage. "Give us a little bit of room so I can speak with General Gates."

The cluster of advisors halted, allowing Connor and Mullins to walk ahead. Several squads of Field Ops and Security personnel formed a perimeter around them as they walked onto fields filled with colonial youth grouped by ages. They were performing certain tasks, some of which were recorded in the student's record while others were purely for experience.

They made their way toward the area where the age group included ten- to fourteen-year-old colonists. There was a wide array of obstacle courses that were designed to challenge the participants—some based on tactical abilities while others were more physical in nature. Participants made their way through the various courses, some of which required the use of various civilian-grade firearms, ranging from sonic hand blasters to hunting rifles. The power regulators on all the equipment used by the participants were dialed down to prevent serious injury. There were team exercises and capture-the-flag scenarios, all designed to teach the colonists that there were times to stand and fight, as well as times to abandon the field and seek cover.

Mullins looked at him. "You're unusually quiet, Connor. Is there anything I should know?"

Connor shook his head. "Nothing CDF-related. I'm going to be a father again."

Mullins lifted his eyebrows a little and smiled. "Congratulations. Did you just find out?"

"I did."

Mullins watched him as if gauging Connor's reaction.

"We're having a boy. Lenora told me this morning."

Mullins nodded. "That's excellent news, Connor. I'm very happy for you."

Mullins was also a father, and Connor could see that familial bonds shared between parents differed from those who'd never had children. It wasn't until he'd become a father for the second time that he'd gained awareness of the profound difference when someone's entire existence was dependent upon him. There were no breaks or putting things off until it was convenient. Children demanded attention. It was a balancing act practiced by parents and was also an experience that had to be lived in order to be understood.

"Thank you," Connor said.

"How old is your daughter?"

"She's four years old now."

Mullins nodded. "That's a great age. I bet she's excited."

"She wants to help name her brother."

Mullins chuckled and turned his gaze toward the activities. More than a few people glanced in their direction, particularly at Connor since he was wearing his CDF uniform.

"I'm curious," Mullins began. "Does being a father affect how you feel about these types of activities?"

"If anything, it further drives the point home," Connor replied. "This training will save lives, especially if the Krake come here. They're not just learning combat scenarios—or very light versions of combat scenarios, in this case. They're also learning how to assess problems, and all of them are required to take basic medical courses. Those are good skills for anyone to have."

Mullins continued to watch the activities and nodded a little. "I'm not questioning the value of what's occurring, but I *am* . . ."

He paused for a moment, trying to find the words. "I just feel like we're stealing their childhood from them, and they're not mature enough to realize it now, but one day they will."

They made their way toward the area designated for the older youth, thirteen to fourteen years old. Adolescence had given some of them a good dose of hormones. They looked healthy and strong.

"I don't like the necessity of this any more than you do, Mullins, but we don't get to decide. I think it would be more of an injustice not to prepare them as best we can. The alternative is a very steep learning curve should the Krake invade, and many more lives would be lost. Future generations are going to judge us regardless, and I think the records will have to show why we chose to do this. I guess it comes down to the fact that if my daughter were out there, I'd much rather she knew how to handle herself. I'd rather give her the best chance of surviving instead of keeping her wrapped in a safety bubble. I think they know what's at stake. They've lived through it before."

"I'd rather they didn't know."

"They're all volunteers. Beyond basic survival, none of them have to do any of these things."

"They view it as exciting," Mullins said. "They're very impressionable. What concerns me is that we're on a path to becoming a militaristic society, and if anything, history has taught us that those societies don't endure for long. I guess my concern is that I don't want us to go too far down this path without being able to get back to where we should be."

"If you'd asked me a couple of years ago, I would've just said that it's my job to make sure we get to a point where we can make those decisions in the future."

Mullins looked at Connor without turning his head and arched an eyebrow. "And now?"

"Kids change you, but that doesn't mean I want to protect them any less. Sure, we teach them survival skills and how to defend themselves, but we also teach them ethics so that if and when they're called upon to take action, they'll understand why and hopefully be able to live with the decisions they make. It's true for all of us," Connor said as he returned a wave to several people. "I can't make it any plainer than this, Mullins. I'd rather my daughter didn't grow up in a world where she had to keep a gun in her hands, but I'm also not going to keep her away from the knowledge of how to use that gun just in case she needs it. The Krake, the Vemus, and even some of the Ovarrow. It doesn't matter. The choice will be hers."

"The Ovarrow are still making the case to become colonial citizens, but they're very rigid. It's going to be a challenge to help them acclimate," Mullins said.

"Senleon understands this, and so do many of the other faction leaders in the Mekaal."

"And the Konus?"

Connor gritted his teeth. The Konus had tried to absorb the Mekaal while testing the CDF's response. Lives had been lost and the Konus had paid a heavy price, but they didn't seem bothered by it. They'd come out of stasis almost forty years ago and chosen to live in secret, preparing for the eventuality that the Krake would return here.

"It might take the Konus longer to learn."

"That's putting it mildly," Mullins said. "I read the reports. They do love to push the envelope and test whether we'll respond. I spoke to Dana the other day, and she seems to feel that there are things we can learn from the Konus. All I keep thinking about is how much I'd rather they migrated far away from us."

Connor smiled a little and sighed. "You know, when I first

started dealing with the Ovarrow, I felt the same way. It took years of working together to build up that trust. I think there's more tolerance for the Ovarrow in the CDF than there is in the colony itself. So, I think it's just going to take time. There are going to be bumps along the way."

"I remember you reporting to Dana about the Mekaal, but more recently I've been looking at the history of the NA Alliance and the European Union, as well as their formation. It took a long time for those unions to emerge in such a way that it didn't entirely make the participating nations lose their identities. So, I agree with you that it's going to take time—probably a lot of time, as in you and I will be old men by the time it's the norm," Mullins said.

The rest of the day, they watched the colonial youth show off their skills and vigor through various activities. Connor recognized the need for the colonial youth to begin learning skills beyond basic survival. They had a say in what their futures would be. Many of them requested various forms of tactical training, and Connor hoped that the balance was there so that the colonists wouldn't become like the Ovarrow—rigidly viewing the world through a lens that required armed conflict to resolve their problems. These thoughts were new for him, and if they survived the conflict with the Krake, this balance would become his focus.

3

THE SALTY SOLDIER—OWNED and operated by one Juan Diaz, Connor's oldest friend on the colony—was the destination of Connor and Lenora's leisurely walk. Lauren was practically pulling them up the long, dark, wooden stairs. A warm glow came from old-style lanterns, lighting up the area over wide planks of dark hardwood that smelled of longevity and good times, as if the restaurant had always been there. Whenever Connor walked toward the front doors, he always caught a healthy whiff of delicious food that made his mouth water.

"Sounds like the celebration has already gotten started," Lenora said.

"Diaz will use any excuse to celebrate," Connor said.

Lenora chuckled.

It was early evening and the sun had started to set, but New Earth's rings shone brightly in the night sky. It was never truly dark here.

There was a sign posted outside that said the restaurant was closed for a private party. One of Diaz's offspring came to collect

Lauren, and she was soon whisked away to play with the other kids.

Diaz was of average height, but barrel-chested and muscular. When he saw them walk through the doors, he ran over and pulled them both into a firm hug.

"Proud papa and mama. Congratulations to both of you," Diaz said.

Lenora kissed Diaz on the cheek and was then called over to a group of women that included Victoria—Diaz's wife—and Ashley Quinn.

Diaz wore a broad smile as he looked at Connor knowingly. "That's number two, Connor. You're going to catch up to me. I know it."

Diaz had five kids and had no plans of slowing down. Connor thought that perhaps Diaz was trying to repopulate the human species with a healthy dose of his own genetic code.

"One rises to the occasion," Connor said, glancing around. "You closed the restaurant for this?"

"Of course. You should've seen the response I got to the invitation I sent out on your behalf."

Connor glanced around the room and saw a lot of familiar faces, as well as some notably absent ones. Sean and Noah were on the lunar base and wouldn't make it down here for this. Nathan and Savannah had sent him another case of bourbon. Nathan couldn't make it, but Savannah was here. She was already speaking with Lenora, and she raised her glass in Connor's direction when he saw her.

The large dining room sported several buffet-style stations that held just about every kind of food imaginable. Diaz had gone all out.

"A son," Diaz said and then gave him a few playful punches to the arm.

Franklin Mallory strode over to him. He stood well over six feet tall and crossed the area in just a few paces. "Connor, congratulations."

"I hear I'm not the only one," Connor said.

Franklin nodded. "Three more months."

A few awkward moments were often shared between Connor and Franklin. The elephant in the room was because of Franklin's son, Lars Mallory, who'd been banished from the colony but had elected to serve in a special infantry division in the CDF. The division was designated for high-risk missions, and because of this, there was always an unspoken question in Franklin's gaze when he saw Connor. Connor gave him an answering nod, conveying that Lars was still alive and well. That was as much as they could hope for. The banished colonists, even with service in the CDF to commute their sentences, could not have any contact with anyone from the colony. Franklin returned the nod with a somewhat somber expression.

Dash DeWitt joined them and raised his glass to Connor.

"That's the next one right there," Diaz said, gesturing toward Dash.

Dash shook his head. "Oh, no. Not now and not anytime soon."

Diaz tilted his head, pursed his lips, and shrugged. "That's what Connor used to say."

Dash's gaze flitted toward Connor and he returned the shrug.

As the evening went on, the celebration was gearing up to full force. There was no shortage of well-wishes and congratulations. Diaz's eldest daughter, Angelina, had taken over organizing all the children with various activities. Connor liked watching Lauren play with the other kids.

"It only gets harder to leave as time goes on," Diaz said to him.

Connor swallowed his bourbon, taking a little more than he'd meant to. It nearly burned his throat. "I know."

Diaz gestured toward Lenora, who smiled and waved toward them. "She might never say it, but *you* know."

Connor nodded. "I know," he agreed again.

The main doors to the restaurant opened, letting in a cool breeze. Connor turned and saw two CDF soldiers scan the room and then stride over to him. They stood at attention and saluted Connor.

"General Gates, I have an alpha priority message from General Hayes. Will you please come with me to the secure terminal I have outside?" Private Jordan said.

Connor set down his glass and it thumped on the table. He glanced at Lenora and saw her smile fade as she watched him follow the CDF soldier out of the restaurant.

The CDF Hellcat had set down nearby, and Connor walked over. There was a secure comms drone active, and he sent his authentication while the two soldiers took up flanking positions a short distance away. The secure terminal generated a communications-dampening field that surrounded Connor so no one else could overhear.

Nathan's head and shoulders appeared on the holoscreen. He was in a command center at the CDF base in Sierra. "I'm sorry to bother you, Connor. I truly am, but this couldn't wait."

"What is it? What's happened?" Connor asked.

"We've received a communication from the Gesora. Warlord Monin wants to meet."

Connor frowned in thought. The Gesora had become an active ally in their search for the Krake. They were helping expand their reach to other universes where the Ovarrow were being manipulated by the Krake.

"Did they find it?" Connor asked.

"Negative. The Krake home world has not been located. Monin asked for you specifically. He wouldn't say much because he felt that communications couldn't be trusted."

"Why does he want to see me?"

"The report indicates that they've seen some patterns among the Ovarrow worlds they've recently visited through the gateway. That's all he'd say, and he wants you to come validate what they've discovered," Nathan said.

Connor glanced behind him at the Salty Soldier. He couldn't hear the goings-on inside the restaurant, not with the communication blackout bubble he was in. He sighed and turned back to Nathan.

"All right, I'll assemble a team and head to the alpha site in the morning," Connor said.

"If there were some other way . . ." Nathan let the unspoken sentence hang between them.

"We all share the same risk, Nathan. Monin isn't an alarmist. If they found something, then it's worth following up. The Gesora know how important it is for us to find the Krake home world. But we need to increase our readiness here," Connor said.

"Agreed. I'll send a briefing over to the CDF base at Sanctuary, but there's one more thing," Nathan said.

Connor raised his eyebrows and waited for Nathan to continue.

"Mullins wants you to bring the diplomatic envoy with you."

Connor shook his head, trying to restrain his irritation. "Civilians have no place—"

"I know what you're gonna say, and I know you don't like to bring civilians on these missions. But I think this qualifies as an exception. Don't make me make this an order," Nathan said.

They were both generals, but Nathan had overall command authority of the entire CDF.

"Understood. Just get whoever Mullins wants to saddle us with to the CDF base here in the morning or I'll leave without them," Connor said. He smiled at the end, trying to take a bit of the sting out of his words. Nathan understood.

Nathan grinned. "I'll relate to Governor Mullins how you're looking forward to working with the diplomatic envoy."

"Thanks," he replied and closed the comlink. The comms drone receded back into the charging station on the CDF Hellcat. He glanced toward the restaurant and saw Dash standing outside, watching him.

Connor waved him over, and the young man joined him. "I've got a job for you."

Dash chuckled. "When you say things like that, I don't really get to say no, do I?"

Connor shook his head. "Nope, and in this case, neither do I. Come on, I'll fill you in."

4

COLONEL SEAN QUINN looked around his apartment on the lunar base. It wasn't exactly a home, but it was where he'd slept for over a year, and most importantly, it was a place he shared with Oriana. Hearing her soft footsteps in their bedroom, he rolled his shoulders and stretched his neck from side to side. His last training session with Boseman had left some of his shoulder muscles a little stiff. Being of average height, Sean had to rely on speed and agility to take on his much larger friend. In the ring or on the mat, rank had no place. It was just you and your opponent.

Sean glanced toward the counter and his eyes flicked upward. Oriana had left her coffee mug on the counter again. He walked over to rack it in the cleaner, then glanced into the sink, sighed, and shook his head a little. He didn't know what it was, but he couldn't stand the sight of dirty dishes being left in the sink or anywhere else for that matter. It must've been a sign of him getting older because it never used to bother him. It wasn't much of an issue when taking his meals on a ship or a base. He used to think Oriana did it just to irritate him—a bit of playful get-your-goat—but she didn't. Sean didn't expect her to clean up after him, so why should the reverse be true? Oriana could let her dishes pile up for days. However, if he mentioned it, she'd take care of them as if they were an afterthought. He'd rather not have to mention it every time. He felt like he was nagging.

Oriana emerged from their bedroom. She was tall and slender, with supple curves that her science-team uniform hugged in all the right ways. Her hair was a deep curtain of velvety black, and her face was sweetly angelic.

She looked at him and smiled, crossing the distance between them and kissing him on the cheek. Dirty mug forgotten, Sean swept her up into the air and set her down.

"You could take the later shuttle," Sean said.

Oriana shook her head. "I can't. I want to inspect the new protector drones before they're sent to the *Vigilant*."

She could inspect them on the ship, but Sean knew better than to suggest it. Being thorough in their respective disciplines was something they shared.

She regarded him for a moment. "Is something wrong?"

Sean leaned back on the counter and rested his hand near the sink. She glanced down at the sink and back up at him, oblivious. "Not a thing. I'll be heading to the *Vigilant* later today."

The CDF heavy cruiser had been rebuilt, utilizing what remained of the severely damaged hull of the old ship. They'd changed the design to allow for a Casimir reactor core, along with many other updates that necessitated giving the warship a series II designation. However, they still referred to the ship by its former name.

"They assigned me separate quarters. Is there something you're trying to tell me?" Oriana asked.

Sean grinned and leaned away from her. "You're smothering me. I've been looking forward to this shakedown cruise for a while just so I can get a break from you."

Oriana leveled her gaze at him, and her dark-eyed stare seemed to hit him in the chest. "You didn't act like you wanted to get away from me earlier," she said with a suggestive glance toward their bedroom.

Sean smiled, and she giggled. "Go on, get out of here before you make us both late."

Oriana left as a comlink chimed on the nearby wallscreen.

Noah's face appeared. He glanced behind Sean, taking in his surroundings. "You're still home? I thought you would've left by now."

"I'm on my way to meet you," Sean said.

There was a knock at the door.

"You better see who that is," Noah said.

Sean opened the door to find Noah grinning in the entrance. He killed the comlink. "You know, it's not as funny as you think it is. It was funny when we were fifteen, maybe even seventeen, but not now."

"Nonsense, it's still funny. There are some jokes that just endure forever," Noah said and stepped back out into the corridor.

Sean took one last glance at the apartment. The dirty mug seemed to mock him, but he turned away and joined Noah in the corridor.

"What's the matter? You look all somber and brooding," Noah said.

"Nothing's the matter."

Noah made an *uh-huh* sound.

"You sure you don't want to join me on the *Vigilant*?" Sean asked.

Noah shook his head. "I'm not even tempted. Commanding warships is your thing. I just don't want to," he said and frowned for a few moments. "Aren't you at the limit of civilians allowed on the ship?"

"That's the beauty of being in charge. I can make exceptions," Sean said.

He knew Noah wouldn't take him up on his offer. Noah was out of the CDF, and while he still might work closely with the colonial military, he'd never join back up.

"No, thank you. You brought me up here under the pretext of this being a six-month stay, and it's been almost a year."

They reached an elevator and climbed aboard, and Sean put in a destination. "Still trying to get your teleporter to work?"

"How many times do I have to tell you? It's not a teleporter. That's not possible."

Sean arched an eyebrow. "We transition between universes, but figuring out a way to teleport matter from one place to another is impossible?"

Noah didn't like to use those terms, and Sean knew it.

"Fine. Granted. However, that's not what I'm trying to do. You don't know how frustrating it is to be on the cusp of something, only to have it remain out of reach." Noah gave him a sidelong glance. "On second thought, you probably do know something about that."

"You'll figure it out. One of these days, you'll crack the code," Sean said.

"You still think that weaponizing the space gates is the best way to engage the Krake?"

The CDF had had to adopt a new strategy for engaging the Krake once they found their home world. Utilizing space gates in combat was incredibly complex, but they had little choice.

"It might not be the most efficient way, but right now, it's our best option," Sean replied.

Noah thought about it and nodded. "That's an interesting way to put it," he said and paused for a moment. "Is Oriana going with you?"

"She's already on her way. I'll be there later today."

The elevator reached their destination, and they both stepped off.

"How long are you guys going to do this?" Noah asked.

Sean frowned. "Do what?"

"You guys have lived together for the better part of a year. Don't you think it's time to kick it up a notch?" Noah said.

Sean smiled. This wasn't the first time Noah had brought this up. "I don't see why we should make it any more complicated."

Noah's mouth opened a little. "Complicated," he said and shook his head. "What's complicated? You guys love each other. Why not take the next step? Marriage. Commitment. All that stuff."

"Why does it matter so much to you?"

"Because it's what you want to do, but for some reason you haven't done it yet."

"So, you gonna tell me what I want?"

"Yes, I am. Especially when you're being foolish."

Noah wasn't usually this direct, and Sean was becoming a little irritated. "Maybe I don't want anything to change."

Noah snorted. "There's a lot of things that we might want, but we don't always get them."

Sean pressed his lips together and regarded Noah for a moment. "What are you saying?"

"What I'm saying is that she's not going to wait around forever."

"Oriana isn't going anywhere."

"Maybe not today or tomorrow, but eventually she might."

"Has she said something to you or to Kara?"

Noah eyed him, then shook his head. "No, at least not with words. Has the subject come up? Getting married, that is."

"No," Sean said.

Noah gave him a look. "Really? No subtle hints or anything like that?"

"We've been kind of busy for the past year, Noah. The Krake and everything else. Anyway, why are you pushing this?"

"I'd hate for you to lose her."

"You think I'm going to lose her if we don't get married? That's no reason to get married. And besides, not everyone is like you and Kara."

"I know that, but relationships need to progress."

"Maybe we're happy with the way things are."

Noah pursed his lips. "Maybe, but have you talked to her about that?"

Sean frowned and inhaled deeply.

"That's all I'm saying. Maybe have a conversation. We all get so caught up with what we're doing that sometimes we forget to take the time to do what's important."

Sean looked away with a slight shake of his head. "I'm sure if Oriana wanted to talk to me about this, she would've."

"Are you sure about that? I mean, really sure?" He paused for a moment. "Think about it."

"I have thought about it. Just now."

Noah sighed. "Yes, some women have no problem moving things along directly, but some do. They want to be pursued. They want to be asked. That hasn't changed, and if you're unwilling to ask, eventually somebody else will. That's all I'm saying, buddy."

Oriana had no shortage of admirers. She was a beautiful

woman and turned a lot of heads wherever she went. Sean had
no illusions about his own appearance, but for some reason, she
was with him. He'd been with other women over the years, but
Oriana was different. Most of his other relationships had lasted
the span of a few months at the most, and that was all he'd ever
wanted. But now he didn't want things to change with Oriana.
She had no problem communicating to him exactly what she
wanted. They fit together, and Sean had just accepted that. Why
fix what clearly wasn't broken?

"There is one more thing," Noah said.

Sean raised his eyebrows. "More relationship advice? You
should open your own clinic."

Noah snorted. "Funny. I need more resources for testing."

"That might be hard to come by. We've already allocated
much of our stockpiles for the CDF."

"I know, but I'm getting pushback."

"Are you surprised? Every time one of your experiments goes
wrong, it destroys your equipment."

"And sometimes we can't recover it, I know, but that doesn't
mean we should stop. Do you know what a breakthrough this
could be?"

"You've mentioned it before, maybe five or six hundred
times. You're going to revolutionize space travel," Sean said.

"You know that saying about reaching for the stars? Well, if I
can get this to work, I'm going to put the stars within reach."

Sean had heard it before. Noah's theory was convincing, but
it was taking considerably more effort to prove, let alone make
work with any kind of reliability. These endeavors had to be
balanced with resource allocation. They'd based their entire
strategy for dealing with the high probability of a Krake invasion
on reliable, proven technology that they could use right now.
They couldn't afford to put huge amounts of time and resources

into something that was going to take years or possibly decades to perfect.

"I'll see what I can do. You also might want to reach out to Connor and see if there is something he can do."

Noah nodded. "I was trying not to bother him."

"*You* won't bother him."

"Okay, I'll do that, then," he said and gave Sean a wry smile. "See how easy that was? Your friend offers you a piece of advice and you take it. Now it's your turn."

Sean rolled his eyes.

"All right, I'll stop now."

"No, you won't," Sean said.

"You're probably right."

5

CONNOR STOOD outside the Salty Soldier. The celebration had been winding down, and the cordoned-off outside dining area was emptying of occupants. He looked up at the night sky. It was clear, bright, and beautiful. Sounds of nocturnal activity from New Earth's creatures were active in a rhythm he enjoyed. The only thing missing was a campfire.

Soft footsteps approached him.

"There you are," Lenora said.

He hadn't told her yet, not that she didn't know something was up. Lenora had a keen sense for that sort of thing. He just hated the thought of doing this to her tonight.

"I was just getting some air," Connor replied.

Lenora nodded and stood next to him, her arms crossed in front of her chest against the chill in the air. Connor wrapped an arm around her shoulders, and she leaned into his side. It felt good. The shape of her body fit with his own.

That's because we're made for each other, he thought. She'd told him that on more than one occasion.

"Are you going to tell me what's going on? I know you've got something on your mind."

"Am I that transparent?" Connor asked.

"Not always, but I know you. Spill it," she said.

Connor told her. They walked over to one of the heating lamps nearby and stood facing each other. The warm amber glow made her eyes appear sapphire, and her gaze was as sharp as any combat knife he'd ever carried.

Lenora breathed in deeply and exhaled. She looked away from him and shook her head as if she were having a silent conversation.

"I have to go," Connor said.

She looked at him, her sapphire eyes stabbing him in the chest. "No, you don't." Connor drew in a breath to form a reply, and she cut him off. "If the Krake are coming, then you need to be here and not off on some world fighting someone else's war."

Connor chose his words carefully. "It's the same war, Lenora. With the Krake, it will always be the same war."

"Then send someone else. I don't care if they want you personally to go there. It doesn't mean you have to go. Send someone else. I don't want you to go. Not this time." Her full lips began to quiver, and he could see the fear in her eyes.

Connor slowly raised his hands and pulled her in. Her head rested on his chest, and he heard a soft cry escape her lips. He tried to think of something he could say to reassure her and couldn't. There wasn't anything he could say. Sometimes the words just wouldn't come. All he wanted was to stay in the moment with her in his arms and forget about the Krake. Forget about the Ovarrow. Forget about everything but the two of them, their daughter, and their unborn son.

Lenora pulled away from him, misty eyes gleaming in the soft amber light of the heater. "Tell Nathan you're not going."

"I wish I could."

Lenora narrowed her gaze. "No, you don't. Don't try to console me. Damn it. Don't you dare try to."

"All right," Connor said, raising his hands in front of his chest in a placating gesture. "I *need* to go. Not because Nathan ordered me to and not because I don't want to delegate it to someone else. *I* need to go, because out there is the only way we can stop them."

Lenora opened her mouth to speak but the words stalled in her throat.

"We all have families. The risk is the same for all of us," Connor said.

"You've done enough. You've done more than everyone else. You're not the only soldier on the colony anymore."

"Lenora."

"No," she said, her mouth forming a grim line as she walked away from him. Her shoulders were rigid, like a coiled spring that was too tightly wound.

Connor followed her. "The only way to defeat the Krake is out *there*. We're not going to do that from here."

She spun around. "You really don't get it, do you?"

"What don't I get?"

"I can't stop you from leaving. Don't think I haven't thought about it. I wish I could . . . I just . . . One of these times, you're going to leave and not come back, and we'll be alone. Your family will be alone without all the pieces that make it whole. And you'll just be gone. That's it. Gone! Who knows where? Probably in some godforsaken place. Alone. Lauren will remember you, but *he* won't," she said, gesturing toward her stomach. "He won't know his own father."

Connor felt the heat flare to his chest and face as his teeth clenched. Why didn't she understand that he did what he did for them? When he'd rejoined the CDF, Lenora had been there to support him. He might not have done it without her support. But this was different, and it hurt. He felt his throat close up as if it had become granite. A piercing ache squeezed his chest and wouldn't let go. It wasn't that Lenora didn't understand. She understood him. She knew him. She just didn't want him to go. It was as simple as that. This was one time too many. He wanted to tell her that he would be back no matter what. Instead, he said, "That's not fair."

Lenora snorted bitterly. "None of this is fair. Not one thing about this is fair. You want to know what isn't fair? Look at me and tell me that if there was a chance you could stop the Krake but it required that you couldn't come home, would you take the chance? Would you do it? You would, wouldn't you? I know you would."

Connor raised his chin. "I'm not going to speculate with you."

"You can't, can you?" Lenora said. She rushed toward him, her hands tightly squeezing his arms. "I don't want you to be a martyr for us. Please, Connor. Don't. People think it's a sense of duty, and sacrifice is required. I know it's selfish, and I don't care. I can't lose you. Not now. Not ever!"

They stared into each other's eyes, the moments stretching out like silent prayers whispered into the night.

"You won't," Connor said and repeated himself.

They stood near each other for a few minutes, not saying anything else. She was so close to him, but it felt as if there were mountains between them.

She backed away from him and wiped her eyes. "You'll need to tell Lauren that you're leaving."

"I was going to."

"Not from a video comlink. You need to come home and do it in person, or do it here if you're leaving right now."

Her words stung him. He'd known she'd be upset, but he hadn't anticipated this level of fury, nor the effect it was having on him.

Connor nodded once.

Lenora's eyebrows knitted together, and she gave him a look that was part pleading, part anger, and part anguish, and all of them cut him deeply. Connor felt something sink inside, weighing him down, knowing that he had caused her pain.

He hated it, and right now, he hated himself. But knowing it didn't change anything, and he could already feel the walls going up to safeguard him from his emotions. It was the only way he'd get through the next few moments.

Connor walked toward the Salty Soldier. The heavy thumps of his boots cut into the ground as he marched inside to say goodbye to his daughter. A few distant sobs stalked him as Lenora walked away.

LAUREN RAN toward him as fast as her little feet could carry her. Connor squatted down and scooped her up in his arms.

"I have to go away for a few days," Connor said.

Lauren looked at him searchingly for a moment, her face serious. Then she closed her eyes and hugged him. She clung to him, and the side of her head pressed into his cheek. Connor was startled by the realization that his daughter knew what it meant that he was leaving for a few days. When had that happened? Some part of him was sickened by how it had become part of her.

She looked at him. Her eyes focused on him intently and she

said, in a tiny voice, "I'll finish the list of names by the time you come back. I'll find the perfect one. I promise, Daddy."

Connor went blind for a few seconds, and he blinked rapidly. "I know you will," he said. It came out in a tight croak, but when he said it, she smiled at him. "I'll be back soon. I promise."

He put her back on the ground and watched her run back to the cluster of children. Diaz was standing off to the side with a knowing look. He gave Connor a single nod of understanding.

All the reasons in the world that were pulling him away seemed to melt for a few moments. Nathan could find someone else to meet with Monin. He wanted to tell Lauren that he wasn't going to leave. He wanted to find Lenora and make things right between them.

Diaz walked over to him and stood quietly by his side.

"Leaving sucks," Connor said.

Diaz nodded. "It only gets worse."

Connor looked at him.

"We'll keep an eye on them. Victoria and Ashley will talk to Lenora."

"I don't know if it's going to help this time."

"She's pregnant, Connor. There's a whole lot of hormones going on there, stirring up all the emotions. Lenora will be all right," Diaz said.

Lenora would be all right. Connor had no doubts about that, but what he kept wondering as he left the Salty Soldier was whether or not *they* would be all right.

***

CONNOR SPENT the next few hours at the CDF base in Sanctuary. Doing the prep work helped distract him from his rocky departure from Lenora. Only a platoon of soldiers would be coming with him to the alpha site. Standard operating procedures regarding the use of gateways required that they only use them on New Earth to transition to one of the forward operating bases they'd established in other universes. These were located on planets not occupied by anyone. They used these vacant planets as a staging ground to launch other missions. This was done to help protect the home universe where New Earth was located.

A comlink chimed on his desk, and he saw Noah's identification on it. He acknowledged the comlink, and Noah's head and shoulders appeared on a small holoscreen in front of him.

"Hi, Connor. Thanks for taking my call," Noah said.

"No problem. How are things on the lunar base going?"

"Everything appears fine, but I wanted to talk to you about one of my side projects."

Connor raised his eyebrows and steepled his fingers below his chin. "All right, which one?"

Over the past year, Noah had had a number of side projects going on.

"Well, it's one that's become the problem child because I'm running into resource constraints," Noah said.

Connor chuckled. "I know which one you mean. You still can't make it work?"

"I only need to make it work once, and then I'll know how to do it. Not only can the space gates be used to allow for the transition between universes, but I also think they can be used to project matter through space and time in our own universe."

"We haven't come across it at all in any of the universes we've explored. And the Krake haven't shown this capability with any of their technology either. Are you sure you're not just chasing a red herring?" Connor asked.

"I'm not. There's sufficient evidence to support that the theory is plausible," Noah said.

"Plausible but not repeatable."

"Not yet."

Connor felt his lips lift a little. "It's something I've always admired about you, Noah. You don't give up."

"Gee, I wonder where I got that from," Noah said and looked at Connor pointedly. "I just need more resources so I can continue experimenting with this. If I can get this to work, it could really give us an advantage and open up opportunities for dealing with the Krake that just aren't available right now."

Connor was no stranger to being required to justify the allocation of resources, but he knew a stretch when he heard one. "Are you promising me the world?"

Noah gave him a guilty look. "Did I come on too strong? Not sorry about that. But I do believe that the potential of this technology will have a tremendous impact on everything."

"I agree with you," Connor said. "And I do think you might figure it out eventually. If anyone can, it's going to be you, especially when you're teamed up with Kara and Dr. Evans. But these things take time."

"Isn't there anything you can do?"

"There's always something we can do, but I'm just not sure it's going to be enough. Have you thought of stepping back for a little while and then going back to it in a couple of months?" Connor asked.

Noah's eyes widened a little. "A couple of months. Come on, you've got to be able to do better than that."

"What about coming to the alpha site and looking at some of the Krake tech we've gathered there? Maybe it'll help put things in a different perspective."

Noah frowned in thought for a few moments. "I hadn't really thought about it. I do read the reports."

Connor tilted his head to the side. "Someone else's reports aren't the same thing as seeing it for yourself. Maybe you'll see something they've missed. Or maybe it'll spark something that might help you solve the problem. It's just a thought. What do you think?"

Noah looked away and exhaled. His head bobbed from side to side as he thought about it. "When did you have in mind?"

"I'm heading to the alpha site in just a few hours. You could meet up with me there," Connor said.

"Today? You mean today as in a few hours from now?"

"That's what I said."

Noah thought about it for a few moments more. "I'll need to get a shuttle back to New Earth. I probably wouldn't be able to get there in time for you to leave."

"No, you won't get here in time, but like I said, you can meet up with us. I'll make sure you have clearance," Connor said.

"Is there something else?"

"Something else?"

"Yes, something else. Why are you going to the alpha site? Is there something that you need my help with?"

Connor told Noah why he was going to the alpha site. "Like I said before, there might be something you'll notice that maybe the rest of us won't."

"I appreciate the vote of confidence, Connor, but you have Dash going with you. I think he's probably better suited than I would be, but I'll come," Noah said.

"Great, I'll see you at the alpha site, then."

The comlink severed and Connor stared at the empty holoscreen for a few moments. Most times, the success of missions depended on having the right people along.

6

As SECTOR CHIEF, Sadoon had ultimate authority over the research experiment involving the Ovarrow. He'd been left alone as long as he made regular reports into the overseer governing body that tracked all research projects. It wasn't a matter of just submitting reports to the overseers who led the Krake empire from the lofty heights of Quadiri. They required proof in the form of evidence that was signed off by his own research team. Sadoon had been stationed here for the better part of fifty years, and he hadn't even realized how tedious the whole effort had been. He was but one researcher among legions that contributed to the great knowable. There were hundreds of similar experiments across Ovarrow worlds—some with direct Krake involvement, but others involved more subterfuge in their execution. However, all research endeavors went toward the perfection of their predictive technology.

Until his own involvement with Aurang and the fifth column, Sadoon had been one of many drones ambling along at the whim of the overseers. The overseers dictated all Krake efforts down to the tiniest of details. Sadoon wasn't a simple-minded worker, but despite all his intelligence and achievements, he was still just a drone. Or he had been until last year. During the time since he'd been assisting the fifth column, he'd learned that he'd been conditioned to seek the approval of the overseers. This behavior was ingrained in the entire Krake society. A hierarchy was needed for their society to thrive. Sadoon still believed that, but knowing his place didn't fulfill him as it once had.

He still felt the urge to seek the approval of the overseers. He'd gone to them seeking alpha resource allocation to study Humans. He wanted to find their home universe and begin their assimilation. Humans were similar to the Ovarrow in that they valued personal attachments. Sadoon had studied this extensively among the Ovarrow they'd brought from multiple universes. He knew how to apply the right amount of pressure to strengthen personal attachments, and he also knew how to tear them down. He'd reduced the Ovarrow to their pure primal roots, making them little more than animals. However, in other ways, the Ovarrow were more Krake-like than the Humans were. Humans seemed to put the value of the individual almost on equal footing in comparison to their society as a whole. Sadoon wondered how they'd achieved so much. In some respects, they were extremely violent creatures that were easy to manipulate, but they were also cunning.

He'd convinced multiple Krake military leaders to support him. They agreed that these Humans were worthy adversaries and that it was worth testing their predictive algorithms, but unlike the Ovarrow, they only existed in one universe.

Over the past year, Sadoon had been gathering resources pilfered from other Krake installations. He'd organized the teams he'd deployed, spreading them apart so they couldn't be traced back to him. The overseers had left him very little choice in the matter. Since they wouldn't give him what he needed, he'd had to take it. This behavior would have appalled him before he'd met Aurang, but he'd come to realize that necessity was the fuel of innovation. He wasn't the obedient drone he'd been. Despite all the current knowledge amassed by the Krake society as a whole, they had become stagnant, and ever since he'd become aware of this, he couldn't go back to what he'd been before. What had initially surprised him was how easy it had been to convince other Krake to join him. There were undercurrents of the Krake society that he'd never thought were possible. How could he have been so blind for so long? But billions of their population still were.

Sadoon stood in the command center that contained not only the feeds for the sector but also the monitors he'd installed for all his efforts off-world.

"You've built quite the following here," Aurang said.

Sadoon looked at the leader of the fifth column. Aurang was the epicenter of their group but also stood apart as if he had plans that only he was privy to. Sadoon wasn't a stranger to that. He had plans of his own too.

"We're close to finding the home universe of the Humans," Sadoon said.

Aurang regarded him. "I told you we could condense the timeline considerably."

"Yes, and the current breakthrough in gateway usage will condense the timeline even further," Sadoon said.

Aurang turned to look at the main holoscreen. "You've managed to garner quite a bit of naval support."

"They've encountered the Human warships and are eager to confront them again. They fight differently than the Ovarrow," Sadoon replied, and then added, "We haven't encountered an

Ovarrow civilization that was capable of spaceflight in over a century."

"A peculiar finding, but not more so than the lack of any other Krake civilization in any part of the multiverse," Aurang replied.

"We're not the only ones," Sadoon said.

"How can you be certain of that? Even the Overseers aren't certain of that."

"No one can be absolutely certain of anything when it comes to things like this. Regardless, what does it matter if we *are* the only Krake civilization in the multiverse?" Sadoon asked.

Sometimes interacting with Aurang became tedious. He'd already had multiple teams out on secret reconnaissance missions utilizing the breakthrough technology.

"I don't think you've given it enough thought," Aurang said. "Why is it that the Ovarrow exist in most universes we explore? Why do our ancient enemies thrive when there isn't a trace of us anywhere? We are the stronger species. Our society endures and theirs is easily manipulated. We should be just as likely to find instances of our own society as we do the Ovarrow, but we don't. There is some universal constant that we're failing to grasp."

"So, we're the exception and not the rule," Sadoon said, becoming agitated with Aurang's condescending tone.

Aurang gave a slight shake of his head. "That's not it. On Quadiri's brother planets in the multiverse, there isn't evidence that life has ever existed at all."

"I do understand that. I just don't allow it to occupy my thoughts as much anymore. Once I trained myself to stop deferring to the overseers, I began to see things differently. I don't care that our civilization hasn't thrived in every universe we explore. It doesn't matter to me, and it shouldn't matter to you. It changes nothing."

Aurang regarded him for a few moments. "You have changed."

Sadoon couldn't decide whether Aurang was giving him a compliment or if he was insulting him. His words might have carried more weight months ago, but not now. Aurang must have sensed this, and his glare conveyed disapproval.

"You're being reckless and moving too quickly," Aurang said.

"That's not how I see it."

"That's not at all surprising. You've become blinded by purpose at the expense of reason."

A deep growl sounded from deep within Sadoon's chest. "And you try to control everyone and everything around you. For someone who opposes the overseers, you're quite proficient at using their practices."

"You have to slow down your pursuit of the Humans," Aurang said.

"I'm not going to do that."

Aurang stepped closer to him, and Sadoon stood his ground. Aurang was unarmed. The weapons systems of Sadoon's power armor were in a ready state.

"Remember the plan," Aurang said. "The Humans have a purpose to fulfill. Rushing to find them gives us nothing."

The weapons systems of Sadoon's power armor shut down, and Aurang tilted his head to the side. "You weren't going to attack me, were you?"

Sadoon tried to reactivate his weapons systems, but they wouldn't respond. He couldn't move. His power armor wouldn't respond to his commands.

"The trouble with armor like that is that it can always be controlled by someone else. I bet the suppression field wasn't even detected," Aurang said, waving a small, palm-sized suppressor. The metallic oval glowed in the center.

The door opened, and Sadoon's soldiers burst inside with their weapons ready.

"You should have shut down the communication systems," Sadoon said.

Aurang glanced at the soldiers, mildly amused. The soldiers leveled their weapons toward him.

"By all means, fire your weapons at me," Aurang said.

The self-destruct protocol activated on Sadoon's armor, and he struggled to reach the abort fail-safe, but he couldn't move.

"Stop this insanity," Sadoon said.

Aurang kept his gaze on the soldiers. "Lower your weapons and get out. If I wanted to kill you, I would have."

The soldiers looked at Sadoon, and he was tempted to tell them to kill Aurang, but that would have been shortsighted and foolish. His power armor's self-destruct was armed and could be initiated at any moment.

"Leave us," Sadoon said.

The soldiers obeyed.

Aurang slowly turned toward him. "We need to work together, Sadoon. If I didn't think we could continue to work together, I would've already replaced you," he said while circling around Sadoon with an unhurried pace.

Sadoon choked back his irritation and forced his thoughts toward calmness. He was at Aurang's mercy, and they both knew it.

Aurang stood in front of him. "Now, do we have an understanding?"

Sadoon raised his chin. "Yes. I will comply with your request," he replied. What he didn't include was the fact that he was going to kill Aurang. Not today, but he had set things in motion.

"Excellent," Aurang said and disarmed the self-destruct sequence.

Sadoon regained motor control of his armor and stepped away from Aurang.

"Now, we have some things to go over," Aurang said.

Sadoon knew his alliance with Aurang was over. He didn't need the leader of the fifth column anymore. He deactivated his armor and it split down the middle, allowing him to step out.

Aurang frowned and stopped speaking. Sadoon charged. Enhanced muscles allowed him to move quickly, but Aurang pivoted to the side, barely getting out of the way in time.

Sadoon stepped toward him and hammered down with both his fists, slamming them onto Aurang's back. Aurang scrambled out of the way, and Sadoon chased him.

"I don't answer to you," Sadoon said.

Aurang dodged out of the way and swept Sadoon's feet out from under him. He hit the ground hard but quickly rolled away, narrowly avoiding Aurang's follow-up blow. The door opened and soldiers raced inside. Molten plasma bolts blazed overhead, and Aurang dove out of the way.

"Kill him!" Sadoon shouted.

Aurang crossed to the other side of the room, and Sadoon grabbed his own weapon. There was no exit. The fool had cornered himself.

"There's no way out," Sadoon said.

Krake soldiers flanked him on either side and fired their weapons, destroying the equipment in the other room. They moved forward, and Sadoon was becoming increasingly aware that Aurang hadn't returned fire.

Sadoon ordered the soldiers to stop firing their weapons and sent one of them up to investigate.

The Krake soldiers crossed the room, with Sadoon bringing up the rear. When they reached the other side of the room, there was a hole in the metallic wall. It looked as if it had been melted away. Something Aurang had with him had melted the armored wall that not even their plasma bolts had. The bolts scorched the surface, but it would have taken significantly longer to burn through.

Sadoon crawled through the hole and the soldiers followed him.

"Call in the other squads," Sadoon ordered. "I don't want him to get away."

The next time Sadoon saw Aurang, he wanted him dead, and he didn't care how it happened.

Alarms blared throughout the fortification, and the hunt began.

7

Six thousand feet beneath the surface of New Earth was the CDF base Hammerholde. The CDF soldiers and civilians stationed there were committed to spending six months on base without physical access to the world above. The base was known among the senior officers of the CDF as Hammerholde, but it had a much more well-known name.

COMCENT.

CDF Command Central had multiple key components that were grouped under the umbrella of COMCENT, consisting of Hammerholde and the lunar base. There were secondary and tertiary installations that could be tasked with the duties of COMCENT, but they were maintained in a semi-permanent state of standby. Those installations would be used under only the direst of circumstances.

Hammerholde wasn't located near any colonial city. Aerial reconnaissance of the planet's surface revealed nothing special about the area other than the sparse ruins of an Ovarrow city nearby that was inexorably being reclaimed by local flora. Nestled in the foothills of ancient mountains, Hammerholde was defensible as well as secret. Additional tunneling efforts had been ongoing to expand the number of colonial citizens who could take refuge there.

Colonel John Randall walked the metallic corridors that branched from the newly finished emergency habitation units, hoping they'd never be used. These habitation units were a major improvement over the hastily constructed bunkers that had been meant to protect the colony's inhabitants during the Vemus War. They now had enough provisions to last them for years. Life in Hammerholde would never be considered luxurious, but it was far from rustic or even from what many would consider the bare essentials.

Hammerholde had access to every satellite in orbit around New Earth, city defenses, and CDF bases, and was tied into both the lunar base and Phoenix Station. Eventually, all CDF communications routed their way through COMCENT. The CDF base was equipped with state-of-the-art technology that was constantly evolving, and they also had one of the most complex computing cores ever created.

Randall had served multiple rotations in command of COMCENT. Standing watch over the colony was a duty he took seriously. When Hammerholde's construction had first been finished, his earliest rotation had been among only CDF soldiers on base, requiring that the soldiers remain apart from their families for six months at a time. But with the colony's burgeoning population, maintaining the status quo wasn't practical, especially when they could easily expand the base to accommodate the families of the men and women who served in the CDF. However, once they arrived at Hammerholde, no one was permitted to leave. They were committed to spending six months at the base without exceptions. There was an adjustment period, but once people made it through that, they adapted to life on the base. That didn't mean they weren't excited to return to the surface when the six-month rotation was over. Hammerholde had expanded beyond that of a CDF base and could be considered a small town in its own right, with twelve hundred residents.

The filtered air was cool and carried just a kiss of spicy evergreen-like scent to it. Randall headed to the command center. He passed the hydroponic gardens, glancing at the green vegetation that gave his gaze a reprieve from gray corridors. He was four months into this rotation and was looking forward to returning to the surface.

The command center was host to multiple teams sitting behind long desks with both personal holoscreens used for specific duties and the main holoscreen that showed prioritized missions. They coordinated with other CDF teams, as well as colonial government agencies, including Field Ops and Security and the Colonial Intelligence Bureau.

Randall had seen a lot of changes at the CIB since former CDF Major Natalia Vassar had taken over the lead position. Like many of the current colonial government organizations, the CIB had been an unplanned entity. So had the CDF, for that matter. The CDF had been established to protect the colony and had its own intelligence apparatus, but it was limited in its access to civilian organizations. The CIB helped bridge the gap, and cooperation between the CDF and the CIB went a long way toward helping to protect the colony.

Randall walked the length of the command center, checking in with various team leaders who were on duty. He stopped at tactical.

"Good morning, Colonel," Lieutenant Amber Wong said.

"What do you hear, Lieutenant Wong?" Randall asked.

Wong smiled. "Nothing but the rain, Colonel."

Randall nodded and glanced at the main holoscreen. "I see the Konus continue to push the envelope."

The Konus were the latest group of Ovarrow to be discovered on New Earth. They'd first come out of stasis nearly forty years ago and had been hiding their presence, hoping to avoid the Krake. They'd cut themselves off from the surface and hence missed the arrival of the first human interstellar colony. They comprised the largest population of Ovarrow on the planet, with their population numbering over a million.

"Yes, sir. They've been increasing their scouting missions, but the groups are small. They know we're watching them, and I'm not sure what's causing the recent uptick in scouting activity," Lieutenant Wong answered.

"Gabriel, is there any anomalous weather activity?" Randall asked the CDF base's artificial intelligence.

"Negative, Colonel. Weather patterns are normal," Gabriel answered.

Last year they had discovered that the Konus possessed certain Krake technologies that allowed them to manipulate the weather. The weather manipulation had provided substantial cloud cover, which had helped conceal their campaign against the Mekaal. The Ovarrow's practice was that the weaker nations were absorbed into the stronger one. The Mekaal were a group of Ovarrow that the colonists had been bringing out of stasis for a number of years. The armed conflict had cost lives, most notably on the Konus side. They'd lost tens of thousands of lives in order to occupy the Mekaal city. Diplomatic relations with the Konus remained on unsteady ground, but there was no misunderstanding that if the Konus fielded an army again, the

CDF would not hesitate to protect colonial cities, as well as the Mekaal.

Randall looked at Lieutenant Wong. "Show me the area they're scouting."

A new window appeared on a nearby holoscreen that showed the region of the Konus city. Icons began to appear where Konus scouting missions had been spotted. Lieutenant Wong added a histogram that showed icons in gray for known scouting missions. The Konus had definitely increased their activity, but it wasn't in any particular direction.

"We received a briefing yesterday based on a Konus report of what they are calling 'strange sightings,' which is the reason for the increased scouting activity," Lieutenant Wong said.

Randall didn't trust the Konus at all. They weren't above outright deception. They knew full well that the CDF was watching them. But what could they gain by increasing patrols in their own territory? He thought about it for a few moments and then shook his head.

"Package up the data and forward it to the CIB per standard protocol," Randall said.

"Yes, Colonel," Lieutenant Wong said.

"I want to send a few reconnaissance drones into the area, as well as send a recommendation to General Hayes for a manual reconnaissance mission. I don't want to take any chances with the Konus," Randall said.

"Understood, sir," Lieutenant Wong said.

The protocol was to send the information to the CIB, but it was a toss-up as to whether the data would reach Natalia or her second. Natalia's second-in-command was a man called Jerry Sherman. Randall had never met him, but he'd heard that Sherman had a different way of approaching the data analytics when it came to intelligence briefings. Randall was concerned that if Sherman received the data, it would just be logged as additional Konus patrols with nothing more to be investigated. That would be the best-case scenario, but Randall didn't like to leave things to chance. It also couldn't hurt to remind the Konus that the CDF was keeping an eye on them.

8

SEAN WALKED onto the bridge of the *Vigilant*. The CDF heavy cruiser had been repaired and its design modified to accommodate new methods of war for engaging the Krake navy. Among the ship design enhancements was a prototype Casimir power core that could be brought online in addition to their main fusion reactor core. Colonial scientists had been attempting to reverse-engineer the Krake power core, which could generate power above and beyond anything they could achieve with their fusion power cores. The potential to fully control Casimir force to access Zero Point Energy was the epitome of propelling humanity to even greater technological achievements. Sean would be satisfied if it just worked reliably. Given a choice, he'd rather not bring unreliable tech onto any of his warships in Trident Battle Group or the home fleet. The prototype Casimir power core worked perfectly until it didn't, and it sometimes required a hard reset in order to bring the system back online. Who didn't have hours to spare in the middle of an enemy engagement?

Trident Battle Group had been expanded to include new destroyer-class ships. Another heavy cruiser wouldn't be completed for another few months, and that didn't include a shakedown cruise to work out all the issues that would inevitably come up. No ship left construction fully operational and without something that needed to be addressed.

They also had additional ships from the CDF home fleet temporarily reassigned to Trident Battle Group. However, there were no plans for them to take the fight to the Krake. Despite wanting to get out there to find the Krake home world, Sean had presented a strategy that enabled them to build up and expand on what was already in their arsenal. Why send an entire battle group when they could use recon drones and scout ships to explore the multiverse? The Krake were an advanced spacefaring race, and a quick survey of the inner planets would indicate whether they were active in a given universe.

The problem with the Krake navy was that they were more powerful than the CDF fleet. Their ships were faster, and their primary weapons were more powerful. In ship-to-ship engagement, the Krake outclassed the CDF fleet. A person without knowledge would incorrectly assume that the CDF fleet was hopelessly outclassed and could not achieve victory in any engagement with the Krake fleet. But what Sean and the rest of Trident Battle Group had proved through their lack of decisive defeat was that there were other ways to stop the Krake. There were many other factors beyond ship-to-ship capabilities that could influence the outcome of a battle. First and foremost was the consideration of who was in command of the warships, and then the experience of the crews. Both were equally important tools at the CDF's disposal.

The Krake navy seemed to forgo a variety of weaponry in favor of their attack drones, and Sean couldn't begin to guess why. Krake attack drones were intelligently controlled, and once armed, they burned at 5000 Kelvin. With enough velocity, they could easily penetrate the armor of any CDF warship. They were highly resistant to energy-based weapons but could be stopped with kinetic weaponry. The Krake more than made up for this vulnerability by launching high numbers of attack drones to overwhelm their target defenses. He wondered how long the attack drones would last once armed. They'd learned that the HADES V missiles could disrupt the Krake attack drones' targeting capabilities, which bought them some time, but the cost of using their most destructive weapon was extremely high. Even if they had an endless supply of HADES V missiles, the computer models showed that the Krake attack drones would eventually outlast the CDF in an armed conflict. HADES V missiles were great for long-range engagement but were limited. The Krake attack drones could also target the HADES V missiles, rendering them less effective in an engagement with Krake warships.

After Sean returned to New Earth, Connor had tasked him to come up with a strategy to either level the field of engagement with the Krake or, better yet, give them an advantage. Sean was only too aware of the disadvantages the CDF faced when coming up with a strategy to defend the colony against a superior foe. Thanks to Oriana, they'd discovered that the use of artificial gravity emitters could disrupt the Krake attack drones, but there was a cost. There was always a cost. The energy requirements to sustain an artificial gravity field sufficient to protect a ship were enormous. However, they weren't unattainable. They'd nearly destroyed the *Vigilant's* fusion power core to escape the Krake, but the artificial gravity field had saved their lives. They just needed a way to accomplish the same thing without exhausting their existing power cores.

The Casimir power cores could, in theory, maintain a substantial gravity field for much longer than any fusion reactor. If only they worked reliably.

Sean expanded the use-case for artificial gravity fields to help protect their missiles so they could reach their intended targets. That didn't mean they could simply install an artificial gravity emitter on every HADES V missile. He wished it was that simple, and it wasn't from lack of trying to make that solution work, but the energy requirements to hold and sustain a powerful artificial gravity field was beyond the capability of a mere HADES V missile. Anything to do with gravity required mass or energy. It was always one or the other. To overcome these limitations, they'd come up with an unmanned escort vehicle that was designed to generate an artificial gravity field to protect their missiles from Krake attack drones. To prove that this was a viable option in their next fleet engagement with the Krake, Sean had organized large-scale drills using live weaponsfire. The loss of equipment would hopefully give them the data they needed to keep pursuing the new tactics. If not, they'd have to come up with something else.

They had moved some of their fully operational CDF defense platforms that would attempt to stop several groups of missiles, along with their escort ships, from reaching them. The defense platforms were restricted to using midrange missiles and kinetic batteries. Both could achieve the velocity that was observed from the Krake attack drones, but none of them were anywhere near as destructive as a swarm of them. This was to be the first of a few large-scale attack drills. Testing the artificial gravity field capabilities was the least complicated of the drills that Sean had scheduled. Nothing was ever easy. If it was, then something had probably gone wrong. Sean was a believer in the maxim that you learned more by doing. There were only so many virtual models you could run before you had to test these things out in the field.

They'd adapted small shuttlecraft to make them entirely unmanned, which allowed them to install additional equipment to sustain the artificial gravity field. This would protect their missiles, but the cost was that they could not travel as fast as the missiles normally could. Sean would rather take the gamble of having a much higher percentage of his missiles reach their targets more slowly than a smaller percentage of them reaching their targets faster. That way, he'd be able to do more damage and level the playing field when they fought the Krake again. Sean had no doubts that he would be facing the Krake at some point in the future. He'd managed to survive by using clever tactics and space gates, but if the Krake came to New Earth, there was no running. There would be no retreat. They would have to fight if New Earth was going to survive.

Sean walked toward the command center. Oriana sat at the science officer's workstation near the commander's chair. She gave him a small nod by way of greeting. Major Vanessa Shelton, his XO, stood up. She was of average height, with dark skin and hair.

"The ship is yours, Colonel," Major Shelton said.

Sean sat down. "Thank you, Major Shelton. Comms, give me the battle group."

"Yes, Colonel," Specialist Sansky said. "Comlink established with the battle group."

"Trident Battle Group, this is Colonel Sean Quinn. Over the next several days, we are going to be testing new combat strategies for helping us defeat the Krake. For those of you who have served with Trident Battle Group before, you already know the enormity of our task. I expect everyone to pay attention and treat these drills as if our lives and the lives of everyone back home depend on it. What we learn from them could very well determine the outcome of our war with the Krake. It's these small steps that give us the momentum to effect the changes we must in order to defend ourselves. The strategies we're going to employ today are built upon our experience and our ingenuity. I expect absolute excellence from all of you. You are here because you are the best at what you do, and over the next several days, I expect each and every one of you to prove it. This is as real as it's going to get until we come face-to-face with the Krake. I urge you to learn all you can from this. Preparing now just might make the difference for everyone in the future. *Vigilant* actual, out."

Sean waited for the comlink to the battle group to sever.

"Colonel, I have an unscheduled shuttle requesting permission to dock with us," Specialist Sansky said.

Sean looked at his personal holoscreen and felt his lips curve slightly. "Permission granted. Inform the deck officer that I want our guest brought to the bridge."

"Yes, Colonel."

Vanessa looked at Sean and lifted her eyebrows.

"One last additional civilian contractor," Sean said.

His XO nodded and turned her attention back to her screen.

Sean looked at the main holoscreen, which showed the deployment of Trident Battle Group. They were conducting their drills near Sagan, the fourth planet in the star system. Sagan was a lifeless sphere near the fringes of the Goldilocks zone. There had been proposals for terraforming the planet because it was within the acceptable limits for sustaining life, which would be quite an endeavor if the project ever got off the ground. However, since no one lived there yet, it would play a part in one of their wargame scenarios.

"Lieutenant Scott," Sean said, "authorize the first attack group."

"Yes, Colonel, attack group alpha authorized," his tactical officer replied.

A few minutes later, the door to the bridge opened and Noah walked toward him. He looked around the bridge, and Sean knew Noah was cataloging the changes since the last time he'd been on a warship. Noah was an engineer to his core, and Sean needed his insight.

Sean gestured to the auxiliary workstation next to him. "Welcome aboard, Mr. Barker."

"I can't believe I let you talk me into this." Noah sank heavily into the seat next to Oriana.

"I'll still get you to the alpha site to meet up with Connor," Sean said.

"You better," Noah said.

"Have you ever been to the alpha site? It's no picnic. This is much better. Just saying."

"Yes, thank you very much, Colonel Quinn. You have the shinier, more impressive ship. However, I need a few minutes to get brought up to speed."

"Honestly, it would be better if we could just get our missiles to their target without the enemy knowing they were coming," Noah said.

A group of them sat in the conference room near the bridge of the *Vigilant*. Several other commanding officers had joined them via a comlink to review the results of the first set of tests.

"If we could do that," Captain Richard Pitts, CO of the

Babylon, said, "we'd already be launching offensive operations against the Krake."

"Do you know how the Krake detect our ships or missiles?" Noah asked.

"We think it's much the same way that we perform our own scans. It's a combination of things, but to answer your question, we don't know exactly what their scanner capabilities are," Sean said.

The artificial gravity emitters did their jobs and held on for quite a long time under intense defensive fire, but there were limits.

Oriana cleared her throat. "If we flew them in tighter formations, that might spread the load that the emitters are under once the enemy tries to take them out. But that doesn't account for evasive maneuvers and anything else our tactical officers come up with."

Sean's gaze darted toward Major Shelton. Then he glanced up at the commanding officers of his senior leadership, whose faces appeared on the holoscreens in the meeting room.

"I agree with Dr. Evans's assessment, Colonel," Captain Jane Russo said. She'd been the former lead tactical officer and acting XO of the *Vigilant* before Sean gave her command of the destroyer *Yorktown*. "Subspace communication has become more reliable, and if we operate within its constraints, that might increase our flexibility."

Sean knew that many people were hoping this would be a slam dunk, as Noah liked to call it. The strategy of grouping HADES V missiles with what they were now calling protector drones did work, but there were limitations. These limitations reduced his envelope for engaging the enemy, which meant they had to be closer when they actually fought the Krake in order for this tactic to work. The CDF fleet doctrine for space warfare had to change. Currently, the doctrine was to engage the enemy while keeping as much distance as possible. Ideally, this was suited for long-range engagements, but this would change to close combat, and Sean shuddered to think of what a broadside-type engagement would do to his ship and crew if it came down to something like that.

"This is exactly why I wanted to do these drills," Sean said. "Now we can adapt our strategy and make it better. It also confirms that in a fleet engagement with the enemy, we might have to get a lot closer than we'd like."

He looked around the room at his officers and science crew, who seemed to be internalizing what he'd just said.

"Gabriel," Sean said. "I'd like you to run some analyses using the current data from these drills in our previous encounters with the Krake. Would it have made a difference in any of those encounters?"

"One moment, Colonel Quinn," the *Vigilant*'s artificial intelligence replied.

Sean looked at Major Shelton. "Any bets as to whether it would be better or worse?"

Vanessa chuckled. "I know better than to gamble against you, Colonel."

"Preliminary analysis indicates that using the current strategy would increase the destructive force against enemy ships," Gabriel said. "However, the end result, if the encounter is allowed to play its course, indicates that the CDF fleet would be destroyed."

"Gabriel, you are assuming that our objective is to destroy the Krake fleet in every engagement," Sean said.

"That is correct, Colonel."

The apprehensive looks from his senior staff dissipated for most of them who knew what that meant.

Noah gestured that he wanted to speak, and Sean nodded for him to do so. "Gabriel, did you include the use of the artificial gravity field to protect the CDF ships in the engagement using the Casimir power core?"

"Negative. This was not one of the variables I was instructed to include."

"Go ahead and rerun your simulations, but this time include current CDF fleet capabilities," Noah said.

"Colonel?" Gabriel asked.

Noah was not in the CDF and therefore could not request the *Vigilant*'s AI to do anything.

"Go ahead, Gabriel," Sean said.

"Understood," Gabriel replied.

"Colonel," Oriana said, "what about using the space gates?"

"It's an option," Sean answered. "For now, I want to keep the drills separate. Coordinating attacks using space gates, even our new offensive space gates, adds a great deal of complexity."

"No one said defeating the Krake would be easy." Oriana arched a dark eyebrow.

"Use of the offensive space gates is designed for first-strike-type engagements. The alternative is a sustained bombardment, but again, it's complicated," Sean replied.

"Colonel Quinn, my analysis is complete," Gabriel said. "I'll put my findings on the holoscreen."

Sean looked at the high-level report. It now showed that the CDF fleet did survive the encounter, but they definitely sustained heavy losses. "I know no one likes having the Casimir power cores on their ships. They've been unreliable, but we need to use them. We need to work out the problems with them because, as you can see, at least in a virtual sandbox, they can really help."

After scheduling them to reconvene tomorrow for the next

set of exercises, he ended the meeting. The conference room emptied out except for Noah and Oriana.

Sean arched an eyebrow toward them. "I sense a trap."

Noah glanced at Oriana for a moment. "It looks like you have things well in hand here. I'm not sure what else you want me to do."

Sean looked at him.

"I told you, I don't like warships," Noah said quickly.

"Have you seen the Casimir power core?" Sean asked.

Noah frowned and then shook his head, his eyebrows raised. "No. Sean, no. You're not doing this to me."

"Doing what?" Sean asked innocently.

Noah shook his head with the hint of a smile. "God, you and Connor do the same thing. You bring me in under the guise of 'please have a look at this,' and then before I know it, I'm fixing something, or I'm neck-deep in something I didn't even want to do in the first place."

Sean glanced at Oriana and then looked at Noah. "You can make it easier by just helping out. Then we wouldn't have to resort to . . . Well, you get it."

Noah grimaced and rolled his eyes.

"Noah, if you want to head to the alpha site or back to New Earth, then just say the word. You'll be on the next shuttle out of here. I'll even assign a shuttle that will get you there fast. Is that really what you want?" Sean asked.

Noah shook his head and sighed. "So, why don't you give me a tour of the ship?"

Sean grinned. "I'll even make sure there's ice cream."

"I need a few minutes before we go," Noah said and left the conference room.

Sean looked at Oriana.

"He's right, you know," she said.

Sean nodded. "I know he is, but we can use a fresh set of eyes on it. I've seen Noah come up with pretty amazing solutions over the years."

Oriana smiled. "That's funny because he says the same thing about you."

"So, what's the problem, then?"

"He doesn't want to be here. He's made that abundantly clear."

Sean glanced toward the door. "If he didn't want to be here, he wouldn't have come."

Oriana tilted her head to the side and gave him that look— the one that said he wasn't fooling anyone. He wasn't trying to, anyway, but sometimes . . .

"Look, that's not how guys operate. Sometimes we need to be pushed or cajoled."

"Oh, I see. You manipulate him to get him to do what you want. That's not being a good friend, Sean."

Her clipped words were sharp with disapproval, and Sean felt the heat rise in his face.

"Noah is here because of you," she said.

"Well, so are you."

Oriana narrowed her gaze.

"Look," Sean said quickly. "You know what I mean."

"Oh no, I'd much rather have you explain it to me."

"Oriana," Sean began, drawing out the sound of her name.

"Sean," she replied in the same tone. "I know you. Once you're on task, you pursue it relentlessly, but sometimes . . ." She paused for a moment and raised her hand, clenching her fingers into a fist with a slight shake. Then her hand came to rest on the table. "Sometimes, you push too hard."

Sean already knew this. "So, what do you want me to do?"

"Noah has been through a lot. He deserves better than to be manipulated by anyone."

Sean inhaled deeply and sighed. "We've all been through a lot. We can't change anything that happened before. Noah doesn't want to be treated differently."

"You're right, he doesn't. But maybe the 'guy' version of tough love isn't the best course of action for you to take. Just think about it," Oriana said.

The door to the conference room opened and Noah walked back in.

Oriana gave Sean a meaningful look.

"I will," Sean said.

She held his gaze a moment longer and then stood up. She smiled at Noah as she left the room.

Noah watched her go and looked at Sean. "Did I interrupt something?" he asked and then shook his head. "You know what, never mind. I don't want to know."

Sean shrugged. "She thinks I'm being too hard on you."

Noah closed his eyes and grinned. "If she only knew what me, you, and Lars used to do."

Sean laughed. "I know, right?"

At the mention of Lars's name, some of the lightheartedness left them.

"Still, you'll let me know if I'm asking too much from you, right?" Sean asked.

"All right, fine. You are. I don't want to be here. However, I also don't want the Krake to kill us all, so I'll just have to grin and get on with it."

"If it makes you feel any better, this is going to be a short trip. We'll be back at Lunar Base in a few days," Sean said.

"When you first showed me all those space gates, I had no idea what you had in mind."

"Well, we figured out how to make them smaller."

"Yeah, but using them to bombard the Krake home world . . ."

"It might be the only option. The other option is sending a fleet there to do it."

"I know. It's just something I hadn't thought of," Noah said.

"Good. We hope the Krake haven't thought of it either."

9

SMOKE ROSE from the Ovarrow city, and Lars Mallory watched the video feed from the reconnaissance drone as it flew over. The city was home to millions of Ovarrow, much larger than any city on New Earth. He couldn't remember which New Earth Candidate (NEC) planet he was on. A new reconnaissance mission every few days tended to make them all blur together.

"How are we supposed to figure out what's going on here?" Duffy asked.

"Perez," Lars said, "any sign of the Krake here?"

Fires burned all over the city, and the smoke was so thick that it was impossible to see where the arch gateway should have been.

"Negative, Corporal. Nothing detected on comms, but we can't see shit in this. If there are Krake here, they're doing a good job of masking their location," Perez answered.

"We have to get out of here," Duffy said.

Lars shook his head. "Not yet," he said and peered through

the gloom, searching. "We need to get to higher ground. The tallest building over there."

"But it's on fire!" Duffy said.

"Yeah, but not that much. Move out," Lars said.

He led the squad farther into the city, moving in from the fringes. Sounds of weaponsfire could be heard in the distance—a mixture of kinetic weapons and small arms explosions. The towns they'd passed on the way had been abandoned, and Lars wondered if the residents had sought shelter in the city.

They reached the towering building, which was over twenty meters tall and constructed of a darkened metal. It was circular, but the roof looked flat. It should give them a good vantage point from which to scout the area.

The building was still under construction and had a support structure on the outside. Lars ordered the squad to climb to the top. The seven of them wore light combat suits designed for quick movement. The suits assisted the wearers' movements, enabling them to quickly climb to the top of the building.

The fires weren't that bad in the immediate area because the buildings were mostly constructed of a metallic framework that offered very little in the way of flammable material. The combat suit's filtration units would be hard-pressed to keep the air they breathed fresh, but it was better than removing their helmets. These combat suits had minimal life support systems. They weren't meant to operate in a place without an atmosphere.

Before they reached the top, one of the CDF soldiers cried out.

"Gah!" Butler blurted. "Damn it! Son of a—My filtration system just stopped working. Oh God, the air tastes like rubbish. Absolute—" Butler began coughing and wheezing, but he managed to keep hold of the support structure.

"Welch," Lars said, "check his suit."

"On it, sir," Welch replied.

Lars reached the roof and climbed to the top. Crouching low, he helped the next person up. He could hear Butler coughing violently, which became gasping as he struggled to breathe.

Lars peered down and watched Welch checking Butler's combat suit. The filtration system was on the back. Welch had opened the hatch, but Butler suddenly jerked away from Welch, struggling to catch a breath.

Lars quickly climbed down to them.

"Hold still," Welch said, but Butler started flailing and let go of the support structure just as Lars arrived.

Lars grabbed Butler's outstretched hand and pulled him toward the wall. His eyes were wide, and his mouth was open as he struggled to inhale.

Lars snaked one of his legs around him and pinned him to the wall. Welch came over and jammed something into the back of Butler's suit and then slammed the hatch shut.

The internal systems of Butler's combat suit reset, and he gasped for breath. He inhaled deeply several times, and Lars waited for him to calm down.

A minute passed.

"You're all right," Lars said.

Butler nodded, his breath coming in shallow gasps before it began to even out. Lars looked at Welch, his eyebrows raised.

"Filters needed to be replaced," Welch said.

Lars looked at Butler.

"First I've heard about it," Butler said.

Lars shook his head. "The alarm system must have shorted out."

"There's a fucking surprise," Butler growled.

Lars glanced at Welch, who was nodding in agreement. The

equipment they were using wasn't exactly the best the CDF had to offer, but that was another matter.

"Let's go," Lars said.

As they started climbing, Lars heard Butler grumble a thanks to Welch. They all knew they had to look out for one another. No one else was going to do it for them—especially them.

Once they reached the top, they stayed low and spread out as Lars tried to make sense of the chaos he was seeing. When they'd arrived at the city, they thought the Ovarrow must have been fighting the Krake, but they hadn't seen or detected any Krake. Now, Lars could see that the Ovarrow were fighting each other in a battle that had spread throughout the entire city.

Lars watched the video feed from the recon drone he'd sent out. These weren't Ovarrow soldiers fighting. They looked like civilian residents of the city—armed but not trained. There were no controlled bursts of fire to conserve ammunition. Instead, there was a barrage of rapid fire as one group attempted to obliterate the other. The Ovarrow moved and fought with the tactics of an angry mob. Lars couldn't see anything that divided the groups. It was anarchy.

"Oh my God. They're just killing each other," Perez said quietly.

"Same thing over here," Rittberg said as she peered east of their location. "They've all gone insane."

Lars watched the horrific spectacle repeat over and over again. Groups of Ovarrow would bludgeon another of their own kind, some of whom were attempting to sneak away. Mobs of them roamed the streets, frantic to find another victim.

Lars checked the recon drones' data feeds, searching for any contaminants in the atmosphere that could cause a mass hallucinogenic effect on a large population. Nothing. There was nothing but a burning city.

Lars's HUD updated with an overlay to show the locations of the other CDF squads of the 3rd Platoon, but only if they were in range. The only squad nearby was being led by Tonya Wagner. He scanned ahead of their location and exhaled sharply.

Lars opened a comlink to Wagner. "You have several large groups of Ovarrow heading toward you. Sending their location to you now."

Lars sent the recon drone data to Wagner.

"Received. They destroyed our only drone," Tonya Wagner said.

No spares for the Phantoms. Officially they were 3rd Platoon, Special Infantry Division of the CDF. Their division was made up of people who'd been banished from the colony and had chosen to join the CDF rather than remain isolated on some island on New Earth. The terms were five years of service and a possible pardon for past crimes when service was up. It had sounded good at the time, but they were a reconnaissance unit that was used for high-risk, low-reward missions. They were expendable. There had been a 1st and 2nd platoon of the SID, but no more. The men and women who served in the SID called themselves Phantoms.

"Have you heard from Miller or Burgess?"

"No. Yours is the only squad in range," Lars replied.

They were limited to short-range communications to avoid Krake detection. Lieutenant Miller and Sergeant Burgess led the other two squads but were coming in from north of the city. And they had the troop carrier transport, which was the only way they'd all make it back to the gateway location at the CDF alpha site.

"I'm going to take my guys and circle north. There's no way we're going into the inner city. We'll never make it out," Wagner said.

"We can head to your location and get out of here together," Lars said.

Several explosions blazed in the distance, and Lars winced at the impact.

". . . can't wait. Follow as best you can," Wagner said, and the comlink went dark.

Perez shook his head. "So much for having each other's backs, or maybe it's just you she hates."

Lars gritted his teeth.

"Hell hath no fury like a woman scorned," Perez said.

"Good guess, but stick to scouting the enemy," Lars said and called the others over. "Are you all right, Butler?"

"Fine, sir."

"Okay, we're heading northeast to get in range of Lieutenant Miller's squad," Lars said.

Rittberg's face broke into a scowl that was shared by a few of the others.

"What?" Lars asked.

"This mission is a shitshow, sir. Miller should be evacuating *us*," Rittberg said.

Loretta Rittberg had the face of an angel but the heart of a killer. She was an excellent scout, and when she spoke her mind, it was clear, concise, and right to the point.

"We can't use long-range comms," Duffy said.

"To hell with protocol," Butler said, which drew a harsh response from the others.

"All right, knock it off," Lars said, and the others became quiet. "I'm not going to reason with you. If you follow orders, you stand a much better chance of getting out of here alive, but I don't need any dissenters here. Got it? None."

There were a few angry glares but nothing that had any teeth to it. Lars had lost track of how many of these missions they'd been on. If there was a bucketful of crap recon missions, it was all theirs.

"Let's go," Lars said.

They climbed back down the scaffolding away from the fighting—at least as far from the conflict as they could get. Lars led them away from the inner city, where the fighting was the worst, keeping to the outskirts. They heard several Ovarrow ships fly overhead but couldn't see them through the smoke. He had the recon drone scouting the area ahead of them. It could be the Krake, but if Duffy had detected Krake communications, he would have told Lars.

"We still don't know what happened here," Perez said.

"Does it really matter? The Ovarrow need very little excuse to start killing each other. We've seen that enough times," Butler replied.

"They're manipulated by the Krake," Kashani said.

Butler looked at her. "So what?"

Kashani shook her head. "It matters."

"They allowed themselves to be manipulated," Perez said.

"It still matters. It's still a factor," Kashani said.

Perez grinned. "What about you, Ritt?"

Rittberg kept her attention ahead of them and glanced toward the upper levels of the surrounding buildings as if someone could be hiding up there. Lars was doing the same thing.

"Ritt," Perez said.

Rittberg sighed. "If the Ovarrow had been smart enough to defeat the Krake, they would have."

Butler grinned, and Perez joined him. Duffy was silent. "Looks like you're in the minority, Kashani."

"Only the minority among idiots. Ritt didn't answer the question," Kashani replied.

She followed Butler, who kept his attention ahead of them.

Lars had heard the same discussion on the other worlds they'd been to, and it was always the same. They'd go round and round the same thing without resolving anything. Sooner or later, they'd ask him. But he didn't care who was to blame. What he cared about was getting his squad through this alive.

"Look around you," Lars said. "Use the translators and look at what's left. See the signs? See the graffiti on the walls of the buildings? The streets? If we went to the inner city, we'd see it on bodies. Someone—maybe it was the Krake, or maybe the Ovarrow did it to themselves—fostered a culture of contempt. This is where it led. We don't know for sure if the Krake did it, and if they did, they might have just left. Regardless, the Ovarrow are still fighting. They can't be reasoned with. There are no allies for us here, so we leave."

They'd all learned early on that they couldn't save everyone. They'd hardly saved anyone. That wasn't their mission, despite the fact that some of them hoped it would be. They had orders, and Lars wouldn't allow them to deviate from them. Get them out alive. That was all he cared about.

Lars increased their pace. The seven-person CDF squad navigated the city streets of burning buildings and vehicles that had served as barricades. The Ovarrow must have been fighting for days or perhaps even weeks before the CDF had arrived. Their mission was simple reconnaissance—search for the Krake, and if there were Ovarrow, determine whether they could be brought into the allied forces against the Krake. The 3rd Platoon, as well as the other platoons that were part of the Special Infantry Division, did the initial contact in universes where it wasn't readily apparent that there was anything worth the CDF's time. Lars knew there were Ovarrow allies who sent out teams of their own to different universes. He'd been concerned that their efforts would overlap, but there had to be some coordination among the allies because that hadn't happened.

The Ovarrow seemed to have developed the same technological base across multiple universes. Appearances might have been slightly altered, but they preferred the same rounded architecture. Ramps connected the multiple levels of their taller buildings. Their aversion to creating anything like a staircase was linked to the physiological development of their legs. They were bipedal and of a similar size to humans, but they had longer limbs, and their skin was akin to certain types of reptiles. But they weren't entirely reptilian. They were warm-blooded like any mammal but still lacked hair. Lars had studied Ovarrow physiology—at least until he'd been captured. If there were new developments resulting from colonial research, he wasn't aware of it.

Rittberg came to a stop and gestured to the others. They crouched down and waited. Lars crept forward to join Rittberg.

"There's a large group of them a short distance that way," Rittberg said, gesturing toward the adjacent street.

Lars peered into the gloom and detected the heat signatures of a large group of Ovarrow. Smaller groups headed into the buildings, followed by weaponsfire. The Ovarrow fanned out along the street, firing their weapons toward the upper levels. The video feed from the recon drone showed that the large group of Ovarrow extended several streets away from them, but they were moving toward the outskirts.

Lars looked at Rittberg and nodded. They couldn't stay there. He gestured toward the others to stay low, indicating that they were going to circle around the Ovarrow.

Several Ovarrow screamed, which was followed by flashes from their weapons. The CDF recon drone exploded.

"They know we're here," Lars said. "Butler, get up here."

Lars peered around the corner and saw Ovarrow racing toward them. "Suppressing fire," he said.

He aimed his AR-74 and began firing three-round bursts into the Ovarrow, dropping them while causing others to stumble. He was joined by Rittberg and Perez. Duffy and Kashani took cover on the other side of the street. Butler carried heavy ordnance and brought up the Hammer—a short-range missile launcher. Once he had one loaded, he came up next to Lars and fired. The missile blazed a path through the smoky ruins of the Ovarrow city just past the Ovarrow front lines. The Ovarrow scattered. The missile detonated, flashing so brightly that Lars squeezed his eyes shut to keep from being blinded.

Lars opened his eyes. "Come on," he said.

The CDF squad ran away from the death and destruction. Lars glanced behind and saw the streets littered with the charred remains of the Ovarrow, but there were more converging on their location.

They had to keep moving. If the Ovarrow managed to pin them down, they were going to die. Random bursts of weaponsfire sounded in the distance, but none of it came anywhere near the fleeing CDF soldiers.

Without a recon drone, Lars had to rely on scouting data that might not be as accurate as he would have liked, but it was all he had. He updated the path to the waypoint and shared it with the others.

They ran through the streets, slowing only to check that the Ovarrow hadn't found them. Sounds of fighting drew steadily nearer to their location, but he couldn't be sure whether the Ovarrow were hunting for them or if they were fighting other Ovarrow.

The CDF soldiers moved quickly through the area, and Lars

couldn't help but think that they were being too reckless. But they didn't have a choice. They had to move quickly.

"Corporal," Duffy said, "I have Cronin. They're pinned down. He gave us their location."

Antwan Cronin served in Wagner's squad. Their location appeared on Lars's internal heads-up display.

"Tell him we're not far from their position. Can they hold out?" Lars asked and looked at the others. "Perez and Rittberg, I want you on point. Wagner's squad is in trouble."

"Yes, sir," they said in unison.

No one had any intention of leaving anyone behind, but sometimes it happened. Sometimes they didn't have a choice, but Lars wouldn't consider it in this case.

"Just told them we're on our way," Duffy said. He looked at Lars and nodded.

They continued onward, with Lars following Perez.

Perez glanced behind him. "Think she'll be a complete bitch to you now?"

"Only if she's lucky," Lars replied.

As they closed in on the other CDF squad, Lars saw hundreds of Ovarrow storming down the street.

"Holy—" Butler said and cut himself off.

Wagner's squad was in trouble. Within a few minutes, they'd be dead. Lars scanned the area and spotted something.

"Butler, stay on me. The rest of you follow," Lars said.

He ran down the street and then cut over to the side.

"Get that last missile ready," Lars said.

Butler secured his rifle and brought up the Hammer.

"We don't have the angle to hit them like we did the others," Perez said.

Butler finished loading the Hammer. "He's right. I'd only take out a few dozen from here."

"I know," Lars said. "See that building at the cross street? The one that's leaning?"

Butler looked and then nodded. "Got it."

Wagner's squad fired their weapons at the oncoming Ovarrow.

"Tell them to take cover," Lars said.

Duffy relayed the message and Butler fired the missile.

The missile raced toward the building that was already leaning precariously to the side, and the missile slammed into the bottom. The ensuing explosion rocked the area, drowning out the sounds of weaponsfire in the area. The building's internal supports gave out and the saucer-shaped roof fell to the side, slamming into the building next to it with such force that the second building also toppled. The buildings collapsed, crushing the Ovarrow in the vicinity and blocking the entire street. The main Ovarrow attack force was cut off. Lars and the others charged forward, firing their weapons at the remaining fighters. Wagner's squad began firing their weapons as well.

They made short work of the remaining Ovarrow, and Lars made it to the others.

Lars peered at where the CDF squad had taken cover. "Kashani, help with the wounded," he said to the medic.

Kashani ran over and began checking the survivors.

Wagner looked at Lars. "I lost Boisvert and Rosenberg on the way here. The Ovarrow came out of nowhere," she said and shook her head. "I should have waited for you."

"Never mind that now. We've got to move," Lars said.

Their combat suits would help the wounded move, but there were limits to how far they could go. Kashani bound the wounds as best she could, and the CDF soldiers quickly left the area.

"Duffy, see if you can get Lieutenant Miller. Boost the signal if you have to," Lars said.

They kept moving away from the fighting, albeit slower than before.

A comlink request came from Duffy. "I have Lieutenant Miller."

"Corporal Mallory, what's your location?" Lieutenant Miller asked.

Lars transmitted his location. "I have Wagner's squad with me," he said and gave him a sitrep.

"Understood. Stand by," Miller said.

Lars waited, and a full minute went by. "Lieutenant Miller, I tried to reach Sergeant Burgess but she's not responding."

"She's dead, Corporal," Miller replied tersely.

Dead? No, not Burgess, Lars thought, and felt a spindly tightness spread across his back. Burgess was the more sensible of the two and normally kept Lieutenant Miller from doing anything foolish.

"Sir," Lars said, trying to think of a diplomatic way to say what he was thinking without stepping on Miller's toes. Sometimes he could be prickly. "Is the troop carrier nearby? We could really use an evac."

"Negative on the evac, Corporal," Miller said, then spoke to someone else for a few moments. "Look, our ship is down. One of their patrols took it out. We need to find another way back to our extraction point. We need a vehicle to get us there. I'm sending coordinates for you to meet us at. Transmitting now," he said and then added, "Get a move on it. We don't have much time. Miller out."

The coordinates came over the comlink, and then it severed. Lars peered at it and gritted his teeth. He glanced down the long city street strewn with rubble, the skeletons of vehicles, and the charred remains of Ovarrow. Ribbons of flame blazed in the smoky air amid the waning sunlight. There had to be a better way. He turned to look at the others, who waited for him.

"Is the troop carrier coming?" Butler asked.

Lars shook his head and the others gathered around him. "The carrier is gone. Miller sent us alternate coordinates to meet up with the other two squads."

Wagner looked at him. "Where?"

Lars exhaled deeply and shared the location. It looked like they were heading to the inner city after all.

"This is bullshit!" Butler exclaimed. "We can't get there. Have they seen what's going on in there? Half of us won't make it."

Several of the others muttered in agreement.

"There has to be a better way, sir," Duffy said.

"Hey, I don't like it either, but we don't have a choice. We need to find a working vehicle and use it to get out of here," Lars said, but he knew going into the city was going to be a death sentence.

The others went silent. There was no use complaining. It wasn't going to change anything, but Lars couldn't help thinking they were leaping out of the frying pan and heading directly into the fire.

10

LARS REALLY COULD HAVE USED a few more recon drones, but there weren't any. One per squad was their allocation. No backups.

"Perez, Rittberg, and Wagner, stay with me. The rest of you, keep watch on our position. I don't want the Ovarrow sneaking up on us," Lars said.

Perez and Rittberg were his scouts, and he kept Wagner there because she commanded what was left of the other squad.

"What are we going to do, sir?" Perez asked.

"Miller wants us to get to the waypoint as quickly as possible, but without any recon drones, we need to survey, and I'd like to find a few alternatives as far as vehicles go."

"Miller must think there are vehicles at the waypoint. Otherwise, why would he send us there?" Wagner said.

"I wouldn't bet on it." Rittberg glanced at the others. "I'm just saying what you're all probably thinking."

"It doesn't matter," Lars said. With Sergeant Burgess dead . . . but he didn't want to chase that line of thinking. "He could be grasping at straws. I don't know. What I do know is that we are going to survey the area and look for alternatives. Is that understood?"

Perez and Rittberg nodded, and after a few moments, Wagner did as well.

They left the area and began making their way to the waypoint. The Ovarrow city was laid out like a grid, much like their other cities. The architecture might change a little, but there must have been some kind of universal constant regarding the layout of cities for there to be such similarities seen in multiple universes.

They were careful to avoid the heated exchanges between the Ovarrow trying to kill each other. Snarling war cries echoed amid the discharge of weaponsfire. It was as if the entire city was one big hot zone. How many Ovarrow had died here?

Both Perez and Rittberg scaled up a building to survey the area. There was no need for them all to go up there. The rest of them remained below to secure the area. After a few minutes, his scouts returned.

"It's more of the same. Burning buildings or Ovarrow trying to kill each other," Perez said.

Rittberg came down from another building a short distance away from them. "I think I found something worth checking, sir. There's an intact building that looks untouched. It's off the path to the waypoint."

Lars nodded. "Good work. That might be just what we need."

"It's away from the waypoint," Wagner said.

"It will put us a few minutes behind, but it might be worth the time," Lars replied.

"That's not what Lieutenant Miller ordered us to do," Wagner said.

Lars couldn't see Wagner's face because they had their helmets in full-armor mode, but he was sure she was glaring. He didn't need this right now. The situation was dangerous enough without them arguing in front of their squads.

"Let's go," Lars said.

His squad immediately began moving, but Wagner's squad waited for her. After a few moments, she jerked her head to the side, indicating that she wanted them to go too.

They kept making their way through the city, but they had to change courses a few times because of fighting that broke out nearby. These groups of Ovarrow wore armor and had more powerful weapons. A couple of soldiers from Wagner's squad were having trouble keeping up. They were wounded, and while the combat suits could help them maintain a steady pace, it was painful. The combat suit AI would only administer enough pain killers to avoid risking the occupant's life, and they needed to be coherent, which also limited how much medicine could be administered. Lars ordered Kashani and Jiang to help them.

They cut down an alleyway, and when they reached the end of it, they found two utility vehicles. They were robust and had thickly treaded tires, making Lars think that they were used for construction. They were much bigger than the other vehicles he'd seen.

"Duffy," Lars said, "see if you can get these running."

They looked like large haulers, but they were empty. There were large scorch marks on the sides, and one of them had damage right in the front where it had slammed into another vehicle.

A few minutes later, amid a flurry of curses and expletives from Duffy, both vehicles were running. The haulers' sidewalls provided a little bit of protection, and the CDF squads climbed aboard. Unfortunately, the vehicles' controls were operated from a place in the middle that was completely exposed.

The haulers' engines were loud and ran on some kind of combustible fuel. Lars ordered them to go quickly. If they couldn't hide their presence, they needed to go as fast as possible.

Lars tried to send a comlink to Lieutenant Miller, but it failed to connect. He didn't get a chance to try again because Ovarrow began firing on them from the nearby buildings. The sounds of the vehicles had drawn them like moths to a flame. The CDF soldiers returned fire with precision and accuracy. But still, the Ovarrow kept coming.

Lars saw Rittberg fire a round, taking an Ovarrow in the head and smoothly moving on to the next one. Each time she fired her weapon, another Ovarrow stumbled to the ground and stayed there. She was by far their best shooter.

Lars fired his AR-74 in three-round bursts and stopped the attacking Ovarrow in their tracks just as easily.

"Duffy, get me somebody from Miller's squads. I can't reach them," Lars said.

Duffy squatted down and opened his personal holoscreen. "Sir, Miller's been wounded, and his combat suit has been damaged. They're pinned down. I was able to reach Flores."

Weaponsfire erupted from the nearby building and Butler went down. He cried out in pain. Kashani hastened over to him and began checking his wounds. Lars raced to the vehicle's controls.

"Give me their coordinates. We're getting them out," Lars said.

He thrust the vehicle controls up, maximizing their velocity. The front of the vehicle slammed into a barricade, knocking it aside, and they gained momentum as they went. More Ovarrow were coming toward them. They all wore different types of uniforms, and it seemed that they'd taken a break from killing each other to team up and hunt the CDF soldiers instead.

Lars turned the vehicle down one of the alleyways and gunned it. They heard sounds of CDF weaponsfire up ahead.

Butler regained his feet and held his weapon. He leaned to the side where his combat suit had taken damage, but he used sidewalls to keep him steady and had his weapon ready.

Flaming debris formed another barricade at the end of the alleyway and Lars increased the vehicle's velocity to punch through it. He jerked the vehicle's controls to avoid a smaller abandoned vehicle, and they leaned to the side, but he quickly adjusted his course and was able to get it righted. A group of Ovarrow soldiers took up positions near the barricade and began firing their weapons. He mowed them down and came to a halt. The two CDF squads hurriedly climbed aboard, carrying the wounded.

Lars glanced behind them and saw hundreds of Ovarrow soldiers running down the street like animals.

"Secure the wounded. We're getting out of here," Lars said.

Ovarrow ran fast. Because of their long limbs, they were able to run much faster than the colonists could on foot without the assistance of their combat suits. Conversely, they weren't fast out of the gate. It took them time to build up speed, but once they got moving, they didn't stop.

"We have to go faster," Butler shouted.

Lars had the vehicle going as fast as it could, but the engines must have taken damage and seemed to be stuck in a particular gear.

"We've got incoming," Perez yelled.

Amid the firelight, a dark shadow flew overhead, squealing in a high tone. Heavy cannons began firing on the vehicles, and Lars jerked the controls to the side to avoid being destroyed. He bounced off the side of a building but managed to keep from being shot. The other hauler did the same thing.

"Get ready for another pass," Lars said.

He kept one hand on the controls and raised his rifle. The rest of the CDF soldiers kept their rifles pointed to the sky, waiting for the ship to return. Waiting was the worst part. They knew it was coming but couldn't see it. All they could do was listen for the squealing sound of the ship as it made another pass. Then out of the darkness, the heavy cannon from the Ovarrow fighter tore into the streets. The CDF soldiers returned fire, and Lars switched his AR-74 to full auto. He would quickly run through his ammunition, but it was either that or death.

The fighter burst into flames overhead, so they must have hit a critical component. The Ovarrow fighter bounced off the walls, tumbling down onto the Ovarrow soldiers that had been racing up toward them. The force of the explosion blew Lars to the side and into a few of the others. He felt pain blossom on his flank, and he clambered to his feet. Duffy raced to the controls and kept them moving.

The streets began to open up as they headed out of the city. They had to keep moving, but the medics made a point of checking the rest of them for injuries. The sounds of pursuit began to fade into the background. There were other Ovarrow fighters flying above the city that didn't pursue them. Instead, they turned their attention toward something else. Lars didn't care. He just wanted to get the hell off this world.

The egress point was several kilometers away from the city, and it wasn't exactly a relaxing drive. It was going to be close. The gateway would be open for only a certain amount of time. Without any recon drones, they couldn't even communicate to the other side that they needed more time. It was a bumpy ride, and they tore ass as fast as they could for the egress point. One of the vehicles died and they couldn't get it started again. The one Lars was in wasn't doing much better.

"Load the wounded into this one and the rest of us will run," Lars said.

They transferred the wounded soldiers onto their remaining hauler.

"Rittberg, Perez, go ahead. Get to the egress point as fast as possible and tell them to keep that gateway open. Don't stop for anything," Lars said.

Rittberg and Perez raced ahead of them in an all-out run toward the egress point.

The hauler was barely moving, but it was better than trying to carry everyone. Lars glanced behind them and saw that the Ovarrow fighters were once more streaking toward them. Apparently, they'd decided they were worth hunting after all. Lars did a quick calculation and swore. They weren't going to make it. If they stayed in the hauler, they were going to die.

"Everybody out," Lars said. "Pair up and head to the egress point."

Lars went to Lieutenant Miller and helped him to his feet. His combat suit had taken severe damage to its legs, leaving parts of Miller's legs exposed. Miller had trouble standing. The wounds on his legs were covered in healing packs. Lars wedged his shoulder under Miller's, and they started hobbling as fast as they could.

The CDF soldiers spread out. Ovarrow fighters flew overhead, buzzing them in a quick flyby. Lars saw the faint shimmer of the gateway in the distance. Perez and Rittberg were almost there.

Lars checked his ammo. Not good. He wasn't out, but he was nearly there.

They kept going. Miller grunted in pain, but he didn't falter.

"We're not going to make it."

"I know," Lars said and kept going.

Kashani raced back to them and came to Miller's other side, helping them go faster. Lars heard the Ovarrow fighter circling around them and gritted his teeth. They'd been on so many missions, and they'd been tasked to evaluate the Ovarrow in each of them. When they found them, it was always the same. More often than not, the Ovarrow were everything Lars had initially thought them to be—untrustworthy, violent, and easily manipulated. These weren't the first Ovarrow he'd killed, and they probably wouldn't be the last.

"Get him to the gateway," Lars said.

He separated himself from the others, brought up his weapon, and updated his ammo configuration for incendiary rounds. They were highly visible and would draw the attention of the pilot in that fighter, which was what he wanted. He ran off to the side and began firing his weapon in bursts but kept moving toward the gateway. Their egress point was in an open field, which would be a shooting gallery for anyone caught out there. The Ovarrow fighter altered its course, heading right for Lars. Incendiary rounds streaked across the sky, but none of them hit the fighter.

Butler screamed nearby and fired his weapon too. Several other soldiers had done the same. They were buying time for the wounded to get to the gateway. The Ovarrow fighter fired back, its heavy cannons chewing up the ground, but hitting a single target was much harder than anyone ever thought, especially when they could move out of the way quickly. They each took turns drawing the fire from the Ovarrow fighter while sneaking their way back toward the gateway. They were slowly moving toward escape, or they'd die trying.

Then a second fighter appeared.

Lars risked a glance back and saw that the wounded were finally making their way through the gateway. He knew there would be no help coming through to them. It was a small, remote site away from the main base on an uninhabited planet where off-world engagements were staged.

They continued to slowly make their way toward the gateway, pausing to return fire at the two fighters trying to take them out. They had no choice but to keep their attention on the fighters and firing back at them, allowing the wounded to get through the gateway.

He had to do something to distract them. Then an idea sprung to his mind, and he realized it might be just enough to give them the seconds they needed to reach the gateway. Lars altered his ammo and fired several flares into the night sky. They gleamed, turning night into day, illuminating the entire area. The remaining CDF soldiers turned and ran toward the gateway. This was their only shot.

Running through a gateway between worlds looked as if it should feel like something. However, when he passed through, he didn't feel anything. He was simply not in the other world anymore, but the enemy fire could also come through the gateway.

"Shut it down! Shut it down!" Lars screamed and rolled to the side. Bolts of molten plasma burst through the gateway and tore into the ground just as Lars rolled away. He came to a kneeling position, his weapon raised, and returned fire. There were several bright flashes, and then the mobile arch gateway shut down, cutting off the bridge between worlds.

Lars gasped for breath and sat down, setting his rifle beside him. He inhaled heavily for a few moments before he felt his wind return to him. His heart was beating rapidly, and his mind clung to the knowledge of just how close he'd come to dying. He looked around, searching for his squad mates.

Perez walked over to him and helped him to his feet. He gave Lars a long look and shook his head.

Lars nodded. "I think we can add that place to the No-Go list. What do you think?"

Perez chuckled.

The CDF retrieval team dismantled the arch gateway and left for their next scheduled extraction. There were multiple CDF retrieval teams that roamed the planet. A pair of troop carriers waited to take them back to base, where they'd be debriefed and allowed to eat and get cleaned up before receiving orders for their next mission. It would be nice if they could get a few hours to sleep, but Lars wasn't counting on it. He knew the stakes. They were racing against the Krake in a search for their home world, as well as looking for potential allies.

Lars walked up the loading ramp and saw Wagner speaking with Lieutenant Miller as medics patched up his leg. He sat down away from them and leaned back. They'd lost some good people back in that hellish world. They deserved better than to be left behind.

The loading ramp closed, and the troop carrier climbed into the air.

Lars looked around. The 3rd Platoon was made up of four squads. His eyebrows raised a little as he realized that his squad was the only one not to lose any lives. Everyone else had suffered losses.

Perez and Duffy were speaking in hushed tones, appearing to disagree on something. Rittberg sat next to them. She'd leaned back in her seat and closed her eyes. Kashani and Butler each sat quietly with an intensity that wouldn't leave them. Lars had learned over the months that everyone dealt with it differently.

They'd just survived a crap mission and the only certainty that any of them faced was that there would be another one tomorrow. Hopefully, it wouldn't be as bad as this one. Lars kept looking for some of the people they'd lost. Sergeant Burgess was prime among them. She'd been a strong leader, if a little dry in personality. But she more than made up for that in tactical acumen.

Lars stood up and walked over to Randy Flores. Flores was a scout and had been in Burgess's squad. He sat away from the others, staring off into space. He glanced up and shifted in his seat as Lars approached.

"What happened over there?" Lars asked, claiming the seat next to him.

Flores drank from his canteen. "Stray shot knocked her and Oravec into a pit. A building close by collapsed on top of them as they tried to climb out."

Lars sighed and shook his head.

"We're not the Phantoms for nothing," Flores said.

An unofficial designation they'd given themselves, the Phantom Platoon was both a part of the CDF and apart from it. They rarely went on missions with CDF regulars, but that didn't stop the scuttlebutt from making the rounds about the Special Infantry Division. Most of them had made a choice between banishment or joining the CDF. There were others who had committed crimes in the colony who'd been offered the same choice. Lars knew that the colony couldn't afford to keep able-bodied people on the sideline, even if they were convicted criminals. He wasn't naive enough to believe that their missions were the only ones that were dangerous, but it did seem like they were provided minimal equipment with which to do the job. They were last in the line of priority for gear, and yet they were still expected to function. They didn't have a choice.

"It's not worth it," Flores muttered more to himself than to Lars.

"We endure. We can outlast this," Lars said.

Flores looked at him. His bleary-eyed gaze was red along the edges.

"Get some rest," Lars said, and taking a page from Rittberg's book, he leaned back and closed his eyes.

He didn't sleep. Mostly he rested with his eyes closed, but he was too amped up to sleep. He knew some soldiers could sleep anywhere at any time, but he wasn't one of them. And so, inevitably, he began to think about home. Thoughts of New Earth seemed to spring unbidden inside him. It was easier to just avoid thinking about home, but sometimes it couldn't be helped. He thought about his father and his half brother. Lars was tall and lean, and though his little brother was . . . he had to think about it. Miles was almost seven years old, and Lars hadn't seen much of him in the past few years. It hadn't bothered him at the time, but it did now. Lars had thought he'd always have the time. Now, he was committed to five years of service in the CDF, and if this war with the Krake persisted that long, there was a good chance that his tour of duty would be extended. Lars knew full well the terms of his enlistment. He was only guaranteed a *chance* for a commuted sentence. All he'd get was a chance and nothing more.

The troop carriers dropped them off at a designated area of the base that had been established for them. They weren't prisoners exactly, but Lars knew they were kept away from the main part of the base.

They returned to their barracks and got cleaned up, turning in their weapons and checking in their other equipment. Lars had been a corporal for months and slept near his squad. He'd just sat down on his bunk when he received a comlink summons.

Lars stood up.

Perez looked over at him from his own bunk. "All of us?"

Lars shook his head. "No, just me. I'm the lucky one."

Perez nodded a little and then rolled onto his side. He'd probably be asleep in less than a minute.

Lars left the barracks and walked over to the command center, entering officer country. Infantry division officers were separate from the main base, so their work areas were shared. Lars sent a check-in message via comlink and waited outside the CO's office. Their commanding officer rotated, and he wasn't sure who'd been assigned to them this time.

He heard a couple of voices speaking inside the office. One of them was deep, and he thought he recognized it.

The door to the office opened and a lieutenant gestured for him to come inside. Lars walked into the room and stood at attention. Lieutenant Miller sat in one of the chairs. His leg was wrapped with healing gels that would quickly mend his wounds. Sitting behind the desk was a large, heavily muscled, dark-skinned man—Major Samson, commanding officer of the 7th Spec Ops Company. A flicker of recognition showed in Samson's gaze and was gone in an instant.

"Mallory," Samson said.

"Major Samson."

Lars wasn't invited to sit.

"Close the door, Matheson," Samson said.

The lieutenant who'd let him into the room shut the door.

"I've just been briefed by Lieutenant Miller about your most recent mission," Samson said.

Since Lars hadn't been asked a specific question, he remained silent.

"Your squad is the only squad to not suffer any losses. How do you explain that?" Samson asked.

"I can't explain that, Major. Everything that happened was in the report," Lars replied.

"There are a couple of reports that indicate a pattern of skirting a thin line for disobeying orders," Samson said.

Lars wanted to look at Lieutenant Miller but kept his gaze locked on a spot on the wall. He knew the value of not volunteering any information.

Samson nodded. "You were ordered to a specific waypoint, and instead, you chose to deviate from that. Why?"

"Sir, we needed to secure transportation to reach our egress point in time. We'd lost our recon drone, so I had Private Perez and Private Rittberg scout the area. Private Rittberg spotted a building that appeared to be in good condition. I thought it was worth investigating."

"And you didn't report this because of the limited communication protocols. There have been reports of disagreements with your orders to head to the waypoint," Samson said.

"Soldiers complain, sir," Lars replied.

Samson's lips twitched.

"His insubordination is unacceptable," Lieutenant Miller said.

"You're right," Samson said, and Miller seemed mollified. "Soldiers do complain, but there's more to it."

This time Lars looked at Samson. "Major, the fighting was worse farther into the city. If we hadn't found those ground vehicles, we wouldn't have made it out of there."

"I believe the term used was 'reckless,'" Samson said and raised his hand. "No one actually reported you using that word, Mallory, but it's implied."

"Sir, I was trying to get us out of there alive."

Miller shifted in his seat.

"Your gamble paid off, and I happen to agree with your actions," Samson said and looked at Miller. "Ordering everyone into the interior of the city? What were you thinking?"

"We saw vehicles near the waypoint. Recon drones spotted a depot that was intact, Major," Miller said.

Samson smiled, unveiling pearly white teeth. "You have to admit, Corporal Mallory's idea of looking for a ride out of that hellhole by searching for stable buildings was a better option. Wouldn't you agree?"

Lars could only see Miller from his peripheral vision, but he thought the lieutenant stiffened.

"It was a good idea. Better than what I'd come up with," Miller finally said.

Samson nodded slowly. "Look, I know what it's like to be in that kind of situation. You're both here. You survived, and you'll be that much more prepared for the next mission." He paused. "We all lose people under our command. This won't be the last time, but you have an open position in 3rd Platoon that must be filled."

"Yes, sir," Miller said. "I can send you a list of candidates."

"Save your list. Corporal Mallory, you're officially promoted to sergeant and will be Lieutenant Miller's second in 3rd Platoon," Samson said.

It took a second for Lars to realize what had happened. "Thank you, Major."

Samson chuckled. "Yeah, right. With promotions comes more work. I don't have a lot of time, but I will say this to both of you: Figure out a way to work together. Otherwise, the soldiers in your platoon will pay the price. Dismissed."

Lars saluted Samson and walked out of the office. A few moments later, Miller joined him in the corridor.

Lars looked at Miller, who seemed to come to grips with his own racing thoughts.

"You heard the man. Congratulations are in order," Miller said.

"Thank you, Lieutenant," Lars replied.

Miller sighed and leveled his gaze at Lars. "You saved our asses back there," he said and shook his head. "Go ahead. Off the record."

"It was a tough situation."

"It was, but you kept a level head." Miller leaned against the wall. "I don't know why they didn't make you a lieutenant."

Lars felt his mouth open in surprise.

"Yeah, I know," Miller continued. "Let's get some rest so we can deal with whatever shithole they send us to next."

Miller started walking, muttering about his leg pain. Lars waited a few moments for Miller to go his way. He'd almost thought they were going to bust him down to private, and instead he'd gotten promoted, though it wasn't really a promotion. They'd given him the rank of sergeant because Burgess died, and he was next in line.

Lars had been kept at a lower rank for much longer than anyone expected. He tried not to have any expectations and just did as he was told. In his previous life, he'd risen among the ranks of Field Ops and Security on New Earth until he'd had the command authority of Major Samson. Most soldiers in the SID knew it too. There was an unspoken deference given to him, even from people like Wagner. Lars didn't encourage it, and always iterated that he wasn't in charge. He believed in preserving the chain of command, but his reputation persisted. It had made some of the officers in the SID reluctant to work with him, and that had been the case until they were reassigned to Major Samson. The major didn't put up with that kind of nonsense.

Samson believed in putting the most capable person in command. No doubt some would see this as Lars trying to rise through the ranks in the service of his own ambition, but his squadmates knew the truth. Lars knew what it took to lead, and they trusted him for it. They trusted him to get them back alive.

11

THEY WERE BEHIND SCHEDULE. The Valkyrie III combat shuttle had left the CDF base at Sanctuary a little over an hour ago, and the diplomatic envoy was late arriving from Sierra. Connor had been tempted to leave without them, but they were late because of a mechanical issue with their C-cat. If not for that, they would have arrived much earlier than Connor had intended to leave, so he thought it was fair that he wait for them. Who said he couldn't be diplomatic?

Franz Holzer was the diplomatic lead. He was a man of slightly above average height and unassuming build. He had blond hair, and crow's feet sprouted at the corners of his pale green eyes. He was joined by Aliza Winfry. She was a junior diplomat fresh from her training in Ovarrow affairs. Connor looked at the assistant they'd brought with them—a young man named Justin Gellner. He was tall, with narrow shoulders and dark skin, and he was timid.

Dash cleared his throat and Connor looked at him. "Is it me, or are the kids getting younger?"

Connor twitched his eyebrows. In his mid-twenties, Dash was little more than a kid himself, but he'd seen a lot in his short life. Dash was born on Earth and had been part of the original *Ark* program. He'd gone into stasis at seven years old, along with his parents. Connor inhaled deeply and sighed. Lauren was four. If he'd had the choice, would he have volunteered for the *Ark* program, taking his family on an interstellar voyage that meant leaving Earth behind forever? He wasn't sure he would have. He hadn't been given a choice, but Dash's family had. Dash himself was an only child, and his parents had died during the Vemus War. Lenora had an eye for young talent and had recruited Dash into the advanced archaeological study program at the Colonial Research Institute. Dash had a thorough understanding of the Ovarrow civilization through years of studying the ruins, as well as a wealth of interactions with the Ovarrow.

Dash had added a number of skills to his repertoire over the years. He'd found himself in a number of situations where he needed knowledge beyond the basics of self-defense, and though Dash would never be a soldier, he was weapons qualified up through the AR-74. He'd also worked closely with Noah, and like anyone who worked within Noah's vicinity, he couldn't help but absorb certain technical skills that couldn't be taught in a classroom. All of these experiences had made Dash somewhat unique among a select few, much like Connor himself had had to become over the years.

"You're five minutes older than he is," Connor replied dryly.

Dash shook his head. "Nah, I was never that young. I don't think he's ever been on a combat shuttle. He probably hasn't been out in the field. Why would they bring along someone who has no field experience?"

Connor arched an eyebrow. "How else will he get field experience? And I bet he's never stolen a C-cat either."

Dash chuckled with a small, guilty lift of his lips at the subtle reminder of his youthful recklessness. Connor could relate, his own checkered past notwithstanding, at least until he joined the military.

Connor saw Holzer look over at them. The diplomat stood up and began heading their way.

Dash gave Connor a wry smile. "Samson told me you'd done worse. Something about—"

"Okay, that's enough reckless youth stories," Connor said quickly while wondering what Samson had told him.

"I'm just glad you don't have me on babysitting duty . . ." Dash's voice trailed off as he noticed Connor looking at someone behind him. The young man turned and saw Holzer gazing at him.

The diplomat smiled in the way a berwolf showed its teeth. "No, I'm afraid we have our own group of babysitters, Mr. DeWitt, so you're off the hook," Holzer said. His accent sounded like he was of Eastern European descent.

Dash glanced at the squad of CDF soldiers that sat near the envoy. "That didn't come out right."

"Oh, I think you were quite succinct in your comments about my colleagues and me," Holzer said.

Much to Dash's credit, he didn't look away or shift in his seat but returned Holzer's gaze. "That wasn't meant for you to hear. I'm sorry if you were offended."

Holzer nodded. "It's not an issue. Now, if you don't mind, I'd like to have a word with General Gates."

Dash looked at Connor.

"Why don't you go give the others some advice about what to expect," Connor said. "Maybe Gellner, since he's never been where we're going. I'm sure he could benefit from some of your experiences."

Dash's lips lifted a little, his eyes gleaming with humor. "I can think of a few things to share," he said. With a quick nod toward Holzer, he went to sit with the others.

Holzer sat down. "Thank you."

"For what?"

"I'm sure having us along isn't what you might have preferred."

"Mullins wants you here."

Holzer nodded. It was a motion that involved his whole upper body rather than just his head. He crossed his arms in front of his chest. "Indeed, but what bothers me is the fact that you don't think you need us here. The Gesora's invitation came to you personally and not the colonial government."

"First, it was a request. The Gesora may have uncovered something important, and they want me to evaluate it. Second, is your office upset that you didn't get an invite?"

"As a matter of fact, we are."

"Why?"

"Because communication with the Ovarrow should come through colonial government channels and not through the CDF," Holzer said.

"Would it change the outcome?" Connor asked.

Holzer's lips flatlined. "Possibly."

"I don't see how."

"This surprises me, General. You of all people are well aware of the importance of the separation of duties," Holzer said.

Connor considered this for a few moments. The colonial government represented the colony, while the purpose of the Colonial Defense Force was to protect the colony.

"I see your point."

Holzer's eyebrows raised a little. "Thank you, General Gates. I'm glad we could work that out."

"Monin wants me to review and validate some of the intelligence they've gathered about the Krake. Other than being part of the conversation, what role do you think is appropriate for this meeting?"

Holzer tilted his head to the side in a slight bob. "Being part of the conversation is a step in the right direction. I should also inform you that Aliza is also part of the Colonial Intelligence Bureau. She's been briefed on the intelligence provided from the CDF reconnaissance missions."

"Briefed?" Connor said.

Holzer nodded. "The CIB prioritizes data as it relates to the Ovarrow and the Krake."

Connor knew about that. The CIB was led by Natalia Vassar, whom Connor had trained in intelligence analysis and reconnaissance. "And Gellner?"

Holzer glanced at the young man. Dash was speaking with both Winfry and Gellner. "He's learning."

"This might not be the best mission for training," Connor replied.

"We have very little choice in the matter. I'll look out for my team, and we have our assigned escorts," Holzer said.

"Okay, just so we're clear. If Sergeant Rowan tells you to do something, then do it. It's for your safety. They'll protect you, but they're not going to throw their lives away because any of you think you know more than they do. Is that understood?" Connor asked.

Holzer nodded slowly. "Crystal clear, General," he said and paused for a moment. "You still think we'll be in the way."

"That remains to be seen. I just don't want anything to happen to you or my soldiers because of you. The Gesora are our allies, but that doesn't mean it's safe to be on their world."

"That's fair. I'll remember your words. There's one more

thing I'd like to point out to you," Holzer said, and Connor inclined his head. "This burden that you have. Really, it's shared by everyone in the CDF. There are some of us who believe the burden of protecting the colony should also be borne by the colony as well."

"We all have a stake in this," Connor said.

Holzer stood up. "Thank you for speaking with me."

"I'm glad we had a chance to talk."

The combat shuttle flew toward a remote location where an arch gateway was temporarily located for the purpose of traveling to the alpha site.

The pilot's voice sounded over a broadcast channel. "Ladies and gentlemen, boys and girls, please pay attention to this important announcement. At this time, I need you all to strap yourselves in and secure your equipment. We are cleared for our final approach to the gateway, and we'll be transitioning in the next five minutes."

Dash walked back and sat next to Connor. "It might not be as bad as we thought," he said and nodded toward the envoy. "Winfry seems to know her stuff."

"That's because she's a CIB agent," Connor said.

Dash's eyes widened. "I had no idea."

"Neither did I, but Holzer just told me."

"I wonder if Gellner is as well. I couldn't get a good bead on him. He's pretty quiet," Dash said.

"One more quick announcement," the pilot said. "I was just informed that there are a couple of you who haven't been through an arch gateway before. There's nothing to worry about, but if this is your first time, I just need to say that the tingling sensation is normal."

Connor chuckled. He recognized the pilot's voice. It was Lieutenant Sykes. There was nothing wrong with a little bit of pilot humor. Connor glanced at Gellner, who spoke to Holzer and then looked at the squad of CDF soldiers sitting nearby. A couple of them looked a bit worried but knew better than to ask.

Sergeant Rowan gave a hearty laugh. "That's right, you're all about to be baptized."

This camaraderie among soldiers was something Connor missed as he'd risen through the ranks. It didn't matter if they were from the Colonial Defense Force or the NA Alliance military. The people were different, but there were things that were the same. He really did miss it sometimes.

Lieutenant Sykes came on the broadcast channel for the combat shuttle. "All right, we'll be transitioning in five, four, three, two, one."

Going through any gateway, be it in space or on the planet, didn't feel like anything. Connor had gone through a gateway quite a few times, and it was always the same. He didn't feel anything, but he couldn't help but think that there was something off about where he was, something that just didn't feel like home. Colonial scientists had speculated that there were different frequencies each universe operated on, but he didn't know about any of that stuff.

The holoscreen flickered on and showed the landscape of the alpha site world. The planet that the alpha site was located on wasn't completely lifeless, but it was close. It had enough of an atmosphere that, while not pleasant to breathe, it could sustain them without any long-term effects for the soldiers who were stationed there.

"This place smells like dirty socks," Dash said.

"You get used to the smell," Connor said.

"That's a lie. I've been here plenty of times, and I never get used to the smell," Dash replied.

"It could be worse. We pick sites like this because the Krake aren't here, and neither are the Ovarrow."

Dash nodded. "What do you think Monin found?"

"He wouldn't say. The Gesora are almost as active with their gateways as we are. They haven't been able to build any of their own, but it's not for lack of trying," Connor said.

"Why wouldn't we just help them build additional gateways?"

"It's better that they try to do it themselves and then come to us with questions, rather than us just handing them the technology. We helped them remove the Krake from power, and there was a brief civil war as a result. Too much change in any society isn't good."

Dash frowned in thought. "I guess if they're smart enough to ask for help, that might make them better allies. Is that what you're saying?"

"Pretty much, but it's not my decision to make," Connor said. "The Gesora have been trying to help us find the Krake home world, and they've been recruiting other allies too."

"I'm surprised we haven't found it by now."

"We will."

"I hope so, but I'd . . ." Dash paused for a moment. "Sometimes, I just wonder if we're looking in the right place. You know what I mean?"

"Yeah, I get it. The same thought has crossed my mind more than once," Connor agreed.

"It's like when we were trying to find Ovarrow bunkers on New Earth. You learn to look for the signs, and it made them easier to find, but I still feel like we're going through the learning part."

"That's why I wanted you along. A fresh perspective. Maybe you'll see something we're missing."

"I appreciate the vote of confidence, Connor, but I've been here before. I've been on some of the reconnaissance missions. It's just that sometimes I don't think it's enough. Like I can't do enough to make a difference." Dash frowned for a moment, then looked at Connor.

"Yeah," Connor said in reply to the unasked question. "That's exactly how I feel sometimes. We do the best we can, Dash. But remember, in all the history books, you only get the highlights. You don't ever really understand all the work that was involved in making those highlights."

In the next half hour, the combat shuttle reached the forward operating base at the alpha site. Establishing a CDF base at locations like this had been a challenge. They'd had to define what was enough of a foothold, but they always had to bear in mind that they needed to keep a minimal presence on the planet, just in case the Krake wanted to pay them a visit. No massive orbital defense stations had been established, although there were a few reconnaissance satellites in orbit and other passive scanning devices farther out in the star system. While nothing like what they had at home, it was sparse enough that if the Krake were detected, they could evacuate the CDF base relatively quickly. Every four months, the base was moved to a different location on the planet or even to another universe. From there, reconnaissance missions were launched and received—at least the missions that were planet-bound. Reconnaissance missions that occurred in space were launched from space gates in their home universe. They were farther enough out in the star system that there was little risk of being detected by the Krake. Their intelligence indicated that the Krake remained in the inner star system. Connor wasn't sure how long those practices would last since the Krake military had encountered the Trident Battle Group. Sean had used every advantage possible to survive those encounters with the Krake.

Everything about the CDF base was temporary, and their breakdown procedures required that they reduce the detectable footprint from any passive scouting missions that might be conducted by the Krake. They couldn't erase their presence here completely, but that didn't mean that they didn't take certain steps to cover it up.

Connor used his comlink to send Lieutenant Sykes updated landing coordinates at the CDF base and received an almost immediate response confirming his orders.

Connor stood up. "Get your things, Dash. We're getting off early."

Dash retrieved his travel pack, securing it over his shoulders. He'd learned the value of traveling light.

Holzer and some of the others looked at him questioningly.

"You're heading to the main base, where you'll be taken to Colonel Ryant's office. I'll meet up with you there," Connor said.

"I thought we would stay together," Holzer said.

"We are, but I need to see to another matter first. It's unrelated to the Gesora."

The combat shuttle made a light touchdown, and the loading ramp lowered for Connor and Dash to exit. They stepped off the loading ramp and cleared the shuttle, which rose back into the air while the loading ramp closed.

Connor and Dash walked off the landing pad and headed to the operations center where the 7th Ranger Company was located. More than a few soldiers glanced in his direction. It wasn't every day that a general of the CDF walked among them.

A young corporal approached him. "General Gates, may I help you, sir?" Corporal Bradley asked.

"I'm looking for Major Samson."

"Of course, General. I'll take you right to him," Bradley replied.

Rows of Nexstar combat suits stood off to the side where members of the 7th maintained their equipment. Several troop carriers were being refueled and resupplied nearby.

Connor had a pretty good idea of where Samson was. They shared a similar work ethic. Samson wasn't one to let time go idly by. Corporal Bradley led them to an operations planning room where Samson was meeting with the senior officers of the 7th Ranger Company. When Connor walked into the room, all conversation ceased. The officers stood up and saluted. He returned the salute.

"General Gates, I didn't expect to see you for another hour. I thought we were meeting with Colonel Ryant," Samson said.

Connor glanced at the holoscreen nearby and saw a mission briefing from the Special Infantry Division. He also spotted Lars Mallory's name there. He looked back at Samson. "You and I need to talk."

"Understood," Samson said and looked at the others. "You have your assignments. Clear the room."

The officers of the 7th Ranger Company quickly left the room, and Dash said that he'd wait for Connor outside. Connor could count on Dash to make himself scarce when he needed to.

"There's something I need to tell you. Permission to speak freely, sir," Samson said.

Connor nodded.

Samson peered at him for a moment. "You look like you have something to say to *me*. Maybe you should go first."

Connor inhaled deeply. "Saul Ashworth."

Ashworth was the leader of the second colony mission. It was a bit of a contingency plan for the colony. Five thousand colonists would be traveling to a star system three light-years away.

"You found out."

"You thought I wouldn't find out? You should've told me. I should've heard this from you."

Samson sighed. "I *just* informed Ashworth that I was on board for the second colony mission. I'm off-world a lot these days. Our paths don't exactly cross that often."

"What about the Krake?" Connor asked.

"What about them?"

"I need you for this fight."

Samson shook his head. "You think you do."

"I know I need you for this fight. Why didn't you talk to me about it?"

"Because I knew you'd react like this. You'd take it personally. I have helped you with the Krake. I trained these soldiers. They're good. They'll get the job done."

Connor clenched his teeth a little. "I just don't understand why you'd want to go. Why would you volunteer to start up another colony with a fraction of the resources?"

Connor had provided a lot of input into establishing the second colony. It was one of the compromises he'd worked out with Mullins.

Samson's gaze became hard. "At least this is something I'm choosing."

"You're choosing," Connor repeated. "You chose to rejoin the CDF. You chose to help me fight the Krake."

"But I didn't choose to be *here*. None of us did," Samson said.

Connor rolled his eyes. "I thought we were past that. It happened. We're here, and we can't do anything about it."

"No, *you* moved past it. I never will. You made a home here.

You started a family here, and I respect that. I can't do it. I just can't," Samson said.

Samson had left the colony before. He'd chosen to roam New Earth by himself for years. When Connor finally caught up with him, he'd been living out in the wilds alone. He wore ryklar skins. The man was a born fighter. It wasn't something that could be trained, only molded. Samson was someone he trusted to fight at his back. Despite their differences . . . Connor let the thought go.

"You still blame me. That's it, isn't it? You still blame me for what happened," Connor said.

Samson shook his head. "No, not anymore."

"Then why are you leaving?"

"Those people need protection too. No one knows what'll happen there. This is how I move forward. This is what you encouraged me to do," Samson said.

"Yeah, I did, but I thought you would stay here."

Samson regarded him for a few moments. "You're not responsible for me anymore, sir."

"I know that," Connor said. "I do know that."

"The Ghosts are gone, Connor. They've either died, or they've moved on and made lives for themselves. I was the last, and I want to do this. I *need* to do this."

Connor felt his throat thicken just a little bit. It was an old guilt he carried inside him. It had been his mission failure that put the Ghosts on the *Ark*. It was either that or languish away in some military prison. The Ghost Platoon was small and highly specialized. They were brothers, all of them—family. And most of them were gone. Samson was right. He still felt responsible for them.

"I heard you're going to be a father again," Samson said.

Connor nodded. "A boy."

"Congratulations. I mean that. I really do."

"You can do it too. You don't have to go light-years away to have a fresh start," Connor said.

"I don't think I can. At least with the second colony, it's something I'm choosing. Maybe then I can really move on. I'm sorry you found out the way you did. I didn't think the news would travel that fast. And . . ."

Connor leaned back against one of the walls. "You're one of the best men I've ever worked with. I don't like it, but I respect your decision."

"Thank you. That means a lot to me."

The *Ark II* was a few months away from embarking upon its journey.

"You could come with me. I could always use a second-in-command," Samson said and grinned. "I'm just playing."

Connor chuckled a little. He tried to think of whom he could get to replace Samson, but his mind came up blank, as if his brain refused to acknowledge what was going to happen.

"How long have you been thinking about this?" Connor asked.

"It's been a while," Samson said. "Honestly, Saul Ashworth sought me out almost a year ago. He wanted to know my thoughts about what they could do to help protect the new colony. There'll be equipment that's going to be built by the auto factories along the way, but we'll be resource-constrained for a long time."

"At least with subspace communications, you won't be completely cut off from us here," Connor said.

Subspace communications would allow them to communicate without any lag at all. Should the worst happen and they lose the colony on New Earth, the second colony would know. It wouldn't be like what had happened on Old Earth where they had to wonder. Samson seemed to guess Connor's thoughts, and they both shared a grim moment of acknowledgment. There wasn't much else either of them could do.

"Well, I've still got you for another mission, right?" Connor said.

"Of course. One more mission," Samson replied.

12

Connor walked out of the conference room, and Samson followed.

"Hey, kid," Samson said by way of greeting Dash.

"Major Samson," Dash acknowledged.

"You still know your way around a rifle?" Samson asked.

"I practice as often as I can," Dash replied.

Samson looked at Connor. "I guess he won't shoot us accidentally."

Dash grinned. "No, unless you shoot me first."

Samson smiled broadly. "Not the same kid I met a few years ago," he said to Connor.

"None of us are the same," Connor replied.

"You got that right."

They left and headed toward the main operations center for the base.

"You promoted Lars?" Connor asked.

Samson nodded. "The kid could lead that platoon. Hell, he

could lead a few platoons if there weren't so many restrictions where Special Infantry Division is concerned."

"Do you call everyone younger than you a kid?" Dash asked.

Samson considered this for a few moments and nodded. "Yeah, pretty much." He gestured around at the CDF base personnel. "They're all kids."

Dash looked around. "What do you call people who are under eighteen?"

Samson leveled a look at him, his face deadpan. "Babies."

Connor chuckled. Old memories bubbled into his mind—memories of Kasey, Wil, and Samson talking about how a majority of the colony was primarily made up of younger people. They were easier to train, easier to turn into soldiers, but Connor had to admit that the older colonists did well too.

"There's nothing worse than man-babies," Connor said.

"What about women? Do you call them woman-babies?" Dash asked, clearly intrigued.

Connor shared a glance with Samson and shook his head. "No, they're just women."

Dash frowned.

"Babies. Kids. Anyone who has a tantrum because they don't get their way can't be anything else," Samson said.

"It doesn't matter which chromosomes they have," Connor said.

Dash smiled and shook his head. "I can't believe this is what you guys talk about."

"What do you think we are? Robots?" Connor asked.

"No, but I just . . ."

"We might be soldiers, but we have layers," Connor said.

"Yeah, we're complex," Samson said and then added, "What do you kids talk about?"

Dash's mouth hung open a little, and he scratched the back of his head. "It depends."

Samson grunted.

"Look, it doesn't matter," Dash said. "Shouldn't we be focusing on something else?"

"The kid has a point." Connor smirked.

Dash laughed. "Oh, God! Enough with the 'kid' thing already!"

Samson arched an eyebrow toward Connor. "I think the kid is getting upset."

Connor grinned, and it felt good to let some of the tension go. "About Lars."

Samson nodded. "I promoted him to sergeant and ordered Lieutenant Miller to make him his second-in-command for 3rd Platoon. Their mission went to hell."

"What happened?" Dash asked.

"They went to a world that was in the middle of some kind of Ovarrow civil war and got caught up in it," Samson replied.

Dash nodded slowly. They all knew how fast a situation could escalate.

"They were being thorough," Connor said.

"The thing about the SID is that they're here under the pretense of having something to prove," Samson said.

"Don't they, though?" Dash said. "They want to rejoin the colony."

"Not all of them," Connor said. "It's not that simple. Some of them do. Others just didn't want to be banished to the island away from everyone else. You're right, though. They do have something to prove. This is how they'll redeem themselves."

"So, you just send them out on reconnaissance missions?"

"There's nothing routine about recon," Connor said.

"I didn't mean to imply that what they're doing has less

value, but they must think that this place is some kind of banishment." Dash gestured toward the ground.

They walked through the doors to the operations center.

"It is," Connor said as they walked down the corridor. "Most of them have had training, and we need that. This is their second chance."

They went inside one of the mission briefing rooms, where members of the diplomatic envoy were speaking with Colonel Ryant, the commanding officer of the base. The officers in the room turned toward Connor and saluted him.

"General Gates, welcome to the alpha site," Colonel Ryant said.

"Thank you, Colonel Ryant," Connor said and looked at the man standing next to him. "Major Kinnear."

"General Gates," Kinnear said.

"Have there been any more communications from the Gesora?" Connor asked as he sat in one of the chairs.

The others took a seat around the table.

"No, sir. After we told them you had agreed to meet with them, they haven't sent any other messages," Colonel Ryant replied.

Franz Holzer cleared his throat. "Is this odd behavior for the Gesora?"

"I think so," Connor said decisively.

"I agree," Ryant said.

"I would have expected that they'd have shared more data beyond the request to meet with me," Connor said. He pursed his lips in thought for a moment. "Did intelligence analysis of their previous interactions indicate anything we should be concerned about?"

"They checked in regularly, and we exchange mission briefings in relation to DOW visits," Ryant replied.

"DOW?" Holzer asked.

"Database of Worlds," Ryant answered.

"Ah, yes. I should have recognized the acronym," Holzer said.

Connor looked across the table at Aliza Winfry. "Does the CIB have anything to add?"

Winfry was an intelligence agent with the CIB, and Connor suspected that she'd been briefed as much as she could be before being tasked with coming here.

Winfry leaned forward and interlaced her fingers in front of her. "The Gesora check-ins occur with regularity, but there isn't any requirement for them to do so."

Connor nodded. "It's a volunteer effort, but I see your point. Without regular check-ins, we don't have an accurate status of our contacts."

"Why not?" Holzer asked.

"Many of them are still coming to grips with the fact that the Krake even exist or can't be trusted," Connor said. "In some cases, the Ovarrow believe that they can't break away from the Krake without losing everything. Each case is complicated, and we categorize them as best we can."

Holzer nodded. "I understand. This is why we attempt to hide the fact that we're not Ovarrow from potential contacts for as long as possible."

"The Gesora know, but Monin must be worried about data security if he won't share what they've found. I can't think of another explanation," Connor said.

There were several head-bobs of agreement from the others in the room.

"General, I must advise you to bring a protection force suitable for the sensitive nature of this mission," Colonel Ryant said.

"Oh, I am," Connor said and looked at Samson. "The 7th Ranger Company will be joining us."

Holzer's eyes widened. "So many soldiers? But these are our allies. Is this show of force necessary?"

Connor simply stared at the diplomat.

"I just thought that perhaps the Gesora were a little more . . . 'Civilized' isn't the right word. Perhaps 'stable' is better," Holzer said.

"The Ovarrow understand a show of force. The Konus drove that point home, and it's a common societal norm that we've observed from the Ovarrow," Connor replied.

"Do you expect to be attacked?" Holzer asked.

"No, but I'd rather have enough soldiers with me to dissuade any opportunists from taking advantage of the situation," Connor said.

Too many times, he'd been caught up in a situation where they'd been unprepared, and each time they'd adapted their tactics so the next engagement would be different.

"I understand. Thank you for answering my questions, General Gates," Holzer said.

"We'll be leaving in the next hour," Connor said.

"I have four troop carrier transports waiting to take you and the 7th to your departure zone, General," Colonel Ryant said.

Connor nodded and then looked at Major Kinnear. "Can you provision Mr. Holzer and his companions with the proper equipment? Also, I've assigned Sergeant Rowan's squad to be their personal protection."

"Yes, sir. I'll see that they've got the full escort provisions and equipment and then get them to the departure zone," Major Kinnear said and looked at Holzer. "If you'll follow me."

Holzer looked at Connor. "What kind of provisions?"

"You'll be wearing a military-grade multipurpose protection suit," Connor said.

Holzer frowned. "We're already wearing MPSs."

"Not like these. The ones you'll be wearing will provide a much more layered protection and will be able to conceal your identities from the Gesora," Connor replied.

Holzer nodded and glanced at Dash. "What about Mr. DeWitt?"

"Mr. DeWitt is field certified for the standard Nexstar combat suit loadout," Connor said.

"Right this way," Major Kinnear said and gestured toward the door.

Holzer and Gellner followed Kinnear. Aliza Winfry looked at Dash for a moment and then at Connor before following the others.

Ryant looked at Connor. "So, Governor Mullins insisted on sending diplomats. Do they know what they're in for?"

Connor tilted his head to the side once. "They're about to find out."

"Is there something else you need from me?" Ryant asked.

"Agent Winfry raised a good point about the irregularities of some of the check-ins without contacts," Connor said.

"We can begin a sweep of the known contacts. Do you want us to just have a peek under the covers, or would you like us to initiate contact?" Ryant asked.

Connor thought about it for a few moments. "How long would it take if we just wanted to have a look?"

Ryant pressed his lips together in thought. "At least seventy-two hours to get to most of them. That's using SRDs and giving them time to make a sweep of the area."

The coordination and monitoring of so many stealth recon drones would require several teams of analysts. Then there were the gateway teams that were in charge of deployment and retrieval.

"Do it. This is a high priority. Log the mission plan with COMCENT," Connor said. "And escalate our state of readiness to orange."

Orange readiness was the equivalent to Condition Two on a CDF warship. Threat probable but not present.

"Understood, General," Ryant said.

They left the meeting room, and Connor looked at Samson.

"The 7th is already assembling. They'll have a kit ready for both of you by the time we get to the hangar," Samson said.

Samson wasn't one to waste a lot of time. Regardless of what Samson thought, Connor knew it was going to be difficult to replace him. There were capable soldiers he could put in command, but there was very little Connor could do to replace all the years of experience that Samson had.

Connor looked at Dash. "Stick close by from here on out."

Dash glanced around, checking to see if anyone could overhear them. "Do you think the Krake are going to attack?" he asked and then frowned. "More than you normally do, I mean."

"I don't know if an attack is imminent, but I'd rather we be as prepared as possible," Connor said.

Dash nodded, his expression serious. This wasn't his first time on a mission like this, but Connor wanted him to stay close.

"If you see anything that you think I should know about, then point it out. I'd rather know about it from you," Connor said.

"I will," Dash replied.

Connor had brought Dash along because the kid was smart. He paid attention to the details and could act accordingly.

Samson looked at Dash. "You're swimming with the big boys now, kid. Don't drown."

"I'll try and keep up."

Connor was already wearing an MPS. It was part of his uniform and his clothing. Even though he would be operating a combat suit, he knew the benefits of additional protection. Doubling up had quite literally saved his life on previous occasions.

They grabbed a quick bite to eat in the mess hall on the way to the assembly area. Connor didn't know when they'd have a chance to eat after they met with the Gesora. He wasn't hungry, but that didn't mean anything. He wolfed down a quick sandwich, as did Dash and Samson.

Then they headed over to the assembly area. About twenty minutes later, both Connor and Dash were outfitted with a standard kit Nexstar combat suit. AR-74s were collapsed and attached to the side panels of the suits. Then they headed out to the hangar bay where CDF troop carriers waited. The 7th Ranger Company was in the process of boarding the troop carriers. Connor was directed to one of the ships, and he walked up the loading ramp. It took him a few minutes to get used to wearing the combat suit again. It wasn't something he used every day, but he was more than proficient at squeezing every ounce of functionality from the Nexstar combat suit.

Connor saw Dash stumble several times, but after a few minutes he, too, was moving around in the combat suit without any issues.

The diplomatic envoy was already aboard, wearing their heavy-duty MPSs. Their faces were covered with helmets to keep their identities from the Gesora.

Samson left them to go brief his officers. It was times like these that reminded Connor that while he commanded the CDF, he didn't have one specific division or company of soldiers that were his to command. It'd taken him a while to get used to it.

Over the years, the more they expanded the CDF, the more he had to keep himself apart. While building the CDF, he'd tried to think of what the NA Alliance generals would have done in his situation.

Connor had long ago adapted to being in charge of the CDF. It was only in recent times that he'd had to share running the CDF with somebody else. Nathan was his superior, at least for now. That was a much easier transition than not having a specific unit. He could be part of Samson's mission briefing to the 7th but decided against it. Samson knew what he was doing, and Connor didn't need to be there. Life was certainly much simpler when he'd had his own unit to command. Sometimes he missed the personal side of sharing a mission.

The four troop carriers sealed the loading ramps and headed to their designated departure zone. The troop carriers were designed for armored protection but could also move soldiers quickly to where they needed to be. It didn't take them long to reach their departure zone, where an arch gateway was already active with the coordinates of the Gesora home world.

The conversations died down to a murmur as they made their final approach to the arch gateway. The pilot announced their departure with a much less colorful and humorous countdown. They flew through the gateway, and the pilot requested that Connor and Samson come to the cockpit.

Connor stood up and headed to the front of the aircraft. Samson and Dash joined him. On the main holoscreen, a large expanse of the jungle showed long stretches of clouds that made for a foggy view of their immediate area. Connor had not returned to the Gesora home world in a long time, but he remembered the heat. He remembered the jungle.

"General," Lieutenant Butcher said, "the arch gateway is gone. It should have been right there."

Connor peered at the video feed on the main holoscreen. "Not just the arch, but the entire facility is gone."

A comlink registered on the main holoscreen. Lieutenant Butcher identified himself.

"CDF troop carrier, this is Redian, Warlord's First of the Gesora. Please confirm that you have General Gates with you."

Connor sent his credentials through the comlink channel. "Redian, I'm Connor Gates. Where is Warlord Monin, and where is your gateway?"

"General Gates, thank you for confirming your identity," Redian said. "I will take you to Warlord Monin. We had to move our arch gateway. Warlord Monin will explain when you arrive. I'm sending coordinates to you now. Please do not deviate from them."

Connor looked at the coordinates, and Lieutenant Butcher put them into the troop carrier's navigation computer.

"They moved it over fifteen hundred kilometers away, General."

"Why would they move it that far?" Dash asked.

"Lieutenant, do a scan of the area. Are there any Krake signals detected?" Connor asked.

Lieutenant Butcher ran the scan and then shook his head. "Negative. No Krake signals detected, General."

"Very well, set a course and give Redian our ETA."

"Yes, sir," Lieutenant Butcher said.

Connor stepped out of the cockpit and looked at Samson. "What do you think?"

"You know me. I don't like surprises. We should keep our eyes open, sir," Samson said.

"I still don't understand why they'd move the gateway. I'm surprised they *could* even move it," Dash said.

"The only reason I can think of is that there might've been a credible threat that required the move," Connor said. "After we helped take control of the gateway from the Krake here, they were moving it to the capital but had decided against it. It appears that they changed their minds."

"Why wouldn't they just tell us that?" Dash said, and his eyebrows raised a little. "Sorry. That's gotta be an obvious question."

"It doesn't mean it's not a pertinent one," Connor said. "Regardless, I don't think they can attack us. But something's definitely off about all this."

He stuck his head back into the cockpit. "Is a gateway back to the alpha site still open?"

"Gateway is still active, General," Lieutenant Butcher said.

"Good. Send an update back to base to let them know our itinerary has changed," Connor said.

He watched as Lieutenant Butcher attempted to send the information back to base, but the gateway had closed. Their check interval must've expired.

"All right, leave a comms drone instead. They'll open another in about six hours," Connor said.

"Yes, General," Lieutenant Butcher said.

Connor left the cockpit.

"Maybe it would be better if they kept the gateways open for a little bit longer," Dash said.

"I was thinking the same thing."

"Connor, I don't like this. I don't have your experience, but I feel like we're being lured away from our only egress point," Dash said.

Connor didn't even think of denying it. Dash had proved that he was capable of handling the pressure. "I don't like it either. And you might be right. Keep an eye out. It might make all the difference."

13

THE FOUR CDF troop carriers flew over the jungles of the Gesora home world—a rainforest planet the likes of which few humans had ever seen. They soared over dark peaks that poked above the low-lying clouds like leviathans waiting in the deep gray of the unknown.

Connor had ordered Butcher to fly them at 60 percent best speed. He wanted to take his time so they could get some insight into the situation awaiting them, keeping some of their capabilities in reserve just in case the Krake had an infiltration force that the Gesora weren't aware of.

Even though the coordinates provided by Redian did lead them to the capital of the Gesora, they arrived at an expanded part of the city they'd never seen before.

They'd left the mountain region where their scanners detected towers and outposts hidden in the jungle.

Holzer stood next to Connor, watching the holoscreen. "How many cities are on the planet?" Holzer asked.

The misty morning began to evaporate as the sun climbed above the horizon. The buildings of the city were multiple levels of large rounded platforms amid a sea of tall ebony-colored spires that reflected a dull lavender gleam.

"We don't know. According to the Gesora, there are hundreds of cities on this continent," Connor replied.

"What about the other continents? Are there Ovarrow there as well?" Holzer asked.

"There are, but none that we've had any interaction with."

"The Krake focused their efforts here," Dash said. "According to the Gesora, there are other Ovarrow on the planet, but they're primitive. Tribal in nature."

Connor nodded and looked at Holzer. "The Krake seem to focus their efforts on the more advanced civilizations."

Holzer frowned in thought. "They don't uplift the lesser societies?"

"Technologically, they're all lesser. We haven't encountered any Ovarrow civilization that's anywhere near the same level of technology as the Krake. I don't know if that's a coincidence or deliberate," Connor said.

"Hmmm," Holzer said and pursed his lips. "Doesn't make sense to me. One of the main drivers for the Krake is to perfect their predictive technology. What better test for that than a competitive species on similar ground? Technologically speaking, that is."

Dash looked pensive. Gellner joined them, and Samson's heavily thudding footfalls sounded as he walked over to them.

"They might have already fought that war," Connor said.

Holzer glanced at the others to see what they thought.

Samson nodded.

"They already fought that war and survived. Maybe multiple times," Connor said.

"Don't you mean won? Wouldn't the Krake have won the war?" Gellner asked.

Connor shook his head. "I meant what I said. We survive a war. We achieve objectives. Just saying that a war was won doesn't give credence to the cost. See the difference?"

Gellner swallowed, his expression somber, and nodded.

"If they already survived a war with the Ovarrow, then why would they do this?" Holzer asked. He looked at the holoscreen while gesturing toward the arch gateway in the distance.

Connor shrugged. "Maybe they almost lost, and this is their way to understand their enemy."

Holzer sighed and shook his head. "This is unbelievable."

"I think there's more to it than the Krake simply wanting to understand the Ovarrow," Dash said.

"I don't doubt it," Connor replied.

"What are the other reasons, then?" Holzer asked.

Samson cleared his throat. "They enjoy it," he said. Both Holzer's and Gellner's eyebrows raised. "Bullies enjoy taunting their targets. You can wrap as much speculation around it as you want. I think they enjoy it. It's a power trip for them."

Holzer looked at Connor.

Connor tilted his head to the side. "That's probably part of it." Sometimes his speculation about the Krake disturbed other people. He drew from a lifetime of experience, hunting down people seeking power. He'd often return to their primal motivations for insight into how to find them and stop them. Thus far, he'd been unsuccessful with the Krake.

"Think about it," Connor said. "Pursuit of their research is only a single layer. I think there are deeper layers to Krake behavior. They want to punish the Ovarrow, in addition to testing out their crazy research experiments."

He recalled his encounter with the Krake sector chief where

they'd staged war games. It was an endless battle cycle where
Ovarrow soldiers fought to reach an arch gateway. They fought
until they died. If they gave up, the Krake killed them. The entire
grotesque, brutal effort was led by a sector chief. Connor had
spoken to him. He'd fought the Krake. He'd looked into the eyes
of the enemy and come away with valuable insight. For all the
Krake's rigid, logical reasoning to justify their actions, they
couldn't separate themselves from their primal instincts. Connor
never used to think in those terms, but he'd had to adapt. He was
assembling the pieces of a puzzle, and he had to complete it
before the Krake found New Earth.

"You think the reason the Krake are doing this is to satiate
some twisted form of vengeance?" Holzer asked.

Even Dash regarded him with a thoughtful frown. Samson
nodded.

"It's part of it," Connor replied.

"What else do you think it could be?" Holzer asked.

Connor snorted bitterly. "If I knew that, I'd have found the
Krake home world already."

Holzer nodded. "You've given me a lot to think about, but
how do you think the Gesora fit into all this?"

"Holzer, there isn't a cut-and-dried way to think about this.
On the one hand, you could say the Ovarrow are victims. They
were manipulated by the Krake, but that doesn't explain
everything. If you're searching for justice, you're not going to find
it. Yes, the Ovarrow were manipulated, but they could have
chosen differently. The Krake don't take away their ability to
choose, so the Ovarrow are still responsible for their own actions,
including not just the Gesora but all the Ovarrow we've
encountered, even on New Earth. The Mekaal recognize this.
The Konus believe it gives them the right to dominate smaller

groups of Ovarrow. All of them are concerned with survival as they struggle with an enemy they can hardly understand. Then you have us. Humanity. We're throwing all the equations the Krake use out the window. We're rocking the boat. It's only a matter of time before they react."

Holzer's mouth hung open a little. His eyes flitted back and forth like a computer that was processing data. "You're goading them. The Krake. You're trying to get them to react. You're using the Ovarrow."

Connor regarded the diplomat for a moment. "Yes."

Holzer licked his lips. "But is that smart? Aren't you worried that . . . well, that you'll . . ."

"Sooner or later, we have to pick a side. Not many people really understand that," Connor said. "It might make you feel better to think that we're enlightening the Ovarrow to what the Krake have been doing. We *are* doing that, but we have our own reasons too. The Gesora aren't ignorant of this fact and neither are the others. Not really. They could go on with their lives, not doing anything about the Krake, but they don't."

"My God," Holzer said, swallowing hard. "I didn't realize it. I never really understood . . ." He looked away from Connor.

"Most people don't understand. They think they do, but they really don't," Samson said.

Holzer exhaled deeply, blowing out a long breath. Gellner looked as if he didn't know what to think.

"How are you so calm about it?" Holzer asked, then shook his head. "Stupid question."

"Believe it or not, it takes a lot for me to leave my family behind. And not just me, but everyone here and everyone back on base," Connor replied.

"What can I do to help?" Holzer asked.

"Just do your job. You're here to communicate with the Gesora and hopefully gain some insight into them."

Holzer considered this for a few moments and nodded. "You've given me a lot to think about. I . . . I might have misjudged you."

An alert chimed from the holoscreen. Butcher was letting them know they were making their final approach to the Gesora capital city.

Holzer and Gellner returned to their seats while Connor studied the video feed on the holoscreen. Mist rose off the dark buildings of the Gesora city, sprawled amid the jungles on an expanse of cleared land. Streams of sunlight cast long shadows in the midmorning sky. The foothills in the distance almost blended into the thick clouds on the horizon. Amid the dark buildings were mirrored windows that reflected the sunlight, which helped dissipate the fog. Ovarrow walked the streets below and traveled the ramps that wound around the other buildings. Walkways connected a group of tall spires, and Connor could see the Ovarrow crossing between them. Their vehicles, which utilized a hybrid of combustion and electric motors, sped along the main thoroughfare.

The CDF troop carriers skirted along the edges of the city as they headed to their designated landing area. A major railway was located nearby.

"Looks like they've given us quite a welcome party," Dash said.

Several hundred Ovarrow soldiers stood in formation near the landing pads. Their uniforms sported deep greens and golds, with metallic plates to protect their chests and backs. They carried long-shafted energy weapons that flared both at the top and the bottom, doubling as a melee weapon at close range. They fired plasma bolts at relatively short range, which were ineffective at a distance beyond a hundred meters.

The troop carriers landed, and the 7th Ranger Company exited their ships, followed by Connor and the others. A detachment of Ovarrow soldiers approached them. Connor didn't see Monin among them.

The Ovarrow of this world retained the pebble-like skin similar to that of a reptile. They had protrusions that stemmed from their shoulders, elbows, and parts of their chins. Their skin ranged in colors from pale gray to dark green. They had long arms and wide hands with four long fingers. Thick brow lines on both sides of their angular heads went all the way back to the base of their craniums. Their nostrils were at the same level as their jade-colored eyes. They were lean and strong but had a bit of a stoop that made their heads bob when they walked.

One of the Ovarrow looked at Connor and walked over to him. "General Gates, I am called Redian. I am the Warlord's First."

"Redian," Connor acknowledged, and introduced the diplomatic envoy and Dash.

"My orders are to escort you and your soldiers to the meeting area where Warlord Monin is waiting," Redian said and gestured toward the elevated train.

Connor's eyes flicked toward the train and then back at Redian. "I expected to meet with Warlord Monin here at your base of operations."

"That was the plan, but Warlord Monin is meeting with governors and visiting leaders from our neighboring districts. Therefore, we are to bring your entire detachment of soldiers there," Redian said.

"I understand," Connor said, and Redian gestured for them

to follow. "One more thing. I will be leaving some of our soldiers with our ships."

"Of course," Redian said.

Connor looked at Samson.

"On it, General," Samson said.

Three squads of soldiers were designated to stay behind with the troop carrier. They'd provide protection and hopefully a bit of a deterrence in case the Gesora wanted to poke around at their ships.

Holzer walked next to Connor. He leaned over and said, "Is this what you expected?"

Connor gave a slight shake of his head. Holzer nodded.

The 7th Ranger Company took up almost three of the large train cars. There were no seats inside them, but there were handholds. The maglev train began to silently move down its track, gaining momentum. The Ovarrow rode in separate train cars.

Dash looked out the windows as the cityscape sped by. The train did not stop at any of the stations on the way.

"They're not taking us to the arch," Dash said.

"Looks like they've moved it again," Connor said.

"Where was it before?"

"It used to be located at a military base outside the city, but they moved it closer to the city for some reason."

As they neared their destination, Samson cleared his throat. "No issues at the troop carriers. Looks like the Gesora are leaving our guys alone."

"Good," Connor said.

"I can't believe they've allowed heavily armed soldiers into their city," Holzer said.

Connor agreed. Armed as they were, he would never green-light anyone's visiting military access to any colonial city. Only a small protection force would have been acceptable to him.

"There are millions of them and fewer than a hundred and fifty of us, but I see your point. I can only assume it's because we helped them against the Krake," Connor said.

CDF weapons were superior to anything the Ovarrow had in their arsenal, but there were limits. He hadn't come here to start a fight.

"Make sure our guys stay calm," Connor said.

"I'll pass the word, General," Samson said.

The train brought them to an outer section of the city several kilometers away from the troop carriers. Connor had long since realized that he habitually kept track of certain types of information after a lifetime in the military. In this circumstance, he was noticing that the Gesora city could fit Sierra within its borders several times over. However, it was still smaller than the sprawling metropolises that were common on Old Earth. It had been a while since Connor had been to a sizable city that was still lived in. New Earth was home to the skeletal remains of Ovarrow cities that had long since been destroyed or abandoned, which was what the colony faced if the Krake found New Earth.

The tracks began descending to an open area surrounded by tall spires amid a backdrop of Ovarrow architecture that was at once both familiar and exotic. Connor glanced at the others and noticed the same silent reverie on their faces.

They'd disclosed their identity to the Gesora. Allowing them to know that the CDF wasn't just another Ovarrow military made the Gesora more open to listening to what they had to say about the Krake. But even before revealing themselves, Monin had made no secret about his suspicions where the CDF were concerned. The warlord had known there was something different about CDF soldiers—something foreign that they hadn't encountered before. The Gesora were among only a few groups of allies who knew that the CDF were humans. It had been a calculated risk, but eventually the Colonial Security Council had authorized Connor to share their identity with the Gesora. Of all the Ovarrow allies in multiple universes, the Gesora had proved to be reliable and cautious in their off-world operations. This hadn't been the case for others.

The train came to a stop, and as the metallic doors opened, the CDF soldiers exited and took note of their surroundings. Redian led them toward a central facility. Hundreds of Ovarrow soldiers stood in formation along both sides of the path to the buildings, quietly regarding the CDF soldiers as they passed.

Connor walked at the front, keeping pace with Redian. Samson and Dash were at his side. Holzer, Gellner, and Winfry followed behind them, along with their personal protection squad of CDF soldiers. Considering how many people and Ovarrow were in close proximity to each other, it was very quiet. The Gesora had seen CDF soldiers in action the year before when they'd assisted in ousting the Krake infiltrators, along with Krake sympathizers. Warlord Monin and the current leadership had consolidated power in order to provide stability to their society.

They reached the outside of the central building that was the base for a tall spire.

Redian came to a stop. "General Gates, I'll need you to select a small group to bring inside to meet with Warlord Monin."

Connor looked at Samson. "Pick a squad to join us."

Samson picked the nearest squad of soldiers led by Sergeant Mason. They positioned themselves next to Sergeant Rowan's squad and followed Connor and the others into the building.

They walked through the entrance, where a series of tall arches lined the path they were to follow. Sunlight shone through the large windows between the arches, giving them a clear view of the outside and the tall, dark spire above them. They entered a central atrium and walked down a ramp to a lower level.

The lower atrium had several offshoots to different areas where Ovarrow were gathered. There were no actual doorways that blocked the entrance to these rooms, but the walled pathway did cut off the most direct view.

"Those walls can move," Dash said.

Connor looked at him.

"I've seen a similar layout like this on New Earth," Dash explained. "It took us a while to understand how it must have worked. It's part of the older architecture, well away from where our cities are located."

Redian regarded Dash for a moment and then gestured toward the interior of one of the open rooms.

"Lead the way," Connor said.

Redian walked toward the entryway and led them inside. Connor heard several Ovarrow speaking and recognized the guttural cadence that he associated with Monin. However, the Krake translators used a monotone to translate the Ovarrow language.

There was a circular room that reminded Connor of an open theater. There were also several speaker podiums interspersed with multiple mesh screens that the Ovarrow used for displaying information.

Warlord Monin wore a military uniform of dark green decorated in gold plating at the shoulders and forearms.

"As you can see, our guests have arrived to validate our findings. Please welcome General Connor Gates of the Colonial Defense Force," Monin said.

Several groups of Ovarrow were separated in cordoned-off areas. Ovarrow greetings would never be what Connor would consider friendly, and he met their silent regard for him in a similar manner. The Ovarrow were highly sensitive to mannerisms that could be construed as weakness, which meant that normal human interaction intending to set someone at ease wouldn't work here.

Connor looked at Monin. "Warlord Monin, I've come as you requested. However, there wasn't much information in your invitation."

Connor saw Holzer shift his feet, about to speak. Dash gestured for him not to.

"I apologize for the lack of information," Monin said and then looked at the others. "There will be time for introductions after. We've made a number of discoveries, and it wasn't safe to send the information to you through our established communication methods."

"What did you find?" Connor asked.

"The Krake have launched multiple military campaigns against the contacts we've made—worlds we've been in contact with for almost a year," Monin said.

"Military campaigns?" Connor said. "What are the Krake doing, exactly?"

"I have reconnaissance videos from our off-world missions. Some worlds show signs of the bombardment you've described for us. In other worlds, there are only smoking ruins of where cities have fallen. Millions of Ovarrow have died. In some cases, there are battles being fought among the Ovarrow, with each side trying to wipe out the other. It's like they've been overruled by an unquenchable bloodlust. They attacked our delegation."

The mesh screens became active, showing various recordings of what their off-world teams had witnessed. The large mesh screens displayed many recordings, each a different form of devastation. Some of the recordings showed Ovarrow lying dead, their faces frozen in agony while blood oozed out of their mouths and ears.

"The Krake released a sickness for which there is no cure. Entire teams of soldiers were lost because they wouldn't return home for fear of spreading the disease," Monin said.

Samson stepped forward and pointed at several of the recordings. "Are those the worlds where Ovarrow were slaughtering each other?"

Monin peered at the recordings. "Yes, those are. They refused to communicate with us. They lost their ability to reason and fought like enraged beasts."

Samson turned to Connor. "This is like what the SID encountered a couple of days ago. Look at the buildings. See the painted symbols?"

Connor looked. The symbols appeared to be slogans, but they didn't make much sense to him, even with the translators. Then he looked at the other recordings. The slogans were different, but there were similarities in their execution, from the colors used to the way the Ovarrow symbols were drawn. "Propaganda," he said.

Samson nodded.

"What do you mean by propaganda? I don't see it," Holzer said.

"It's on multiple screens. Do you see it?" Connor said.

"None of it is the same," Holzer replied.

"The messages are different, but how they're delivered is the same. They're meant to elicit an emotional response—anger, frustration, anxiety," Connor said.

Human history was filled with the effective use of propaganda to entice people toward a belief.

"Are you saying the Krake made them destroy themselves through sensationalism?" Holzer asked.

"We've seen evidence that the Krake maliciously use misinformation to test Ovarrow behavior," Connor said.

"I realize that, but on this scale? And not just on one world. There are multiple worlds that . . ." Holzer went silent.

"We've experienced this method of mind warfare here among the Gesora. It was the Krake attempting to divide us," Monin said.

Connor looked at all the recordings on the large mesh screens. Monin activated several more. Each showed a subset of recordings, but the method of destruction was different.

Connor walked toward them and studied the videos. Samson and Dash came to his side. "These are different."

"They're all dead," Dash said quietly.

Dash had witnessed a lot of violence during his young life, but while Connor could compartmentalize what he was seeing, Dash had to first acknowledge the death toll. It wasn't that Connor didn't see death in the same way, but his instincts were to evaluate what he saw with as little emotion as possible. This caused some people to believe that Connor didn't care enough, that he was some kind of robot who was devoid of empathy or emotion, but it was quite the opposite. In the deepest parts of him, his worst nightmares waited. They were his battleground, but he focused on understanding and problem-solving because that was the best way to protect his home.

"The Krake are cleaning house," Samson said.

Holzer hastened over to them. "What did you say?" he asked. Samson repeated himself.

Holzer's eyes went wide and he looked at Connor.

"The Krake must have realized that we were using the gateways to fight them," Connor said, then turned to Monin. "You've been in contact with all of these worlds?"

"That is incorrect. These recordings are several months old

and are from worlds we've never been to. We began finding more and more of them. Then we decided to revisit other worlds, contacts we've made. The devastation we found, and others have found, is beyond words."

Connor swallowed hard, his gaze taking in all the recorded desolation. His mind jumped to a realization he didn't want to come to, but the truth couldn't wait. The Gesora must have suspected what this meant.

"We'd like you to validate our findings," Monin said.

Connor exhaled a long breath. "We need to establish a pattern of activity across time. We need to know when the Krake began their attacks."

"You don't think it's random?" Holzer asked.

Connor shook his head. "The Krake's actions are never random. They can't be. This is deliberate."

"They're targeting our allies," Monin said.

"No, it's worse than that. They're targeting everything. Every world they've been to is being purged," Connor explained.

"Holy shit," Samson said. "Why scrap their operations now? What changed?"

"You wanted a response from the Krake. I think you've got it," Holzer said.

"Maybe," Connor replied. "But there's got to be more to it. Look at it. This is their entire operation on every world they've been to, but the attack isn't the same. There aren't any Krake soldiers. How are they doing it?"

There were a few moments of silence.

"Warlord Monin," Dash said, "are the recordings' dates and times from when they were logged by your off-world teams?"

"This is accurate," Monin said.

Dash took a few steps away from the others and opened his

personal holoscreen to capture the information shown on the Ovarrow screens.

"Is there a problem?" Monin asked.

Dash didn't reply. His hands were a blur of gestures while he navigated the holo-interface.

"Just give him a moment," Connor said, watching what Dash was doing.

Dash stopped and then turned toward Connor. "The Krake are tracking gateway uses."

Connor frowned, not understanding how this could be possible, but he wanted to believe. "Show me what you've got."

"Here is a histogram that shows the timing from when the Gesora first visited a world to when they returned" Dash said. "Some of them were recently visited, as in within the past few months, but when the Gesora returned, the Krake had already been there. I tagged them. It's not concise, but there *is* a pattern."

Connor peered at the data.

"That shouldn't be possible," Samson said.

"We don't know what's possible about the gateways," Connor replied.

"There's too much variance in the data. You're making an assumption," Holzer said.

"I must agree with your companion," Monin said.

"It's not exact, but each contact you make through the gateway results in those Ovarrow making other contacts. We spread information about the Krake and get information in return," Dash said.

At last, Connor understood. "It's spreading. Contact between worlds spreads."

Monin looked up at the mesh screens and then turned his gaze downward. "We must fight this. The Krake could attack us at any moment."

An Ovarrow ran into the chamber and rushed toward them. He handed a message to Monin.

The warlord turned toward Connor. "We've just received information that one of our new allies has knowledge of the Krake core worlds."

Connor frowned in thought. Core worlds? "Do you mean their home world?"

"Yes, but according to this, there might be more than one of them," Monin replied.

14

CONNOR LOOKED at Samson for a moment before turning back to Monin. "How many worlds do the Krake have? Did they give you their locations?"

"According to this report, there are two core worlds where the Krake have a significant presence. They didn't share the locations, but they did open an invitation for us to meet with them," Monin replied.

"Who are they?" Connor asked.

"They call themselves the Bhatdin."

"How long have you been in contact with them? Can they be trusted?"

"We've never met with them. This intelligence has come through another group, an intermediary," Monin said.

"That's a thin lead," Samson said.

"It's one we can't ignore." Connor turned his attention to Monin. "Can we meet with them?"

"Yes, of course. But I thought you had already made contact with them. Their message refers to a mutual ally," Monin said.

Connor looked at Dash. "Do we have any records of the Bhatdin?"

"Checking," Dash replied.

Samson took a few steps away and began speaking to someone on the comlink.

Connor looked at Monin and the other Gesora leadership. "If the Krake are attacking Ovarrow worlds, you need to prepare. What's your state of readiness?"

"We maintain a military presence in all the provinces, but it is impossible to deploy them to every city," Monin said.

"But you have a significant military presence here," Connor said and gestured toward a grouping of the video recordings on the mesh screens nearby. "This looks to me like an attack force came to these places."

Several of the Ovarrow leaders spoke at once, and the translator was unable to decipher them all. Connor was able to understand only snippets of their conversations.

Samson walked over to Connor. "There's some kind of disturbance near the troop carriers."

"What kind of disturbance?"

"Butcher isn't sure. He just said there are a lot of creatures coming out of the jungles and entering the city," Samson said and paused for a moment, listening to his comlink. "He said the Gesora . . . Something's going on, sir."

Several bright flashes streaked overhead. Connor looked up, but whatever it had been was gone. The open skylights showed a clear day.

"Tell Butcher and the other pilots I want them to take off," Connor said. "I want one of them to go to the lower atmosphere and see if they can detect any Krake ships. The others I want to make a sweep over the city to look for anything out of the ordinary."

"Yes, sir," Samson said and took a few steps away to speak with his men.

Connor saw that Monin was in deep conversation with the Gesora leadership. "Warlord Monin," he said.

Monin stopped speaking and looked at Connor.

"We've received reports from the landing field of increased animal activity. Large creatures coming from the nearby jungles," Connor said.

Several more flashes lit up the skylights overhead, drawing their attention.

"What is that?" Holzer asked.

Connor took a few steps toward the middle of the chamber to get a better look. He saw a bright light dart into view and then slam into the central spire above them. It burst out the other side, changed course, and flew back into the building.

"It's a Krake attack drone. We're under attack!"

There was a brief but intense buildup of silence as more attack drones flew overhead.

"We have to get out of here," Connor said and gestured for Holzer and the others to head to the exit.

Warlord Monin began shouting orders, and the Gesora leadership also started heading toward another exit. The Gesora used a specialized version of comlink that had been given to them by the CDF. It replaced the bulky transmitters they had been using to communicate with. Monin was using one now, as were several of his senior officers, calling for troop deployments in the city.

They left the room and ascended to the floor above to find Ovarrow scrambling to exit the building. Dash stayed by Connor's side. Sergeant Rowan and his squad kept Holzer and the others together as they followed. As they neared the exit, Connor could hear the sounds of weapons being fired. They emerged from the building and saw that the 7th Ranger Company had gathered along a mobile barrier that had just been erected. In the middle of the vast courtyard, there was a slight shimmer in the air, indicating that a gateway was opening. For a moment it appeared as if it was just a gathering mist in the area, but then it coalesced.

Several more Krake attack drones flew overhead as Connor watched. There were only a dozen of them in the sky, but they were striking buildings—bursting through the upper levels and working their way down. Ovarrow tried to flee out of them, but the Krake attack drones relentlessly pursued them. The drones burned like tiny stars and could melt through the battle-steel armor of CDF warships. The buildings in the Ovarrow city didn't stand a chance.

Connor opened a comlink to Lieutenant Lafferty, who commanded the 3rd Platoon. "Lieutenant, I need you to have one of your squads target the Krake attack drones. The attack drones can be broken apart by high-density ammunition, but check your fire because you'll use up more ammunition that way."

"Yes, General Gates," Lafferty replied. "Dixon—"

Connor cut the comlink.

Across the courtyard, just beyond the gateway, large predators the size of a berwolf burst through at a run. The thickly muscular quadrupeds galloped on all fours. Their pinkish-gray armored plating was akin to a crustacean or large shellfish, and they moved with an agility and speed that Connor had only seen with the use of a CDF combat suit. They had long, thick tails with an armored, wedged-shaped tip. Their feet spread out wide, grasping like an eagle's talons. They scrambled in every direction—some headed away from them, while dozens came through the gateway right toward them and into the weaponsfire from the CDF soldiers and the Gesora.

Bolts that were shot from the Gesora long rifles were absorbed by the creatures' armored plating and hardly slowed them down.

They weren't completely covered with armor. There was plenty of exposed grayish skin along the underbelly and parts of their heavily muscled thighs. Connor aimed his weapon and fired at the exposed flesh of one creature. Hardened high-velocity darts tore into it, shredding flesh, muscle, and sinew. The creature was in mid-leap and tumbled to the side, trying to scramble back to its feet, but one of its legs was broken. The Gesora soldiers finished it off.

The creatures continued to pour out of the gateway. They had to scramble over the dead and dying, but they kept coming. The Gesora military adapted their tactics to match the CDF's, firing their weapons at the vulnerable underbellies of the creatures coming through the gateway.

Connor looked at Samson. "We need to plug up that hole."

"On it," Samson replied.

A CDF soldier in a combat suit heavy, equipped with a quad-barrel M547 gauss cannon, fired at the gateway. It tore up everything in its path regardless of armor. Sergeant Collier's name appeared on Connor's internal heads-up display.

Dash sprang up from behind the barricade, fired a few rounds, and then ducked back down. He looked at Connor. "Is it me, or are they getting bigger?"

Dash was right. The creatures coming through the gateway were nearly twice the size as the ones that were dying in the courtyard.

Several CDF combat suit heavies stepped around the barricade, and their weapons tore into the enemy lines.

A CDF troop carrier flew overhead and fired scorpion missiles right at the threshold of the gateway. The explosion shook the ground at Connor's feet, and he ducked instinctively. Rock and debris blew in all directions and rained down on them. When it cleared, Connor stood back up. There was a large crater where the gateway had been, but the gateway was now closed. It was gone. The creatures stuck on this side of the gateway scrambled away from them. They were trying to leave the complex.

Gesora soldiers moved forward and tried to stop them. Connor heard the shot of a Viper sniper rifle, and one of the creatures arched its back in pain, falling off the wall. It took them almost ten minutes to clear the courtyard.

Monin deployed his troops into the city. There were reports coming in of multiple gateways being opened and creatures flooding the streets, attacking anything that moved.

Connor wanted to deploy his troops also, but this wasn't a colonial city. They'd use their weapons to defend themselves.

"I have confirmation of multiple gateways open in the city," Samson said. They appear to come at random. Some of the gateways stay open for longer durations, while others don't stay long at all. The same creatures are coming through, though."

"We need to know if this is happening everywhere or if it's just here because of the arch gateway," Connor said. Samson nodded. "Has there been confirmation of Krake ships?"

"Not yet. Troop carriers are slower. We should hear something within the next fifteen minutes," Samson replied.

Connor made his way to where Monin was issuing orders to his own officers.

"Thank you for your help," Monin said. "We've had reports from other parts of the city. Those damn creatures are everywhere."

"What about other cities?" Connor asked.

"We've sent out warnings to the other provinces. It's going to take a little bit of time to hear back from them," Monin said.

The creatures' roars ended with high-pitched squeals like rocks being dragged over battle steel. Several tall spires burned about half a kilometer from their position. The creatures were climbing up the spires, looking for a way inside.

"My God," Holzer said, his eyes wide. Gellner looked as if he were about to run away. One of the CDF soldiers was trying to get him to calm down.

Warlord Monin sent multiple groups of soldiers into the city. They were to engage the enemy. The creatures were heading toward the arch gateway that was near the center of the city. It was as if they were being directed, but they hadn't detected any type of broadcast that was controlling them. They would attack anything that moved, but they also seemed to be directed toward a common goal.

Redian, the Warlord's First, ran over to Monin and spoke so quickly that Connor's translator was unable to provide a clear translation. The translator only spoke words that it determined it could interpret with a high degree of accuracy.

"Order everyone to the gateway," Monin said to Redian. "We can't secure this location for long. Everyone is to go to the gateway. We need to use our emergency site location to clear out civilians."

Redian left them and began issuing orders to other Gesora officers.

Monin turned to Connor. "They're attacking us everywhere. There are reports of attacks coming in from the other provinces. These damn creatures are murdering my people. How could the Krake hit us all at once like this?"

Samson walked over to Connor. "You need to hear this, General."

Connor nodded and was patched into a comlink with Lieutenant Butcher.

"I'm currently located north of the city in lower orbit. Confirm the presence of three Krake warships. They've split off. They might be heading to the other cities. I don't know," Butcher said.

"What else, Lieutenant?" Connor asked.

"I've seen some attack drones come away from the ships, but I'm not sure where they're going—Oh my God!" Butcher shouted. "Sir, I don't believe it! The Krake are using WMDs. They're using WMDs on the cities. We just saw two huge explosions. Oh man, there's a third. Confirm the distance," he said, speaking to his copilot. "Sir, I can't tell how bad it is, but it looks bad enough. Recommend immediate evac."

The Krake were using weapons of mass destruction to obliterate the cities. This was a coordinated attack, but where were they coming from? Connor tried to think of a way the Gesora could effectively defend themselves against this kind of attack. Instead of focusing on what the Gesora didn't have, he thought of their assets. They had a large military, which would help them defend against the creatures coming through the gateways.

"They didn't send a fleet," Samson said.

Connor shook his head. "Why would they? The Gesora don't have orbital defense capabilities. They have fighters, but they're limited to the atmosphere. The Krake are coordinating the attack from another staging location, some other world. Where else would the creatures come from?"

"Shit!" Butcher said and repeated himself a few times, the

tension building in his voice. "Here they come. Krake attack drones are flying right toward us." His voice sounded strained.

Connor and Samson turned in the direction of the troop carrier. It was too far away for them to see, even with the enhanced vision from their combat suits.

"We're not gonna make it—" Butcher was saying when the comlink cut off. The troop carrier had been destroyed.

Connor ground his teeth. They'd never stood a chance. Troop carriers couldn't outrun Krake attack drones.

Holzer was shouting at Sergeant Rowan. "We have to get out of here! We can't stay here! Let me go!" The diplomat ran toward Connor. Rowan hastened behind.

"What do you want to do?" Samson asked.

"We can't leave. If they have data on the Krake home world, we need to find out what it is. We need to make it to that arch gateway before it's destroyed," Connor said.

"What about them?" Samson asked and inclined his head toward Holzer and the others.

"They have to come with us. There's no safe place to put them, and splitting up isn't an option. We're too far inside the city. We have to stick together," Connor said, and hated the necessity of it. They were down at least one troop carrier. He thought of sending the others to the egress point, but it was too risky with this kind of attack. He needed to keep the troop carriers close, to provide air support and escape.

Connor told Monin that they were going with him. "We need to find the Krake home world. It's the only way we can end this attack. Will you be able to hold on?"

"The Gesora will endure. We can survive this," Monin said.

"Let's move out," Connor said.

15

THE GESORA MILITARY had atmospheric fighters that used liquid fuel the equivalent of the late twenty-first-century technology that had been common at the formation of Old Earth's global alliances. They carried more powerful plasma cannons near the underbelly of the aircraft.

The Gesora military had armored vehicles with mounted weapons. Dozens of them scouted the area away from the complex.

The CDF 7th Ranger Company surrounded Connor and the diplomatic envoy. Dash stayed near Connor and was quiet. Gesora fighters flew overhead, making surgical strikes in areas where the otherworldly predators came through seemingly random gateways. Krake attack drones blazed a path. The Gesora fighters tried to destroy them, but their weapons were ineffective.

The heavy gauss cannons on the CDF troop carriers could destroy the Krake attack drones because the high-density rounds were shot with such force that they could break the attack drones apart before they could melt their way through the ship. The downside was that they would use their nanorobotic ammunition much faster in order to produce a round with enough mass to destroy the Krake's weapons. And the attack drones' agility made them extremely difficult to hit.

Connor ordered the troop carriers to provide air support but to limit their presence as much as possible. Let the Gesora defend their city. Connor couldn't be sure if the Krake would assume the CDF was here based on the presence of the one troop carrier they'd destroyed. He had to presume that the Krake would prioritize CDF targets because they were as eager to find New Earth as the CDF was to find the Krake home world.

Using their combat suits to travel required significantly less effort than if they'd been walking. The MPS was no different, but it took some time for Holzer and his assistant Gellner to become comfortable with that fact. Agent Winfry didn't complain. She must have had training with the MPS. She carried her weapon but hadn't fired it. The 7th Ranger Company was surrounded by the Gesora military, which provided a protective bubble around them.

They moved quickly through the streets. Monin reassigned soldiers to protect and help guide Ovarrow civilians to safety. This slowed them down, but they had very little choice.

Fighting throughout the Gesora capital city intensified as the Krake invasion force rampaged throughout the city. They were there to wreak havoc and mayhem, and their losses didn't appear to affect them. It reminded Connor of ryklars being controlled by the activation signal.

"The orders haven't changed. Stick to the perimeter of the city and we'll call you when we need you," Samson said, speaking over comlink to the troop carrier pilots. He paused and was quiet for a moment. "Roger that," he said.

A gateway shimmered to life right in the middle of the

convoy, and Connor pulled Dash to the side. He saw Sergeant Rowan ushering Holzer and the others to the other side of the street. They had to clear the area.

"Check your fire," Connor shouted.

They were more in danger of shooting each other than what was about to come out of the gateway. He ordered a platoon to take a position in front of the gateway and fire into it. The remaining people in the convoy split down side streets to get away.

Connor watched the gateway as they retreated. He couldn't see clearly. It was as if the other side of the gateway was shrouded in a thick fog, and he could only see hints of shapes behind it. Then the body of a creature fell at the threshold. It was quickly joined by others.

Farther down the street, another gateway shimmered into existence, followed by another and then another. They were staggered.

Connor yelled for them to retreat. They couldn't afford to get caught out there. The Krake had updated their tactics and were attempting to pin them down by scattering them, and it was working.

Several armored Gesora vehicles turned down the street just as creatures burst from all the different gateways. By the force of sheer numbers alone, they tore those vehicles apart. The Gesora fought and fired their weapons until they were overwhelmed.

"This isn't a battle. It's a slaughter," Samson said on their private comlink channel.

"I know," Connor replied.

He glanced up toward the buildings nearby and could see the top of the arch gateway in the distance. They had to keep going because of the slightest chance that they could gain some kind of intel about where the Krake home world was.

"Watch out!" Samson shouted and shoved Connor.

Connor stumbled off-balance for a moment, but the combat suit helped him regain his footing. He spun around and saw the armored predators crawling over the tops of the buildings. He brought up his AR-74 and fired it on full auto. CDF soldiers nearby took up positions and provided covering fire.

There weren't that many of the creatures. They must have been a smaller group, roaming around and causing havoc. Maybe a scout force.

The soldiers moved out of the area, but now they kept watch on the rooftops of the buildings as they ran below them—the ones that had been left intact, anyway. As they kept going, Connor began to believe that they were doing exactly what the enemy wanted them to do. They wanted them to try and hold the city. They were being occupied. Krake ships must have been on the way here. But why? Why stage an invasion this way when they could just use their ships to knock out an inferior opponent?

"Stop!" Connor ordered. "It's a trap. They want us to go to the gateway."

"What's the trap?" Samson asked.

"Everything."

Monin was far ahead of them, but Connor opened a comlink to him.

"We can't go to the gateway. It's a trap," Connor said.

"What do you mean? Data for the Krake home world is there," Monin said.

"The timing of all this is suspicious, don't you think? The Krake might not have known that we would be here, but you can be damn sure they know we want to find their home world. All of us do. They're conducting multiple invasions across who knows how many worlds. They want to kill us all in the most efficient way possible."

"But the data could be real. We could stop them if we could find their home world," Monin said.

"Monin, you have to listen to me," Connor said. "The arch is located in the central part of the city. The Krake want us to go there because then when they use their WMDs, they'll knock out all resistance in one strike. We need to flee the city. You need to get everyone out as fast as you can."

Monin went quiet. He'd paused the comlink while speaking with somebody else.

Connor looked at Samson. "Are any of our troop carriers near the arch gateway?"

"Yes," Samson said and patched Connor into the video feeds from the troop carrier.

The arch gateway was active, and Connor could see the Gesora running through it to escape the city. The skies around it glowed in an unsettling white light.

"General Gates," Monin said, "the Krake might want us to go to the arch gateway, but we have no choice. We can escape through the arch and regroup. You are welcome to join us."

The comlink severed. Monin hadn't waited for an answer, and Connor couldn't really blame him. Monin had to do what he thought was best for his people.

Connor took a few moments to study the video feeds from the troop carriers. There was fighting in all parts of the city, and the skies were becoming filled with Krake attack drones. The Gesora fighters tried to stop them, but their weapons were ineffective. They even tried suicide runs, but the military vehicles had no effect on the Krake attack drones. They just punched through them and kept speeding toward their targets. Samson was right. This was a slaughter.

"Connor," Dash said, "I've been monitoring Gesora comlink channels. I used one of my language filters and an analysis AI to help. The reports coming in from the other provinces are all similar to what's happening here. More Krake ships have been spotted. More bombs. More gateways. More everything. Everything that's happening here is happening on a global scale."

Connor regarded Dash for a few moments. The attack was happening everywhere. "Damn it," he hissed and then nodded at Dash.

They needed to get out of the city, and the closest exit was at that damn arch gateway. He ground his teeth in frustration. Going to the arch was a mistake. He knew it.

"What do you want to do, sir?" Samson asked.

"We need a spot to bring the troop carriers in," Connor said.

"Getting in is one thing, but getting out again is something else."

"I know," Connor said and glanced up at one of the nearby buildings. A rooftop extraction was extremely risky. "If we split up and each group takes a rooftop to meet a troop carrier, an extraction might work."

Samson thought about it for a second. "We're almost to the arch. They could meet us there and we can stick together. I think we should stick together, sir."

Connor nodded and choked off a curse. "You're right. What am I going to do without you?"

Samson grinned. "I know a few people who'll watch your back like I do."

They regrouped and followed the Gesora soldiers and civilians heading to the arch. The different-size gateways kept appearing at random. Some were small enough that only a few of the creatures leaped through, and others were much bigger. It couldn't be random if they were being herded, but how would the Krake know the layout of the city?

The skies above them blazed as if another star had come into existence. The combat suit's systems polarized the view to protect the wearers from being blinded.

"Incoming!" a CDF soldier shouted.

Hundreds of Krake attack drones flew in an attack pattern, forming a massive spearhead that flew toward the arch gateway. Connor heard the sounds of the troop carriers' heavy gauss cannon fire, but it wasn't enough. He watched in horror as the Krake attack drones ripped through one side of the arch, executed a sharp turn that would have overwhelmed the inertia dampeners of any CDF ship, and cut through the other side of the arch. The giant structure teetered for a moment and then slid down, crushing the Gesora nearby. The gateway was gone.

The Krake attack drones wheeled around. The remaining Gesora fighters tried to flee but couldn't outrun the drones. Connor watched the skies as the CDF troop carriers attempted to elude the attack drones by flying low, using the buildings as cover. It was the tactic Connor would have used if he were piloting, but it didn't work. Krake attack drones punched through the buildings and then ripped through the main fuselage of the troop carriers. The engines fell away in a burst of flame, and the remains of the carriers crashed into buildings before falling out of view. The attack had been so sudden that it took Connor a few seconds to realize that all the troop carriers had been destroyed. Without them, they had no chance of reaching their own egress location to return to the alpha site within the next check-in period. And if the Krake could track gateways, he didn't want anyone else from the alpha site to send more soldiers through.

Samson came over to him. "Are you all right?"

Connor exhaled explosively. "Yeah, we're in the shit now."

"It gets worse. There's a Krake warship heading for the city. This is the last location and speed detected," Samson said.

Connor muttered a curse, trying to force his mind to think, and ideas rushed out like the flood gates had been opened in his brain. They didn't have hours to fight through hordes of creatures. The Gesora couldn't reach a minimal safe distance, and neither could any of them.

A comlink from Warlord Monin registered with Connor's combat suit.

"It is over. The gateway was our only way out of here. Now my scouts have informed me that there is a Krake warship flying toward us. I've ordered an evacuation," Monin said.

"They're going to use their WMD to destroy the city. You won't have time to get away," Connor said.

"There has to be something we can do."

Connor looked around. The skies were filled with fumes. Flashes of light from gateways could be seen reflecting off the low-lying smoke. He frowned as another thought occurred to him. The reasoning part of his brain shouted in defiance, but the more reckless part of him knew it was their only option.

"There's only one way out of this. We have to use the Krake gateways," Connor said.

Samson shook his head. "That's crazy. Those creatures will kill us."

Monin said the same thing.

"It's our only option. We're dead if we stay. We might die if we go through, but there also might be a place we can regroup," Connor said.

"This is crazy, but we need crazy." Samson then cut over to the officers' broadcast channel.

"Monin, we're going. It's our only option. I hope I see you on the other side," Connor said.

"How do you know there aren't Krake soldiers on the other side of that gateway?" Monin asked.

"I don't. All I know is that the Krake warship is heading here, and there's nothing you or I can do to stop it. The only unknown is through that gateway. We don't have much time."

"But those creatures," Monin said.

"The Krake control the creatures. They're going to be recalled. The Krake don't waste resources," Connor said.

The comlink went silent. Connor glanced at Samson, who was filling the others in. Monin made a sound that the translator couldn't decipher. "We'll follow you."

Finding gateways nearby was the easy part. Predicting how long they would stay active was almost impossible, but they didn't have a choice. They had to take a chance and roll the dice. They followed the armored creatures. The predators had stopped their rampaging and were heading toward active gateways as if they'd been summoned. The whole operation was ruthlessly efficient. Krake attack drones moved out of the area. The CDF soldiers followed as closely as they dared, but sometimes the creatures spun about and attacked. It couldn't be helped. They needed to close the distance, and Connor was sure the Krake had accounted for some loss of their attack force. In fact, they'd probably planned for it, so the CDF harassed the creatures right up to the gateway. There were shouts for them to hurry. One of the soldiers spotted the Krake warship flying toward the city. They were out of time.

CDF soldiers ran through the gateway and Gesora soldiers with them. Connor wasn't sure where Monin had gone, but he hoped the warlord had made it to a gateway. Any gateway. He had no illusions that Monin would needlessly sacrifice himself.

Most Ovarrow were pragmatic. They'd rather live to fight another day.

"It's our turn, sir. I'm not going without you," Dash said.

Connor ran through the Krake gateway with Dash at his side.

16

CONNOR EMERGED from the gateway and dropped several feet to the ground. He stumbled. The ground was uneven and shifted beneath his feet as if he were standing on a mound of rocky debris. The skies were almost pitch black but for the lights of a large, glowing platform. Connor glanced upward and saw an arch atop the platform. Howling winds blasted across the landscape, carrying dirt and debris that bounced off his combat suit. Dash stumbled into him, and both slid down the pile of debris.

A CDF soldier helped Connor to his feet. "General Gates, are you all right?"

It took Connor a few moments to untangle his thoughts. They were surrounded by large mounds. Lights flashed overhead, and the wind . . . The wind gusts were brutal. "Yeah," he said and looked at the soldier. His name and rank appeared on Connor's internal heads-up display. "Sergeant, thanks for the assist."

Sergeant Mason leaned down to help Dash.

"I'm all right," Dash said and looked upward. "I think we dropped five meters before we hit the top of that mound."

"You were both lucky you landed on it. Some of us didn't," Mason said.

Connor watched the platforms flying nearby. There were so many of them. They slowed down when a gateway became active, and dark shapes plowed through. The creatures hit the ground at a run, their thick, muscular bodies absorbing the impact as they headed away.

The soldiers scouted the area, as well as helped other soldiers and Gesora. The Nexstar combat suits had protected them, but the soldiers had still gotten bumped and bruised. The Gesora wore less effective armor and had sustained more serious injuries.

Connor looked up at the sky. The winds still gusted, but the skies were clear. There were no moons, and no rings circled the planet. The few stars he was able to see shone dimly, which was caused by some kind of atmospheric effect.

Survivors gathered in tight clusters. The CDF soldiers had night vision capabilities through their combat suits, but the Ovarrow didn't. They used bioluminescent sticks to light the area in a deep amber glow.

Connor found Sergeant Rowan's squad, along with Holzer, Gellner, and Winfry.

"General, Gellner might have cracked a rib. He took a bad fall. Holzer and Winfry are fine, considering," Rowan said.

"Good job," Connor said and looked at the rest of the squad. Gellner was wincing as Winfry checked his ribs.

"She said she was a field medic in Field Ops, sir," Rowan explained.

Connor nodded and watched Gellner.

Winfry glanced up at Connor. "Definitely a broken rib, and he probably bruised a few more. I'll get him patched up."

Gellner's eyes were wide. "Don't leave me behind. Please don't leave me behind."

Connor squatted down so he was eye level with Gellner. "Sit tight. Let Winfry get you situated. We're not leaving *anyone* behind, all right? Just sit tight. One thing at a time, now."

Gellner swallowed hard and blinked his eyes a few times, nodding. He exhaled forcefully. "All right."

Connor stood up, and Holzer walked with him a short distance.

"Where did those creatures go?" Holzer asked.

"They headed away from us, probably to wherever the recall signal ordered," Dash answered.

Holzer glanced in the direction Dash had gestured. "I can't see anything. What are we going to do if they come back? They could turn around at any moment and attack." The words came out in a rush, along with a wave of fear and anxiety.

"Listen to me," Connor said. "I know this isn't what you were expecting. None of us were. We're going to do everything we can. If they come back here, we'll deal with it. We've made it this far, and we can go further. Just stay calm. Listen to Sergeant Rowan. Do what you're told and you'll be fine. All right?"

"What about the Gesora?" Holzer asked.

"I'm on my way to find out what their status is," Connor said.

"Do you mind if I come with you?"

The last thing Connor needed was Holzer looking over his shoulder. The man was scared, but he also just wanted to be kept informed. "You can come, but I want you to remember that we all have a job to do. Don't make it harder on us."

Holzer regarded Connor for a moment and nodded. He began to speak but then thought better of it.

The 7th Ranger Company was made up of three platoons

comprising 160 soldiers, but they'd sustained losses. Samson joined him, along with his second-in-command, Lieutenant Lafferty.

"I've sent out two SRDs to scout the area," Samson said.

Stealth recon drones would give them an immediate layout of the area.

"Can you grant me access to them?" Dash asked. Samson made a passing motion from his holoscreen to Dash. "Thanks," he said and focused his attention on his own holoscreen.

Connor looked around at some of the Gesora. "Where's Monin?"

Samson shook his head. "I'm not sure."

"How many did we lose?"

"Twenty-two. Between the loss of the troop carriers and in the city, we lost twenty-two," Samson replied.

The number wasn't especially high, but the cost was. It always was, where lives were concerned. The Colonial Defense Force wasn't such a large military that lives could get lost in the shuffle. They weren't like the militaries of Old Earth where there were billions of people to draw from. As a result, Connor refused to allow the life of a soldier to become a number. This would never stop him from making hard decisions where human cost was unavoidable, but it still mattered. The lives of his soldiers would always matter to him.

"Understood," Connor said. "Try to find Monin, and if we can't find him, look for Redian. Keep working down the chain of command until we find someone in charge. Otherwise, I don't know what the Gesora are going to do."

Samson looked at Lafferty. "You got all that, Lieutenant?"

"I'm on it, sir," Lafferty said and left them.

"What the hell is this place?" Samson asked.

"They're staging invasions from here," Connor said. He

Invasion

165

brought up his own holoscreen, and the SRD video feed came to prominence.

"It just goes on and on," Samson said.

The platforms that carried arch gateways were moving steadily away from them. The scope of the Krake invasion operation was mindbogglingly huge. Connor couldn't easily count how many platforms were out there.

"I need to see this for myself," Connor said.

He climbed up to the top of the nearest mound of rocky debris, which looked to be a collection of rubble. None of the pieces seemed to go together, but he was able to get a secure foothold and climb to the top with relative ease. Samson came with him and then Dash joined them.

When Connor reached the top, he inhaled deeply and sighed. Sometimes when looking at things through a reconnaissance drone video feed, one could lose perspective. Training could help with that, but no amount of training could've prepared Connor for what he saw. It was just an ever-expanding landscape of the same kinds of things they were already seeing—mounds of debris and shadows moving in the pale light of the platforms leaving the area. The barren landscape wasn't completely devoid of life. He could make out some kind of shrubbery in the distance, but it was barely clinging to life.

Connor turned and glanced down at their camp. Gesora soldiers were coming toward them. How many hadn't made it? Over the years, Connor had developed an eye for judging the emotional state of the Ovarrow, and the Gesora were no different. Their movements were quick and seemingly agitated. They argued among themselves. Connor could see it even though he couldn't hear what they were saying. The Gesora had just witnessed the loss of their capital city and possibly their entire world. They were no doubt wondering if there were any survivors, and Connor had to believe there were. There might be Gesora in the countryside still fighting, but who knew what else the Krake would do to the planet. If he could somehow get back to the alpha site, he could send ships to help, but it could already be too late.

What if the Krake had already invaded New Earth? He'd been thinking it ever since the attack had begun. It was there in the back of his mind, and he knew it was in the back of the minds of his soldiers. They couldn't stay where they were. Nothing good would happen if they stayed. Either the Krake would discover them and wipe them out, or discipline would break down among their ranks. The CDF soldiers would look to him to lead them, but what would the Gesora do?

"Have they found Monin yet?" Connor asked.

"The message just came through. They found Monin and he's alive," Samson said. Then he added, "You need to be careful with him."

"What do you mean?"

"Connor, the Gesora might not have a home to go back to. They're not stupid. They'll figure it out."

"I know that."

"I know you do, but I just wanted to remind you that Monin and the other Gesora might not be rational," Samson said.

"Noted. Now, we'll go find out."

They found Monin arguing with a group of civilians that had somehow made it through the gateway with them. When the warlord saw Connor, he dismissed the civilians. A few refused to leave, and he had his soldiers forcibly remove them. The Ovarrow weren't a gentle species.

There was a hard glint to Monin's gaze. He didn't offer an explanation, and Connor wouldn't comment. They stood a much better chance at surviving the situation if they worked together.

"We've begun scouting the area," Connor said and showed him the SRD's video feeds.

"What is this place?" Monin asked.

"I think it's some kind of staging world for invasions," Connor replied.

Dash cleared his throat. "This was an Ovarrow world."

Monin turned his harsh gaze to the young man. "No Ovarrow could live here."

"A long time ago, they did. About five hundred years to be exact," Dash said and looked at Connor. He tapped a storage container on the side of his combat suit. "My field kit."

Connor nodded, understanding. "Never go anywhere without it." He looked at Monin. "He's right. He can date the area."

"These mounds look like they are from other worlds. How accurate could the dating method be?" Monin asked.

"There are structures around us amid the mounds. It's hard to see. I had our drones run a scan with specialized protocols to identify partial architectural structures," Dash said and showed them an image from the scan. It displayed a mound of rubble but also a partial wall. There was a grid overlay on the image, and the analysis done by Dash's computer showed where it projected that part of a building had once been. There was enough data to make a fairly accurate assumption. Connor had used earlier renditions of these analysis protocols when he'd searched for hidden bunkers on New Earth.

"Another world was taken from us," Monin said. "I don't know why the Krake hate us so much. We've done nothing to them." He glanced at where the Gesora citizens huddled together, seeking whatever shelter they could get against the gusting winds. Then he looked at Connor. "I want the Krake to suffer for this. All of them. Every single one of them."

"I want to stop them too, but first we need to find a way out of here. We need to find where those arch gateways went," Connor said.

"We can use the gateways to get home and come back to help them," Holzer said.

Connor shook his head. "No, we can use them to return to the alpha site. If the Krake can somehow trace gateways, then we can't use the ones here to get home."

"They might already be there," Holzer said.

"There's no way to know that, and I'm not going to put our home in any more danger than it already is."

Holzer frowned. "But they have to be warned. What if this happens to them?"

"We're prepared."

Monin gave him a sharp look.

Holzer shook his head. "The attack came without warning."

"Yes, it did, and they knew the layout of the city. The Krake haven't been to New Earth. They certainly don't know the layout of our cities. They don't even know where our cities are. They'll have their work cut out for them. We have defenses in place and people watching out for them."

Holzer pressed his lips together but didn't say anything else.

"You could defend yourself from an attack like this?" Monin asked.

"An attack like this, yes," Connor said. "But the Krake would come back with more. They'd bring more ships. They'd bring their soldiers, and they'd use those predators. I don't know if we could survive all that while trying to find their home world."

All of this was assuming the Krake would come to New Earth to wipe out the colonists, but Connor knew better. He'd spent two years trying to build up the colony's defenses. Even given the immense scale at which the Krake operated, he knew the CDF would make the Krake pay a terrible price to destroy New Earth. But the Krake wouldn't want to simply destroy them. They'd want to capture them and subject the colonists to malicious experiments that would go on for years. There had to be a way to stop them. Where was their damn home world?

"I'll use their gateways to return home and then search for survivors. They couldn't have killed everyone. I can't abandon them," Monin said.

"What about your contact that had information about the Krake home world? The Bhatdin," Connor asked.

Monin thought about it. "We should try to find them." He looked away for a few moments. "I have more than just soldiers here. I can't leave them."

Connor thought Monin left a lot unsaid. The Gesora warlord was still coming to grips with what had just happened.

"What about bringing them to our alpha site? They'll be safe there, and then you can figure it out," Connor said. It was best not to make well-defined plans but to take smaller steps. Smaller steps were easier to wrap one's mind around, but Connor already had something else in mind. And he knew no one else was going to like it.

"First, we need to find the gateways," Monin said.

"The creatures used in the attack are in the same direction as the gateways," Dash said.

"It makes sense. I don't like it, but it makes sense," Connor said. "There's gotta be some kind of command center. Somehow, they're being controlled, but they're also controlling the platforms. We might need just one of those platforms. It must have a controller unit. We find that and then we can use it to open a gateway."

Dash frowned in thought for a few moments. "There might

be others in the area, other Ovarrow who came through the gateways. We should look for them."

Connor nodded and looked at Monin. "We should search the immediate area and then start making our way in that direction." He pointed toward the disappearing platforms.

"Give me a few minutes to coordinate with my soldiers. We have wounded and they'll need to be carried," Monin said.

The Gesora warlord stomped away from them, leaving Connor with Samson, Dash, and Holzer nearby. He gestured for them to come closer. He'd rather Holzer wasn't close by for this, but it couldn't be helped.

"We need to figure out what this place is," Connor said.

"You said it before. It's some kind of staging world for the Krake invasion force," Holzer said.

"That's what they're using it for, but we still don't know what this place is." Connor looked at Dash. "You stumbled onto something when you dated the architecture here. This place is old, which means it must be from the early days of when the Krake started exploring multiple universes. I don't think we've ever been closer to finding the Krake home world than we are right here."

"General Gates," Holzer began, "you said we'd return to the alpha site."

"We will, but we should also learn what we can about this place and maybe bring a division of our own soldiers back with us. Maybe even a battle group from our own fleet as well."

Samson nodded, and then his brows knitted into a thoughtful frown. "This has to be more widespread than we thought. These attacks. Our away teams could be in trouble."

Connor nodded. He couldn't do anything about it. Those teams were on their own until they could warn them. They had protocols in place, and those CDF soldiers had their training.

But how many would they lose? They'd scouted hundreds of worlds and still hadn't found the Krake home world. It didn't make sense, considering that there were supposed to be limits on how many worlds they could access. Connor had the gnawing feeling that they were looking for the Krake home world in the wrong place. He didn't know why, and he didn't know where else to look, but the feeling was there.

He looked at the others. "We have our objectives. Let's get moving."

They did have their objectives, but the situation wasn't good. There were so many things that stood in their way. Connor had to project a stance of strength, but he was afraid, though that wouldn't stop him from doing what they had to do. Samson wouldn't be fooled. He knew. There were so many things that could go wrong. Those creatures could attack at any moment, or the Krake could detect their presence and come to destroy them. But they couldn't be paralyzed with fear. If that happened, they were as good as dead, so Connor wasn't going to let that happen. They had to keep moving.

The mental images of the attack on the Gesora home world kept coming to his mind. He tried to imagine the same thing happening in any one of the colonial cities. They did have defenses and had conducted drills to prepare colonial citizens, but if they were blindsided like the Gesora had been, there would be losses. He thought of his home at Sanctuary—Lenora, Lauren, his son. His gut tightened and he ground his teeth. He had to stop it from happening. He had to stop the Krake. He'd do whatever it took, but would it be enough?

17

As they searched the area, they kept finding refugees who were disoriented, bedraggled, and all too many times, wounded. Monin sent out his soldiers to help find his people, many of whom were frightened and in pain. Connor watched as more wounded Ovarrow were brought back to the area. The Ovarrow who'd made it here were the lucky ones. Reports came in where groups of Gesora were found dead. Their wounds were fresh, meaning that they'd been killed after they came through the gateway. It was assumed at first that they'd been killed by the predators used in the invasion, but not always. Their wounds were inconsistent with the predators' vicious attacks. Large puncture wounds in the backs of the victims had struck vital organs with incredible precision.

Connor shook his head and looked at Samson. "This isn't going to work. We can't take all of them with us. There are too many wounded."

"There's been a lot of infighting among them," Samson replied.

Connor nodded. "And we're stuck in the middle of it."

He'd ordered the CDF soldiers to remain on the outer fringe of their temporary camp. If there was a breakdown of command and the Gesora began fighting among themselves, he didn't want CDF soldiers caught in the middle of it. He knew what they needed to do. The most recent recon drone data had confirmed it.

"Send out a broadcast that we're moving out soon. I'm going to speak to Monin before we do. I doubt that what I'm going to say to him will come as a surprise," Connor said.

"We're always ready, General," Samson said and sent out a broadcast update to his officers.

Connor walked to where Monin was organizing his people. There were both Gesora military and civilians alike. Dash followed him but remained quiet.

Gesora soldiers looked at Connor and Dash as they walked past. Ovarrow facial expressions would never be considered friendly. They were a completely different species, but the burning anger in the soldiers' gazes was unmistakable. The Gesora's entire society had been forced to adapt to a threat that, in some ways, they understood better than Connor did, but not in all ways. They'd thought they were prepared. They'd believed that they could fight the Krake and defeat them. The invasion of their world had brought with it a reality the Gesora had feared but didn't expect. They couldn't defeat the Krake despite everything they'd done to prepare—building up their military, searching for the Krake home world, finding allies. It hadn't been enough. They hadn't just come up short. They'd been completely outmatched, and he saw the shock of it in their haunted gazes. Some of the Gesora soldiers looked at Connor with an almost accusatory stare, as if he were the reason the Krake had invaded their home world in the first place. Other soldiers kept their angry brethren in check by reminding them who the real enemies were.

The squad of CDF soldiers that followed him kept an eye on their surroundings, looking for potential threats. They were seasoned soldiers, and the likelihood that any of them would accidentally cause an issue was almost nonexistent.

Monin was speaking to multiple Ovarrow, receiving their reports. He glanced at Connor. "General Gates, we keep finding survivors. It's taken us longer to get ready to leave than I thought."

"I understand. It's one of the reasons I came."

A small group of survivors walked by, some stopping to stare.

"It's not safe to move all these people," Connor said.

"Do you suggest I leave them behind?"

The Gesora in the area turned their attention toward them.

"Warlord Monin, the situation has changed. We can't take all of the wounded and civilians to find the Krake command center. It's better that they stay here away from danger," Connor said.

Monin drew himself up to his full height. "There isn't a safe place for us here."

"There are degrees of safety. You need to keep searching for survivors. We might have found a command center worth checking. It could lead us to where the platforms with the arches are."

"What's to stop you from leaving us all behind? I trust your intentions, General Gates, but the Krake put us all in a precarious position. Show me what you've found."

Gesora soldiers gathered around. They looked as if they were waiting for Monin to give them an order to force Connor to give them what they wanted.

Connor met Monin's gaze. Showing weakness or uncertainty

would embolden the Gesora, who were becoming less rational by the second. He activated his personal holoscreen and showed Monin the recon drone's video feed.

"I'm not going to leave you behind. We can get there faster than you," Connor said. "Look at the ground."

Thousands of creatures lay on the ground. The recon drone flew high above them, and with the high winds, it was doubtful that the creatures were aware of it.

Monin peered at the video feed. "Why would they do that?"

"They're sleeping. The Krake control them. They probably forced them to go to sleep to conserve energy. This is why you can't take your wounded there. A smaller group might be able to slip through," Connor said.

Monin watched the video feed and looked as if he were weighing his options. "How will you get past them?"

"I don't know. We'll learn more as we get closer. I need you to trust me."

Monin looked away and regarded his soldiers for a few moments. "What if you fail?"

Connor powered off his holoscreen. "Then I'll send you whatever we learn. Maybe you'll be able to come up with something. I'm taking my soldiers and I'm going there. I'm not going to wait for you, but if you try to follow us, you'll be putting your people in more danger than they already are. There's a good chance the Krake are going to find out we're here. I'd rather them target us away from you."

"If you believe the Krake are going to detect us, then why not bring a bigger fighting force?" Monin asked.

Connor inhaled and sighed. "There aren't enough of us to make a difference. Not in a standup fight. We need to out-think them. That's how we'll defeat the Krake."

Monin considered this for a few moments. "We must return to our home. I thought we'd go with you to your alpha site, but I can't."

Were he in Monin's shoes, Connor would have thought the same thing. He'd also return home to search for survivors.

"I understand. First, we find one of those platforms, and then I'll send it to your location. But you'll need to move out of the area," Connor said.

This location on the Gesora home world was right in the middle of their capital city, which had most likely been leveled by a Krake WMD.

"I will keep my comlink active so you can track us," Monin said and stepped closer to Connor. "Do you still believe there is a way to stop the Krake?"

"I don't give up. We need to hit the Krake where they live, and we need to take out places like this so they can't invade anyone else," Connor replied.

"I hope you succeed for all our sakes. I really hope you succeed," Monin said.

Connor and the others left the Gesora camp.

"For a few seconds there, I thought they were going to attack us," Dash said.

"You're not wrong about that," Connor replied.

"What would you have done?"

"It doesn't matter. Monin will focus on finding survivors and moving his people to another location. We get to figure out a way past thousands of those creatures."

"I hope you have a few ideas about that because I'm coming up blank."

"I doubt that," Connor said, and Dash stared at him. "The 'coming up blank' part."

Dash didn't reply and kept walking next to him. There was only so much information they could glean from recon drones. They needed to get closer to the area. Connor was glad Monin was going to focus on his people. That was what he needed to do, and it also freed Connor up to do what *he* needed to do.

18

A FEW HOURS LATER, Connor and the 7th Ranger Company had made their way to a Krake facility. The gusts of wind had significantly lessened but still came unexpectedly at times. They walked among the corpse of an Ovarrow civilization. Dash had done a few more scans as they traversed toward their objective, and his findings were consistent. The rubbled remains of Ovarrow buildings were at least five hundred years old. There were piles of rubble clustered along the landscape. Their formations were as if someone had dumped broken remnants of buildings from other worlds. The fields of debris had a burst pattern to them as if an arch gateway had been active when an explosion occurred. The result was a scarred landscape amid the bones of an already devastated world.

They saw clusters of predators that were asleep and seemingly hibernating, immune to their surroundings. Connor looked at a group of them half a kilometer away. They lay in a gaggle of dark shadows, and their armor dully reflected what little twilight there was. The creatures were completely vulnerable to attack if Connor had wanted to initiate one, which he didn't.

"I don't get it. Don't they need to eat?" Winfry asked.

"Maybe they already did," Gellner replied quietly, sounding a little bit sick at the thought.

Holzer and the diplomatic envoy followed nearby, but Connor was able to hear their hushed conversations via the combat suit's detectors.

Dash glanced at Connor for a moment. He'd heard the others as well. "I was thinking the same thing."

"I didn't see them eat the Ovarrow," Connor said, dismissing his vivid memories of the attack. These creatures killed with their claws, teeth, and an armored stinger on their tails. They were meant to kill, not to feed.

They were heading to what they hoped was a Krake command center. A complex of buildings near a tower had been found by their recon drones. They'd detected various power sources, but they hadn't seen any Krake in the area. Given the limited number of SRDs they had, Connor didn't want to waste any by having them take a closer look at the complex. He also didn't want to risk alerting the Krake until they were closer, which would decrease their response time.

"They have to eat something. Normally predators are carnivorous and require more food," Dash said.

"Assuming . . . I don't know. They're probably engineered to perform their function with less upkeep," Connor replied.

"And they just happened to have millions of these creatures available?"

Dash made a good point. "Apparently, but if you really want to twist your mind up in knots, start thinking about the ryklars," Connor said.

Dash frowned in thought for a few seconds and then shook

his head. "I can't believe you just did that. Now I can't stop thinking about it."

"There are a lot of similarities. Both species were engineered to be lethal and controlled. It's as if someone was trying to come up with an effective defense against an invasion from creatures like the ones here."

"What about the berwolves?"

"You tell me," Connor said.

Dash was quiet while he thought about it. "There aren't any berwolf control signals, but they could have been next. They're the ryklars' natural enemies, but that's probably because they're both apex predators vying for control."

The CDF soldiers ahead of them stopped, and Connor made his way toward the front. They'd managed to avoid clusters of hibernating predators until now. He accessed the drone video feed as it hovered in the air high above them. The landscape was flat, without any plant life. Anything that had grown here was long since dead. What had once been a wide-open plain was a giant field of debris from who knew how many worlds. The mounds had become steadily smaller, and they could see the tower in the distance.

"No platforms here," Samson said.

Connor pressed his lips together in disappointment. He'd hoped they'd find some kind of facility where the platforms carrying the arches would be located. All equipment required maintenance. The platforms must have needed to be recharged at some point. "That might have been too easy."

"Is it still worth heading to that tower, then?" Holzer asked.

"Absolutely. We don't have time to explore the whole countryside," Connor replied.

Holzer went silent.

"How do you want to proceed, General?" Samson asked.

"We need to get past the sleeping beauties down there, and after that, figure out a way to get inside that tower without alerting anyone," Connor said.

"Look at them all. There isn't a way past them," Holzer said.

Samson nodded. "We could go through them. Punch a hole through them, but that would blow our chances of remaining undetected."

"What about a diversion, General?" Lieutenant Lafferty said.

Connor looked at him.

"Go on, Alphonzo, you got our attention. Spit it out," Samson said.

"I could take a few squads away from here and make a bit of noise. Something the beasties can't ignore, clearing the way for you to reach the tower. We can regroup after you're finished in there."

"That's insane," Holzer said. "Those things are fast."

"So are we," Lafferty replied and looked at Connor. "General, we're not as restricted out here as we were in the Gesora capital city. We can take several positions a few hundred meters away. That would give us some lead time to keep the pressure on and keep our distance at the same time. Draw them away so you can reach the tower."

Connor considered it. Lafferty's plan wasn't bad, and he'd already been considering something similar.

"This is reckless. You'll get us all killed," Holzer said.

Connor glared at the diplomat. "Holzer, I let you stay here, but you don't have a say in how we achieve our objectives. If you can't handle that, I'll have you removed. Continue to be a problem, and I'll have you gagged. If you can't think of a way to help, that's fine, but don't get in the way of the people who are. Ideas are good. Is that understood?"

Holzer's gaze darted to the others as if he was seeking support. Getting none, he shook his head.

"Why don't we give General Gates some room," Sergeant Rowan said, and the diplomat allowed himself to be led away.

Lafferty looked pleased with himself. "Shall I give it a go, General?"

"Excuse me," Dash said.

"Yeah, Dash, what is it?" Connor asked.

"We don't know if they're light sleepers."

Lafferty arched an eyebrow and looked at Samson. "What's he talking about, sir?"

Samson shook his head.

"We think they're hibernating," Dash said, "and the lack of movement would suggest it. What we don't know is how deeply they're hibernating. What if we could sneak past them without them waking up?"

Lafferty snorted. "Would you like to go down there and test that theory of yours?"

Dash glanced at Connor for scarcely a second and then looked back at Lafferty. "I'd do it. I've sneaked by my fair share of predators before. Want to race to the other side?"

Samson chuckled. "I'd actually place a wager on that myself."

"Dash has got a point," Connor said, and the others went quiet.

"General, that could be a death sentence to whomever we send down there. If those things wake up, we give ourselves away. Especially if all of them wake up," Samson said.

Connor grinned a little and tilted his head to the side, arching an eyebrow. "I expected more, Major."

Samson looked at him in stunned silence. "You expected more?"

"Yup, and right now, I bet you can figure it out," Connor replied.

"I'm glad someone can because I'm lost," Dash said.

Lieutenant Lafferty knew better than to make a comment. He just looked at Samson and waited.

Samson exhaled through his nose and looked at Lafferty. "Looks like you're up, Lieutenant. Take three squads over to these coordinates. Don't do anything until you're ordered to do so," Samson said.

"Yes, Major," Lafferty said and then looked at Dash. "Maybe next time, kid." He saluted Connor and left them.

"So how are we going to test the kid's theory, sir?" Samson asked.

Dash rolled his eyes. "Again with this."

Samson smiled with one side of his mouth.

"I'd rather not send a scout in there, but we might not have a choice," Connor said, and his eyebrows knitted together in thought. "All right, hang on. I've got it. I need . . . Who's on drone operations?"

"Specialist Ruo," Samson answered immediately.

"Is he any good?"

Samson looked at him, his face deadpan.

"I'll take that as a yes. Get Specialist Ruo up here. I've got a job for him," Connor said.

Samson opened a comlink to Lieutenant Martin, requesting Specialist Ruo to join them front and center.

Dash looked at Connor. "I can get past them. I've gotten through nests of ryklars before."

"I appreciate the enthusiasm, Dash. It won't be necessary, and I wouldn't send you out there by yourself," Connor said.

"I just want to help. You know, be useful."

"You are helping," Connor said. Dash nodded and looked

away. "Look at me. Not everyone has to put their life on the line to prove they're useful. We have scouts that are trained for this. It's their job to do something like this. All right?"

"I know," Dash said and winced. "I mean, I understand. I just feel like I should be doing more."

Connor leaned in closer. "I know what you mean. Smaller steps get the job done. We're gonna get through this."

A CDF soldier hastened over to them as quietly as he could.

"General Gates, you wanted to see me," Specialist Ruo said.

"I did. How are your tactical drone warfare skills, Specialist?" Connor asked.

"I can hit any target you give me, General. Just say the word," Specialist Ruo answered.

Connor nodded. "I don't want you to hit anything. I want you to fly by something," he said, then explained what he wanted.

Specialist Ruo thought about it for a moment and nodded, as if working things out in his mind. "You want me to buzz the predators, sir."

"That about sums it up. First, a series of flybys to see if we get any response. Then, I want to get progressively closer to them. We'll proceed from there," Connor said.

"Understood, General. I'll need a minute to move my drones into position," Specialist Ruo said. The young man took a few steps away from them and opened a couple of holoscreens with drone control interfaces active and ready.

Connor looked at Samson. "Let's get our guys deployed. Defensive positions. If we do kick a hornet's nest, we might have to get out of here, quick."

"Defensive positions. Understood, sir."

For the next few minutes, the CDF soldiers moved into defensive positions. Specialist Ruo organized nine SRDs into position away from them. Lieutenant Lafferty had taken three squads and was already heading toward a location five hundred meters away. Combat suit heavies were the core of the squads Lieutenant Lafferty commanded. They could certainly make a lot of noise and deliver death and destruction from their weapons.

Everyone had their weapons ready as they waited. Specialist Ruo tasked three drones to be observers. Stealth recon drones were meant to minimize their presence by design. This was accomplished by additional shielding to reduce heat to the angle of the synthetic alloy, which was meant to limit being detected by active scans. They operated in different modes that gave them versatility for different situations. They could operate in quiet mode, but there were costs to the various configurations. Connor watched as the drones carried out a flyover of the sleeping predators. Ruo began twenty meters over their heads, and there was no reaction from the sleeping predators at all. He proceeded to fly the recon drones lower and lower while also reducing their stealth capabilities. The creatures should have been able to hear the drones flying over them. When they didn't respond, Connor looked at Dash.

"That was the easy stuff. Let's see how far we can push it," Specialist Ruo said.

Several of the recon drones descended until they hovered barely a meter off the ground. A pair of drones spun around as if they were chasing each other. Spotlights were enabled, and there was flashing in the area. The creatures did not react at all. Specialist Ruo turned off the spotlights, and the drones stopped spinning in the three locations they were running the tests. Then the specialist flew the drones less than a meter above the sleeping creatures. All pretense of hiding their abilities was gone.

"All right, let's give them a little poke," Connor said.

"Yes, General," Specialist Ruo said.

The drone video feed showed the drone land on top of one of the creatures' armored bodies. Then it rose up into the air. Next, Specialist Ruo had the drone bump the creature with a light tap.

"Well, they're not light sleepers," Dash said.

"No, they're not," Connor said.

"General Gates, how far do you want me to push it?" Specialist Ruo asked.

"I don't think we need to try to wake them up. Try a path that will take us to the tower. Let's see if they're all as deeply asleep as we think they are, or let's see if they're all in as deep a hibernation as we think they are."

"Yes, General," Specialist Ruo said.

Connor looked at Samson. "Okay, we're heading toward the tower. Tell Lafferty to sit tight and keep an eye on us. If it looks like those creatures are starting to wake up, he's clear to engage. But otherwise, I want him to just observe."

"I'll let him know. I have scout teams ready to go first and then we'll follow. I'm assuming you don't want any of us to stay behind," Samson said.

"I thought about it, but I'd rather keep us all together. I don't think we could do much to minimize the risk of what we're about to do," Connor said.

"You got that right," Samson said and began issuing orders.

"I've made it to within two hundred meters of the tower, General. No reaction from those creatures at all," Specialist Ruo said.

"Good. Engage all stealth protocols. Let's see what's at the tower," Connor said.

Specialist Ruo didn't have to pilot all nine reconnaissance drones in order to recon the Krake tower. There were protocols the drones would follow to perform a tactical assessment. The combat AI computers on the drones would highlight any defenses in place and monitor for Krake communication signals. It was Specialist Ruo's job to monitor the drones for feedback.

"Thanks for your help, Specialist Ruo. You can go back to your unit. Let us know if you find anything," Connor said.

Specialist Ruo saluted Connor and returned to his squad.

They made their way slowly, snaking past clusters of creatures and hills of debris from previous invasions.

The creatures were so deep in hibernation that their breaths had slowed to only one breath a minute. Even their body temperatures had dropped, and their heartbeats had slowed. The soldiers moved slowly and steadily past the creatures. It wasn't lost on any of them that only a few short hours ago, these beasts had been wreaking mayhem and destruction at the Gesora capital city. And now they looked almost dead.

Connor checked the SRD's signal detection data, looking for some kind of control signal. There wasn't any, or at least it wasn't something that was maintained. The Krake must have controlled these creatures somehow. They might've been bred with some kind of implant using devices they couldn't detect. Or perhaps it required a signal that didn't need to be maintained, which meant that a signal could be transmitted at any moment and all these creatures would come out of hibernation. Connor didn't think they would suddenly just wake up and be fully operational and ready to take action, but he didn't want to wait around and find out.

More than a few soldiers kept careful watch on the sleeping creatures. The movement of the clouds above cast shadows that made it almost seem as if some of them were moving. They weren't, but Connor wasn't immune to the illusion. They didn't talk. They merely marched toward their objective.

The tower loomed in the distance, with a few smaller

buildings nearby. Finally, they'd made it to within two hundred meters of the Krake command center.

"No enemy presence detected," Samson said.

"There aren't any defenses either," Connor replied.

"Makes sense. I mean, look where we are," Samson said and gestured behind them.

There wasn't anything in the way of active communications, other than a scheduled periodic check-in. There were short intervals of time between check-ins, but they didn't know where the signal was going.

"The Krake found a way to automate their invasion force. How long are these creatures going to be dormant before the next invasion is ordered?" Connor asked mostly to himself, thinking aloud.

Sometimes the pragmatism of the Krake scared him. There were constant reminders that everything the Krake did, they'd been doing for a very long time. This wasn't the first effort by the Krake to invade worlds or anything else like that. It was well-thought-out, practiced, and efficient. Why hadn't they anticipated an infiltration force like the CDF ever coming here? Was it because the Ovarrow had never done it before? Were the Krake blinded to this possibility? Or were they just simply too arrogant to care?

As they neared the tower, Connor ordered a few squads to check out the smaller buildings nearby. At the base of the tower, they found an entryway door. Using the Krake translator, they were able to gain entry. There was little security, which just reaffirmed Connor's belief that the Krake had never anticipated anyone but themselves coming here. And by the looks of it, the Krake hadn't come to this place in a very long time.

"Looks like those smaller buildings hold nutrient-dense bio

matter. It must be the food supply for these creatures," Samson said.

"I wonder how they distribute it," Dash said.

Once they were inside the tower, they made their way to a central command room. A few tech specialists set up shop and quickly gained access to the Krake's computer systems. Dash went to one of the workstations, planted his feet in a wide stance, and started working.

Connor used his implants to open his own link to the Krake computer system and began running a search query. He used a search protocol he'd gotten from Sean when Trident Battle Group had returned from its mission.

Samson came to his side. "It looks like everything is running on a schedule, if you can believe that."

"Looks like we have a few hours before some of these countdowns recycle. If it weren't for the fact that we're looking at an attack schedule, it could just as easily be a schedule for almost anything else," Connor said.

Samson shook his head. "If I hadn't seen it, I wouldn't have believed it. The Krake automate and schedule invasions."

"They think they've accounted for every conceivable outcome, and they're doing it without excessive personnel overseeing it all. The logistics of it on such a scale are something else."

"What do you mean?"

"It's arrogant and well thought-out at the same time," Connor said.

"We're not a threat to them from here."

"That's where you're wrong. We're inside. We're beyond the battle lines, and we need to go deeper."

The tech specialists had multiple holoscreens set up that showed data feeds coming into the Krake command center. It took a little bit of time for their translator to interface with the system, but before they knew it, they had a visual of what was going on there.

Dash sighed explosively and cursed. "You've got to see this."

Connor and Samson walked over to him.

"We knew the creatures were hibernating, but it looks like it's a rest cycle, and it's not hours. These are minutes."

Connor looked at the data. The creatures weren't about to wake up, but they would have to cut their time short. "We need to find where the platforms went."

"My guys are still searching," Samson replied.

"That's not the only thing," Dash said. "It looks like this is part of an ongoing schedule. If each of these data points represents an Ovarrow world, it looks like they're working through a huge list of worlds."

Connor peered at the data. The Krake designation for the different universes was something they were still trying to match up with what they knew. They hadn't been able to find a designation that matched New Earth. But it wasn't as simple as doing a search for whether the Krake were about to come to New Earth. It was on this list, and Connor still didn't know how the Krake coordinated this command center with others across the planet and in other universes.

"It doesn't make any sense," Samson said.

"I might be missing something," Dash replied.

"No, you're not," Connor said. "The Krake aren't purging *some* worlds. They're purging *all* worlds. Every single one of them, and they even have a schedule for it. Damn it."

He gritted his teeth. The others were quiet for a few moments. Connor could see that they were conflicted. Dash looked as if he wanted to deny it but couldn't.

Connor glanced over at the group of CDF soldiers working

on the Krake computer systems. "I need those platforms, now. Where are they?"

"We found a platform control interface," Specialist Ruo said. "I think we can recall some, but I don't know how long it will take them to get here."

Connor lowered his brows in thought. If he ordered the platforms to come here, would some kind of Krake detection system recognize the anomaly? With a schedule as complex as the one they were seeing, he had to wonder just how many red flags recalling one or two platforms would really be noticed by the Krake. "Recall the platforms, but don't initiate the connection. Allow the command to go through the regular check-in intervals. That should minimize our exposure to their anomalous detection systems."

"Yes, General," Specialist Ruo said.

A communications window appeared on one of the Krake holoscreens. The jade-colored interface flashed, followed by an audible chime to draw their attention. Everyone in the command center froze.

"What the hell is that?" Samson asked.

"Someone's initiating a comlink," Dash said.

"Specialist Ruo, do you need physical access to the system?" Connor asked.

"Negative, General. I can set up a remote access point," Specialist Ruo answered.

"Do that, and then let's clear the room."

Samson stepped closer to Connor. "You're not surprised someone is calling. Who is it?"

"That's what I want to find out."

"You don't know?" Dash asked.

"Not for sure," Connor said. "During Sean's mission, he came across a group of rebels within the Krake civilization.

They're known as the fifth column. They gave Sean a few ways to contact them, which included protocols to find their signal within the Krake systems. When we got here, I started a search and initiated contact. Someone replied."

The Krake comlink screen flashed again. Samson ordered the CDF soldiers to clear the room. Connor told Samson and Dash to wait just out of view but wanted them to listen in.

He walked up to the Krake holoscreen and acknowledged the comlink.

An image of a Krake appeared. He had an elongated, wedge-shaped head with twin cranial lobes. A jagged scar went from the top of his right lobe down toward his neck. His azure eyes were framed under a thick brow and cheekbones. The Krake's skin had a bluish hue, and the thick flesh sprouting from his chin appeared like a beard that vibrated when he spoke.

The Krake stared at Connor for a few moments. Connor wore a Nexstar combat suit and helmet, which hid his identity.

"Colonel Quinn, is that you?"

"No, it's not," Connor replied.

"But you are of the Colonial Defense Force. The CDF. You are Human," the Krake said.

"Yes. Colonel Quinn told me how to contact you. Can you confirm your identity?"

"I am Aurang. The information I gave to Colonel Quinn was to contact me personally."

"Good, then maybe you can tell me what's going on."

"You're not going to tell me who you are?"

"It doesn't matter who I am. You know what you need to know," Connor said.

"Is this how you would treat a potential ally?"

"We're not allies."

Aurang considered this for a few seconds. "You contacted me. I can go ahead and sever this connection."

Connor shook his head. "You're not going to do that."

"Why wouldn't I?"

"Let's get on with it. We both need something from the other. That's enough, isn't it?"

"What are you doing inside an automated control tower on the staging world?" Aurang asked.

"Why are the Krake purging entire worlds?"

Aurang looked away at another holoscreen that Connor couldn't see. "There is no such operation happening."

Connor tried to guess whether Aurang was lying to him and couldn't decide. "It's right here. I'm sure you're in the system right now, looking at the same information I am."

Aurang's gaze darted to the side for a moment, and then he looked back at Connor with a flicker of irritation on his face.

Connor inhaled deeply. "You *didn't* know. I can see it. You didn't know this was happening." He turned as if to leave.

"I can help you get off that world," Aurang said quickly.

"Not a chance. By the time you get here, we'll be gone," Connor said. His hand hovered over the comlink control system, about to sever the connection.

Aurang seemed to sense this. "Wait, General Gates. I think that's you. I found records of you from one of your ships. The *Vigilant*. You are General Gates, is that correct?"

Connor's face was hidden within the confines of the Nexstar combat suit. He hadn't known Aurang had been able to steal any information from the *Vigilant's* computer systems. Neither had Sean, although he'd suspected it.

"Tell me where the Krake home world is. It's not here, and I don't think it's on any of these worlds," Connor said.

"You cannot reach Quadiri from your location. It is impossible," Aurang said.

Connor thought he sounded certain of it, but the Krake could be telling him whatever he wanted to hear.

"Then I don't see the point in continuing this conversation. If you're not going to tell me where Quadiri is, what's the point. I know you're trying to use us, but maybe we're not the only ones being used here. You didn't even know that these invasions were occurring. That's a pretty big thing to miss. What else don't you know?"

Aurang turned away, and Connor saw another recent wound on the Krake's neck.

"My time is up, and you can't help me," Connor said.

"I can't help you right now. But give me a way to contact you, and I will."

"Why?"

"Because we want the same thing, General Gates. You want to find Quadiri, and I want you to find it."

"Then tell me where it is. Give me the coordinates."

"It's not that simple," Aurang said. "Even if I gave them to you, you couldn't reach it."

"Giving them to me now would prove your intentions."

"There will never be trust between us."

"Give me the location!" Connor snarled. He stepped closer to the holoscreen, an armored fist raised in front of his chest. "Tell me! Tell me where your home world is."

Aurang frowned and he looked off-screen again. "Transferring the location—"

The comlink to Aurang suddenly severed.

"No!"

Several other Krake holographic windows came to life. It looked like an automated system process had just engaged.

Connor tried to open another comlink. Aurang had been about to tell him. Damn it! He'd been so close. The Krake communication system wouldn't respond. He wanted to smash the console. He'd been so close. All he'd needed was a few more seconds.

Dash came to his side. "Connor, we have to go. Time is running out. I think the creatures are being brought out of hibernation."

Connor glared at the holoscreens, searching for some kind of override. Maybe they could delay the cycle. He looked at Samson and shook his head. "He was about to tell me."

"I know. He knows we're here," Samson said.

"He didn't know any of this was happening," Connor said and then tried to realign his thoughts.

Another world was going to be invaded. They had to move.

19

"Why would they lock out the communication systems?" Dash asked as they walked through the corridors of the Krake command center.

"It's a lockout protocol, meaning that once an operation has received a green light, they lock the system down to reduce discrepancies or anything that could interfere with the scheduled operation moving forward. We do something similar," Connor said.

"That's probably why they weren't too concerned with us accessing their system. Assuming they knew we were in there," Dash said.

Connor looked at Samson. "What's the status on the platform recall?"

"There are two platforms on their way to the Gesora camp right now," Samson replied.

They stepped outside, leaving the Krake command center behind after authorizing CDF access points so they could still receive status updates from the Krake systems.

"Have Specialist Ruo keep trying to bypass the lockout," Connor said.

Samson relayed Connor's orders and then directed other soldiers to take up positions on either side of Specialist Ruo. They would watch out for him while he tried to get into the system.

The creatures were still in deep hibernation as the CDF soldiers quickly made their way past. Connor kept going over his conversation with Aurang. Why would the Krake keep this a secret? It didn't make any sense to him. The Krake fifth column must've had an extensive network of infiltration teams embedded within the various levels of the Krake government. Connor kept coming up with more questions than he had answers for. He clenched his teeth. What happened to make the Krake decide to purge all worlds? Was this their reaction to what the CDF had done? Why not just leave them if they wanted to withdraw from them? He thought he knew the answer. He understood part of what motivated the Krake. There was a deep level of hatred that was obvious, but what fueled such hatred was what Connor didn't understand. How had the Ovarrow wronged the Krake in such a way that it had shaped their entire society?

He caught sight of movement off to the side where clusters of the predators were hibernating on the ground. Something caused them all to shudder at the same time. At first, Connor wasn't sure what he was seeing. Had they moved? Then the shudder happened again. It was a big wave, and it happened to all of them almost at the same time. There were thousands of those creatures surrounding them.

The CDF soldiers noticed the movement, and they halted.

"Keep moving," Connor said.

The line of CDF soldiers began to move.

He looked at Dash. "What's happening? Are they coming out of hibernation?"

"No, there's still time. I think it's like a pre-wake-up call," Dash replied.

They quickened their pace, making their way through an open field filled with deadly predators. The gusting winds had mostly died down and there was nothing to cover the sounds of their armored feet as they continued onward.

They didn't talk. They just kept moving. Specialist Ruo had been unable to bypass the lockout, but he did inform them that their platforms were en route to the Gesora camp. They quickly made it to the outer edges, where the creatures were still clustered in groups but more spread out. Once they were beyond the area of the hibernating creatures, they went even faster. The CDF combat suits enabled the wearers to move at speeds that were equivalent to that of any ground-based transportation over rough terrain. Even the MPSs the diplomatic envoy wore allowed them to keep up. Connor had sent word to Monin that they were headed back with a way off this world.

They made it back to the Gesora encampment to find that the Gesora soldiers had explored the area, looking for Ovarrow who had somehow come through one of the gateways. They did find survivors, but they also found many dead bodies. Some of the Ovarrow were dead or dying, but the ones who survived seemed to be in a perpetual state of shock.

After moving the encampment away from its original location, Connor shared what they'd discovered at the Krake command center.

"That means there are no safe places for us to go," Monin said.

"We were able to retrieve a lot of Krake data from the

command center. We need to get it back to the alpha site so we can analyze it. We can't give up," Connor said.

"I have no intentions of giving up. When will the platforms arrive?"

"They should be here in a few minutes," Connor replied.

"We'll need to establish a perimeter for when those creatures come out of hibernation," Monin said.

"I have my own scouts on it, but we can always use more people watching our flanks."

Monin left them to confer with his soldiers.

"Why didn't you tell him?" Dash asked.

"Because we don't know if there's a problem or not," Connor replied. "I think we'll be able to control the gateway, even if it's not part of the same system that controls the platform. The platform is just providing transportation, and that's all we need right now. Once it gets here, then we can worry about opening a gateway."

Dash shook his head. "I'm sorry, Connor. I should know better."

Connor received an alert broadcast from one of their scout groups. The platforms were almost there, and they could see their bases glowing near the thrusters at the edges. He watched as the individual thrusters moved on the base to keep the arch stable across a thirty-meter span. Specialist Ruo had them land side by side.

Several CDF tech specialists climbed up and started checking the base of the arch. They found a maintenance access point and began opening a control interface.

The Gesora gathered closer to the platforms.

Connor looked at Samson.

"Recon drones are on standby. Scanning on all available frequencies," Samson said.

They didn't know what was going to happen when they activated the gateway. Would it transmit something back to the central command that managed the platforms and gateways? Connor didn't know, but he was pretty sure they could get through it and be away from here before the Krake could generate any kind of response.

"Open a gateway to the alpha site," Connor said.

A gateway materialized, filling the space of the arch down to the platform. It wasn't bright, but there was definitely a shimmer that gave a hazy view of the other side as the CDF reconnaissance drone flew through the gateway. The Gesora were getting restless and tried to press closer, but soldiers held them back, requesting that they remain calm.

"Connection established to the drone," Specialist Ruo said. A few seconds later, he frowned and looked at Connor. "General, I'm not getting any—emergency Zulu protocol. Automated beacon, and it repeats."

"Close gateway now!"

The shimmering gateway dissipated and went dark.

Emergency protocol, Connor thought. He and Samson shared a knowing look.

"What is that? What's emergency Zulu protocol?" Dash asked.

Monin watched Connor, waiting for his answer.

Connor's gut clenched. "The alpha site has been attacked. Those beacons were activated to warn the away teams to stay away."

Holzer stepped toward them. "The alpha site has been attacked?"

"Yes, and it's been destroyed. The alpha site is gone," Connor said, unable to believe it.

"Destroyed? But how could—" Holzer began.

"General Gates, there's a broadcast coming from the platform," Specialist Ruo said.

"Shut it down," Connor said.

"I'm trying, but it's already checked in with something. There's an acknowledgment here," Specialist Ruo replied.

Connor brought up the Krake mission control schedule. The timeline had changed. The creatures were coming out of hibernation, and they were heading for them.

"What are we going to do?" Holzer asked.

Connor's mind raced. The alpha site had been destroyed by the Krake, and the creatures were heading toward them. All those soldiers who'd been stationed there . . . Had they all been killed? They would have fought. They would not abandon their posts. And what about all the away teams?

"We need to return home," Holzer said.

Connor shook his head. "No."

"What do you mean 'no'? Where are we going to go? We can't stay here, and we can't go to the alpha site," Holzer said.

Just then, various scout reports came in, tracking movement from the creatures. They were still far away, but they were heading here. Connor looked around at the others.

Holzer was about to speak again.

"Just wait for a second," Connor said. "Specialist Ruo, can you remote control the gateway now?"

"Yes, General," Ruo answered.

"Good. Send that platform away from us toward the creatures. Activate it and pick a world at random. I don't care. Just do it as quickly as possible," Connor said, then frowned. "Wait, Specialist. I have an idea where to send them."

Monin stormed toward him. "What's the meaning of this. You're sending away a means for our escape."

The Gesora soldiers readied their weapons. The CDF soldiers did the same, aiming at the Gesora soldiers.

"Monin, you have to trust me," Connor replied. "Activating the gateway is somehow linked to whatever system is controlling those creatures. They get activated. They come out of hibernation and they're heading here right now. We still have the other platform."

"We can't stay here," Monin said.

The platform began to rise into the air.

"Bring the platform back down," Monin said.

"It's not going to happen. If we don't move that platform, those creatures will be here in minutes. If you want to stop me, you're going to have to shoot me," Connor said.

As the platform continued to rise into the air, Connor wasn't sure whether the Gesora were going to open fire. This was getting out of control too quickly.

"Stand down," Monin said at last.

The Gesora soldiers reluctantly lowered their weapons, and Connor ordered the CDF soldiers to do the same.

He couldn't open a gateway to New Earth from here. The Krake would be able to track them, and he wouldn't put New Earth in any more danger than they were already in. The platform flew away from them, but they still had one more.

Samson came over to him. "The alpha site is destroyed. New Earth may already be under attack."

"We don't know that."

"Fine, but what do you want to do? If we don't do something, someone else is going to do something stupid," Samson said.

He wasn't wrong, and Connor knew it.

20

Lars Mallory glanced up at the clear skies overhead. This world wasn't as bad as some of the others. At least the air was breathable, but the gravity was 23 percent higher than normal. The Nexstar combat suits helped compensate for the increased gravity. Without them, they would've tired out much more quickly.

For the past thirty-six hours, they'd been on this world doing reconnaissance of the Ovarrow who lived here. The Ovarrow of this world had evolved differently than what they'd seen on the other worlds. They were much shorter, which was attributed to the higher gravitational pull of their larger planet. The Ovarrow of New Earth were tall and lean, and seemed to share an ancestry with both reptiles and mammals. The Ovarrow here were shorter and more muscular, but beyond the differences in appearances, Lars had observed similarities that seemed to be evident in every universe they'd been to. He suspected that the Krake had contributed to this cycle they'd seen over and over again.

"You know, this place isn't so bad," Perez said.

The rocky desert landscape was a sea of deep reds, with a terrain that had baked under the powerful sun since forever.

"Thirty-one-hour days? No thank you. Like every one of these places we go to, I can't wait to get out of here," Butler said.

"At least we can breathe the air here," Perez replied.

They were just over a kilometer outside the city, which had been founded because of an oasis. Lars couldn't think of another reason why anybody would settle out here. But this was just another place for him, just something else that he had to do.

Lieutenant Miller gestured for him to come over. "They're late. Are we sure about the egress point?"

Lars double-checked the coordinates and confirmed their location. "Yes, sir. This is the place."

"Maybe somebody decided that we're not going home this time," Perez said.

Miller looked away and scanned the area.

"No, seriously, this is our reward," Perez said.

"Shut up, Perez," Lars said.

"Geez, I was just joking, Sergeant."

"I know you are. It's just not helping. Why don't you go make sure no one's sneaking up on us," Lars said.

Perez left them with only minimal grumbling.

Lars walked over to Miller. "I think we're a little exposed here, Lieutenant."

Miller shook his head. "Something's not right. I know it."

"They could just be having a mechanical issue with the arch on their end. I say we find some cover and maintain a visual of the area, sir," Lars said.

Miller nodded. "I hope you're right, Sergeant, I really do."

A comlink registered from Perez. "I'm seeing movement out here. There's something—Damn! There are a lot of things crossing the desert."

"I'll be right there," Lars said, and Miller raised his eyebrows. "Perez saw something. I'm going to see what it is."

As Lars crossed their small camp, he noted that others were seeing something in the desert too. He climbed to the top of a hill and peered into the distance. It only took him a few moments to see what Perez had been talking about. There were creatures appearing out of nowhere and heading toward the Ovarrow city in an all-out run. There were so many of them that they left clouds of dust in their wake.

Lars engaged the high-res optics of his combat suit. The creatures had pinkish-gray armor, craggy and rough. They galloped on all fours. A group of them broke off from the others and headed toward a small fuel station where several Ovarrow were working. One of the Ovarrow gestured toward the others, and they spun toward the creatures.

"Holy shit! Those things just killed them," Perez said.

Lars looked at Miller. "We should send out our SRDs."

"Do it," Miller replied.

In less than a minute, they had four SRDs heading toward the city at an accelerated rate. More creatures appeared, but Lars couldn't find where they were coming from. They were all heading toward the city. He saw a slight distortion near the ground. As the SRD flew toward it, Lars got a better look.

"These are gateways. They're coming through gateways," Lars said.

"It's the Krake. It has to be," Miller said.

"Shouldn't we warn the Ovarrow?" Perez asked.

"What for? Who's going to listen to us?" Butler said.

"I don't know. Somebody might."

"No communication," Miller said. "Recall the drones now."

Perez looked like he was about to say something else, but Lars glared at him, and he shut up for once. The SRDs were quickly recalled, but not before the video feed showed multiple gateways opening inside the city.

"Lieutenant, can we talk?" Lars asked.

Miller nodded and they walked back down the hill. "What is it, Sergeant?"

"We've seen an uptick in Krake attacks. This might be part of a larger campaign. I'm wondering if the Krake have attacked the alpha site and that's why they're late," Lars said and glanced at the soldiers on top of the hill. "Maybe no one is coming for us."

Miller thinned his lips, and his eyes took on the cast of just having learned something he'd rather not consider. "Damn it. I hate to say it, but I think you're right. They've never missed a rendezvous time. Something's wrong. What the hell are we going to do? We're stranded here."

Lars glanced up at the top of the hill where most of the 3rd Platoon had gathered.

"It's right in front of us," Perez said.

The CDF soldiers brought up their weapons, and Lars and Miller raced up the hill.

"Hold your fire," Miller said.

A short distance from them was a gateway, and those creatures were coming out of it. They didn't look behind them, running toward the city as if they knew where they had to go. Lars hissed for the others to be quiet. He glanced toward the city and saw a Krake warship flying toward it. There was no question about it now. The Krake were here, and they were invading this place.

"Sir, I have an idea, but you're not going to like it," Lars said.

Miller looked at him. "What have you got?"

"We can't stay here, and we don't have a way home. We need to use that gateway to get out of here."

Miller's eyes widened. "You can't be serious."

"It's the only option. We shouldn't stay here. Those creatures are going to find us, or the Krake are going to find us. Something happened back at the alpha site. That's the only reason they're late. They would've brought another arch in for us by now." Lars gestured toward the gateway a short distance away. "But there's a way out of here. We wait for the creatures to stop coming through, and then we slip in."

"We've no idea what's on the other side. There could be thousands of those things waiting for us," Miller said.

"Send a drone through, have a look around, and report back to us. I think this is our best option, sir. But it's your call," Lars said.

Miller regarded him for a few moments and then nodded. "Send a drone to the gateway."

"I'm on it, sir," Private Derek Duffy said.

An SRD flew above them, heading toward the gateway. It slipped in overtop of the creatures thundering through and disappeared from view. Less than a minute later it came back, and Lars looked at the video feed data it had recorded. It showed a darkened landscape. As the video panned around, he saw hundreds of arches on floating platforms, moving from place to place. Miller was right. There were thousands of creatures there, but not in the immediate area.

Lars looked at him. "Out of the frying pan, sir."

Miller shook his head. "3rd Platoon, we're going to that gateway. Wait for my order."

When it came time to work, the 3rd Platoon was all business. What had been a peaceful reconnaissance mission had become something else, and they all knew it.

"I'll go through first," Lars said.

"I knew you would," Miller said.

Lars gestured for his squad to follow him and they

approached the gateway. The number of creatures running through had slowed down to a trickle. He counted to five and then circled around the gateway, stepping through. Going through a gateway never felt like anything, but this time he stumbled forward because he'd found himself a meter off the ground. He cleared the area and waited for the others. Lars had his weapon up, checking the vicinity. The rest of the squad came through and took up positions on both sides of the gateway. Dull, shimmering light came from the other gateways spread out around them.

Several creatures ran toward them, and the soldiers fired their weapons, stopping them in their tracks. The rest of the platoon came through, and Lars led them away from the gateway. The creatures continued to head toward the gateway as if they were drawn to it.

The soldiers cleared the area, moving a good distance from any of the other gateways, and regrouped. Lars checked his comlink and saw there was a broadcast signal. He frowned. It was a CDF broadcast.

Lars acknowledged the broadcast, and a comlink opened.

"This is Corporal Bradley, 7th Ranger Company. Who is this?"

"I'm Sergeant Lars Mallory, 3rd Platoon Special Infantry Division. We just came through a gateway. The Krake are attacking that world. Our rendezvous from the alpha site didn't happen."

"Understood, Sergeant. I have your location. I'm connecting you to General Gates now," Corporal Bradley said.

A few moments later, Lars heard Connor's voice, and Lars told him what had happened. Lieutenant Miller joined the comms channel.

"The alpha site is gone," Connor said. "You're luckier than you realize."

"I'll take your word for it, General," Miller said. "Honestly, it was Mallory. He's the one whose quick thinking brought us here, but we're surrounded by those creatures. The weird thing is that they seem more concerned with getting to the gateways than they are about us."

"Understood, and good work," Connor said. Lars thought he sounded like he meant it. "Sit tight for a minute. I'm going to transmit our location and send a waypoint for you to meet us."

"General, what's going on?" Miller asked.

There was a brief moment of silence. "The Krake are staging multiple attacks on Ovarrow worlds. We don't know if they've attacked New Earth, but they did reach the alpha site."

Miller looked at Lars and exhaled a puff of breath. "How'd they find the alpha site?" he asked.

"We think the Krake can track gateway use and are tracing its use to all our allies. They attacked the Gesora while we were on their world. That's all we have time for now. Sending the waypoint to you. Travel fast and silent. Gates out."

21

SEAN SAT in his room aboard the *Vigilant*. His quarters were more like an apartment. He had a bedroom, a private bathroom, and a small meeting area. The wallscreen showed a distant view of Sagan's mustard-colored surface. Long gashes marked the planet's northern hemisphere where great chasms expanded like cracks on a sheet of ice. The planet had no atmosphere and no signs of life having ever been there. The rocky inner planet was of a similar size to that of New Earth but lacked a magnetic field strong enough to protect its surface from powerfully charged particles.

Sagan had two small moons and a small asteroid field that orbited the planet. The moons had given Sagan enough of a tilt that if it had a more solid iron core and an abundance of water, there would've been a better than average chance that life would flourish there. Planetary tilt was necessary to provide movement on the surface of a planet in order for life to thrive. Because they'd discovered salt deposits, colonial scientists believed there'd once been oceans of water on the planet. Sean wasn't sure why he found that so interesting, but he did. This planet was an example of just how fragile the chance was that not just life, but intelligent life, could exist in the galaxy.

"You're awfully quiet," Oriana said. "At times like these, I don't know whether to be worried or just leave you alone to enjoy the silence."

Sean looked at her and smiled. "You can always come over here and join me."

Oriana approached him, and his gaze slid down to take in the sway of her hips as she walked.

"Eyes up here, mister."

Sean chuckled as she sat down, but she looked at him intently.

"You *do* have something on your mind."

He shrugged. He did, but he wasn't sure how to ask the question. She leaned into him, and he wrapped an arm around her shoulders.

"I will never get tired of this," she said.

"Me either."

He felt the tension drain out of him, but there was still a good bit gathered in his stomach. He inhaled and felt the heat rise in his chest. Oriana sat up and looked at him, waiting.

"Do you ever think about—"

A klaxon alarm sounded.

"Action stations. Action stations. Set condition one throughout the ship. This is not a drill," Gabriel said over a broadcast comlink.

Sean's eyes widened and he inhaled sharply. Both Sean and Oriana stood and raced out of his quarters, which were in close proximity to the central bridge. As they ran down a stretch of corridor, the CDF soldiers on duty spotted them coming and opened the doors.

Sean hastened toward the command center. "Sitrep."

"Multiple Krake contacts. Destroyer class, Colonel," Major Shelton said.

She moved to the auxiliary workstation, and Sean sat in the commander's chair.

He looked at the tactical plot on the main holoscreen. Lieutenant Scott was already coming up with firing solutions. There were four groups of Krake ships, and their emergence point was closer to Sagan than to the Trident Battle Group. Between them were rows of space gates that the CDF had been using in a mock bombardment exercise.

"Gamma burst detected, Colonel," Major Shelton said.

"Can we lock in the origin point?" Sean asked.

He needed to take out the Krake warships, but he also wanted to shut down their space gates. The only way they could be detected was from gamma bursts when a gateway was opened in space.

"Two definite and two partials," Major Shelton replied.

"Tactical," Sean said, "I want Alpha and Bravo firing solutions. HADES Vs with protector drone escorts. Targeting priority is the two confirmed gateways we can detect."

"Yes, Colonel, firing solution ready," Lieutenant Scott said.

"Execute," Sean said.

The *Vigilant* was the flagship of the battle group. Targeting priorities were instantly communicated to the rest of the battle group, and the combat AIs across multiple CDF ships presented the data to their commanding officers. Ultimately, it was up to the commanding officers to execute firing solutions. The twelve CDF warships fired their HADES V missiles, along with the protector drones, achieving near synchrony.

The tactical plot on the main holoscreen split into four quadrants. Gabriel, the *Vigilant's* AI, highlighted a high-res image of the Krake warships in the distance. There were green flashes of light.

"They've launched attack drones," Lieutenant Scott said.

"What's the status on the location of the partial gateways?" Sean asked.

"The sensors can't get a definitive lock, Colonel," Major Shelton said.

In a perfect world, Sean could wait for a target lock, but he didn't have time for that. "Tactical, I need a targeting solution for the partial gateway locations. We'll need to update targeting as they go."

"Yes, Colonel. Firing solution ready."

"Execute," Sean said.

The ammunition stores on the Trident Battle Group warships weren't fully stocked. They had expended more than half of their ammunition on the war game drills they'd been performing. The situation wasn't ideal. He had to hit the Krake hard and fast. He didn't have time to be worried about how the Krake had found them. They were here.

Sean looked at the tactical plot on the main holoscreen and frowned. The Krake combat drones weren't heading toward them. They were on an intercept course for the colonial space gates.

"Ops, what's the status of the alert squadrons?" Sean asked.

"Six Lancer groups are refueling. Eight Stinger groups are on standby, sir," Lieutenant Hoffman said.

"Green-light the Stingers. They are to defend the space gates, best speed."

Talon-V Stinger-class fighters were a single-occupant, quick-response, light attack craft with three forward-facing cannons. They were highly maneuverable, which would assist them when avoiding destruction by the Krake attack drones, and they could help defend the space gates, buying Trident Battle Group time to get into position. They would've been overwhelmed if the Talon-V Lancer-class fighter hadn't joined them on the field.

Lancer-class fighter was also a light attack craft with three occupants. It carried more in the way of weapons and point defense systems.

"Ops, I don't care who you have to kick in the ass. I need Lancer squadrons launched ASAP," Sean said.

Lieutenant Hoffman acknowledged.

"Helm, plot a course to our space gates."

"Yes, Colonel," Lieutenant Aaron Edwards replied.

As Trident Battle Group moved in to defend the colonial space gates, the Krake attack drones approached at high speed. They were going to beat the CDF to the space gates. The tactical plot now showed squadrons of Talon-V Stinger-class speeding ahead. A few minutes later, the Lancer squadron began to show up on the tactical plot. Ahead of them all were clusters of HADES V missiles, along with their protector drone escorts. The protector drones had not activated the artificial gravity field and wouldn't do so unless the Krake attack drones targeted them.

The Krake destroyers had moved away from their emergence point and were heading toward the rows of space gates. This was an aggressive tactic, and Sean ground his teeth in frustration. He didn't have enough HADES Vs to engage the Krake at a distance, and they couldn't survive a broadside with them. The artificial gravity field powered by the Casimir power core could protect them in an emergency, but not with the sustained barrage that a broadside would give them.

The first group of Krake attack drones reached a colonial space gate, and within moments it went off-line. The Krake attack drones spiraled around and headed toward the next space gate in the line.

Their active sensors detected more Krake attack drones, and these were heading on an intercept course for their missile groups. The new targeting information had already been transmitted to the protector drones.

"Artificial gravity fields have gone active on protector drones," Lieutenant Scott confirmed.

Because of the recent war game drills, they'd learned which HADES V formation gave them maximum protection by the protector drones. The tactical plot on the main holoscreen of the *Vigilant* showed that the attack drones were within close proximity to the first wave of missiles. Video feeds from several protector drones confirmed that the attack drones had tried to collide with the HADES V missiles, but they slid off course when they contacted the artificial gravity field. The attack drones attempted to course correct, but the same thing happened. Sean watched as the power levels for the protector drones went down.

The first set of HADES V missile groups put on a last burst of speed as they closed in on the Krake warships.

"Direct hit. Confirm detonation," Lieutenant Scott said.

The fusion warheads exploded, temporarily blinding their sensors, but Sean knew that the destructive force was tearing the Krake warships apart.

"Four confirmed kills, Colonel," Lieutenant Scott said.

Sean clenched his fists. "Yes!"

The Krake warships began to execute evasive maneuvers. More attack drones were launched.

Sean looked at the tactical plot where the Krake gateways were. Two HADES V missiles left the cover of the protector drones and executed a full burn. They reached the two gateways as a gamma burst was building up. The missiles must've slammed into another Krake warship as it was transitioning. The HADES Vs detonated, but their sensors only detected a partial detonation, which meant that a bulk of the warhead had ignited in the alternate universe.

The HADES V missiles from the Charlie firing solution blazed a path to the vicinity where the third and fourth Krake gateways were, but several Krake destroyers had altered their courses and were heading on an intercept trajectory. Krake destroyers were fast. A wave of attack drones raced toward the unprotected HADES V missiles at speeds the CDF couldn't match. The HADES V missiles were destroyed before they could detonate.

"They're on to us now," Sean said.

The battle was far from over, but if Sean couldn't take out the other space gates, their situation was dire. He had no way of knowing just how much of a supply line the Krake had in whatever alternate universe they were coming from.

This was only the beginning.

22

Ne ws of the Krake attack reached Nathan while he was en route to a Security Council meeting with Governor Mullins. He'd immediately ordered the pilot to take him to the CDF base. There, he opened a comlink to Mullins using the secure emergency network protocol.

Governor Mullins's face appeared on the holoscreen in front of him.

"Trident Battle Group has discovered Krake warships near planet Sagan. The Krake are here, Governor," Nathan said.

Mullins blinked rapidly as if he wasn't sure what he'd just heard. "My God. Are they anywhere else? Are they here as well?"

"Nothing has been reported yet. I've ordered Phoenix Station and Lunar Base to high alert, as well as the home fleet. The Krake are coming here. If they're in any part of the star system, they're going to be coming here as well. It's just a matter of time. I need your authorization to enact a Cavalier."

Project Cavalier was the defensive measures and plans that

both he and Connor had put together after the Vemus invasion. They had made it part of their rebuilding efforts.

"Project Cavalier is authorized," Governor Mullins said without preamble.

"Thank you, Governor. I'll update you within the next fifteen minutes. I urge you and your staff to get to your secure location," Nathan said.

"May God have mercy on us," Governor Mullins said.

The video comlink severed.

Emergency communication protocols were in place for just this event. Nathan now had all the authorization he needed, and he executed Project Cavalier. Automated systems would begin activating throughout all colonial cities. Emergency communication networks went live. Civilian flights were grounded, and passengers were ordered to return to their cities of origin. Project Cavalier also put all CDF bases on high alert, as well as notified the Mekaal that they'd received an imminent threat from the Krake. The Ovarrow would follow their own safety measures, which Nathan had reviewed. They would sequester the population of Ovarrow who could not fight into a safe location, but everyone else would be armed.

Years ago, when the Vemus invaded New Earth and Sean Quinn had defended the cities, he had done so with limited armed soldiers. Field Ops only had light weaponry, and Sean had chosen to lure the Vemus into the city. Then, using a WMD, he'd blown them up. The CDF had had their backs against the wall then, and it had fallen to Nathan as part of their rebuilding efforts to prevent such a catastrophe from happening again. Nathan had never faulted Sean's tactics. He'd have done the same, but this time would be different. They were better prepared. The more they learned about the Krake, the more

Connor and Nathan had pushed for additional preparations to be made for their safety. Stockpiles of weapons, survival gear, medicine, and anything else they could possibly need were safely tucked away. The Vemus had been an unknown threat, and they'd only been able to guess at how they could prepare for it, but the Krake were different. They'd known the Krake were coming. Nathan had never doubted it. In this, both he and Connor agreed. And they had worked to convince everyone else of the validity of the threat. He just hoped that their hard work had been enough.

As he flew over the city, he glanced down and saw that Field Ops had been deployed and was helping to guide civilians to a safe location. Governor Mullins was broadcasting a warning to everyone. People would be scared, probably more frightened by what they didn't know. Nathan checked the data feeds from COMCENT, and so far no Krake presence had been detected near New Earth.

The pilot flew them to the CDF base and landed at the emergency landing pad just outside central command. As Nathan was exiting the shuttle, he received a comlink from Savannah.

"Where are you?" Nathan asked.

"I'm at the CDF base at New Haven. I saw that Cavalier has gone active. Where are the Krake?"

"Sean has engaged them out near Sagan," Nathan said.

Savannah frowned. "Sagan?" she said in disbelief. "We always thought they'd show up right here. How did they find us?" Her gaze darted to the side as she read a quick message. "The children are on their way to the secure bunker."

Nathan thought of young Oliver and little Liv. Their daughter was only two years old and probably didn't really understand what was happening, but Oliver was older. Nathan expected that all he'd want was to be by his parents, but he couldn't have that. Pangs of guilt thickened the back of his throat for a few moments. He wanted to protect them himself.

At the command center in New Haven, Savannah acknowledged somebody speaking to her off-screen and then looked back at him. Her eyes were tense. "I want them with me, but I know it's . . ."

"Me too," Nathan said. "Me too, and you as well."

Savannah smiled, and they shared a brief moment where they were just husband and wife. All too soon, it was gone.

"I'm entering the command center now. Time to go to work," Nathan said.

Savannah gave him a crisp nod and the comlink severed.

The command center at the CDF base at Sierra was much like the base at Hammerholde. COMCENT duties were shared between the two. Data links to the two bases, as well as Lunar Base, were synced so that any one of them could perform the duties of the other. Nathan was general of the CDF and therefore had command authority wherever he was at the moment.

He walked over to the central holotank and sent his authorization. A shield emblem presented itself and then scattered into multiple vid-comm windows. Nathan looked at them. His wife represented the commanding officer at the CDF base at New Haven. Colonel John Randall was on for Hammerholde. Colonel Celeste Belonét was stationed at Phoenix Station. Colonel Jenna Watts was on the bridge of a heavy cruiser leading the CDF home fleet. There were others as various colonial government agencies joined, but there was one face missing. Nathan noticed right away, and it was probably on more than one person's mind. That absence was something he wished he hadn't noticed. He would have preferred someone else who could shoulder the burden with him, but Connor was nowhere to be found.

"The Krake are here and we need to be on full alert," Nathan said. "I'm authorizing the mobilization of all CDF forces. We will begin patrols in addition to our current defensive measures. We cannot afford to leave any stone unturned. The Krake are coming here, and we will be ready. Defensive networks will be engaged and coordinated with Field Ops. The Mekaal have been notified and should join us shortly. I also want a comms drone dispatched to the Konus."

At some point, the Security Council had joined the meeting. No one trusted the Konus. They had attacked the Mekaal, and CDF lives had been lost as part of their test of the CDF military.

"The past is the past," Nathan continued. "The Krake are coming for us all, and that includes the Konus. They have a sizable fighting force, and I intend to use every tool at our disposal to fight the Krake. It's as simple as that."

"General Hayes, what is General Gates's current status?" Mullins asked.

"I have an update for that," Colonel Randall said. Nathan gestured for him to keep going. "As part of Project Cavalier, we requested an update status from all CDF bases, and the alpha site has failed to check in. They're on a twenty-four-hour check-in interval. We opened a gateway to the alpha site and sent a message through that was not acknowledged. We then sent an SRD. I've just seen the image myself right now, and the alpha site is gone. It's been destroyed."

Shocked silence took hold of everyone at the command center in Sierra and everywhere else on the call.

"Did you find any survivors?" Nathan asked.

"Not yet, General. We're still searching. The CDF base there is completely gone," Colonel Randall replied.

Nathan's mouth went dry. "We need a rescue op to the alpha site. We have away teams scheduled to return there, and right now they're all stranded. Colonel Randall, I'm putting you in charge of that."

"Yes, General Hayes. I'll see to it right now," Colonel Randall said, and his comlink shut down.

Even as Nathan focused on what he had to do, in the back of his mind was a faint, gnawing whisper that Connor was dead. He didn't want to believe that or even acknowledge the thought. He needed to focus. There were too many moving parts depending on him.

"Colonel Watts, the fleet deployment will need to be done by you. Stay within the vicinity of New Earth, but make sure we have adequate coverage of the planet," Nathan said, and went through their defensive posture with the various CDF locations.

The last update they'd received from Sean Quinn had to do with the success of the protector drones. Nathan wanted whatever stockpile of the prototype drones they had deployed to the home fleet. The logistics were being coordinated by Colonel Hughes of Lunar Base. They'd also need to start building more of the protector drones as soon as possible.

They tried to cover all their contingency plans, but they didn't know what the Krake's intentions were or what type of invasion force they'd bring here. If they wanted to wipe them out, they'd come with an overwhelming fleet to bombard the planet. Perhaps the Krake fighting force at Sagan was just a scout force. They still had a little bit of time. Nathan felt that they were going to invade somewhere near New Earth. Governor Mullins asked him what he expected.

"We've talked about this," Nathan said. "It could be anything. I'd first want to get a foothold and then start planet-side operations. Coordinate my attacks with wherever my supply lines were coming from. When the Krake attack, it will escalate quickly, and it will get much worse as time goes on."

"What about finding the Krake home world?" Mullins asked.

"Connor was working on that very thing. That's why he went to the Gesora. With the alpha site destroyed, we don't know where Connor is. But I can assure you that will be part of the main rescue op," Nathan replied.

With Project Cavalier engaged, there would always be somebody commanding these communication calls, so they didn't all have to stay there. Representatives from various government agencies would keep the lines of communication open. Nathan stepped away from the holotank and opened a commlink on his personal holoscreen. He owed his friend this much.

Lenora Bishop answered. "Nathan, where's Connor?"

"I'm sorry, Lenora. I don't know. I just learned that the alpha site has been destroyed by the Krake. We're starting rescue operations, and as soon as I know more, I'll contact you. I'll do everything I can to find him. Please believe me."

Lenora inhaled and swallowed, squeezing her eyes shut for a moment. Then she shook her head. "I believe you, Nathan. I know you'll do everything you can. I know you don't have any time to talk to me, and I appreciate you contacting me anyway. I just want to say one thing. Connor believes in you. He always has. You know him. He always said the CDF was in good hands with you leading it."

Nathan felt the heat rise in his face. He swallowed hard and couldn't think of what else to say. He'd rather have his friend here with him. Lenora said goodbye and the comlink closed.

Connor had decades of experience in the military. He'd attempted to impart that knowledge to everyone in the CDF, but it was different. The men who had served with Connor in the

NA Alliance military were different. Now, it would be up to the men and women of the CDF to defend the colony.

Nathan pushed his personal angst aside and returned to the holotank. One thing at a time, he told himself. That's what Connor would tell him.

23

AURANG HAD DEVOTED his life to removing the overseers from power. After his conversation with the CDF general, Connor Gates, he decided to investigate something he had thought was beyond the overseers' reach—the fifth column network. It was a fragile thing, segmented to avoid detection and compromise. Sadoon had betrayed him, and there had been others, but he'd always been able to neutralize those threats. The most useful tools were the ones that only he could influence, but the more control he exerted, the less useful those tools became. Sadoon's treachery meant that he had to change his plans.

It hadn't been difficult for Aurang to track the CDF soldiers to the staging world. He didn't need their exact location. All he needed was a general region where they were located. They'd either discovered one of the staging worlds on their own or gone through a gateway that had originated from that world. He soon figured out how they had come to be there.

Long ago, Aurang had established automated protocols to

validate the fifth column network and all its participants. Those checks never failed, and yet he'd missed that Prime Overseer Ersevin had launched a major operation to purge all Ovarrow worlds. Fifth column agents often worked in isolation, which was their strength. But when Aurang had checked on his agents' current statuses using alternative means, he'd learned that they were no longer active. Someone had eliminated them, or they'd betrayed him, and yet the check-in protocols he had established didn't reflect this fact.

He'd returned to Quadiri and was in one of his safe houses, a location no one else had ever known about. Doubtless, everything else that had been recorded was now compromised.

He stood before multiple green holoscreens, and each showed that his life's work was coming undone. He'd clung to the belief that the Humans would eventually find Quadiri and bring the war here, but they were out of time. He had to act. Tools that he'd accumulated over the years would have to be used. He worked quickly, knowing that his current level of access was likely being tracked by Prime Overseer Ersevin. If he was lucky, what he was setting in motion wouldn't be stopped.

All the holoscreens powered off at once. The door to the warehouse opened, and Krake soldiers stormed the area. Suppression shackles flew through the air and Aurang scrambled out of the way, activating a small defense turret. A panel in the ceiling opened and a high-energy plasma turret descended. Several Krake soldiers went down in a barrage of fire from the turret. The other soldiers scrambled out of the way.

As Aurang ran toward the back of the room, he heard the soldiers' weapons firing back at the turret. He reached the door and tried to access the controls. They were unresponsive. He was locked out. The turret went silent and he heard the suppression shackles flying toward him. They slammed onto his wrists and lifted him into the air. The shackles spun him around and flew back toward the soldiers, then raised him into the air and let him fall to the ground. This cycle repeated, and each time, the shackles raised him to a height that, enhancements notwithstanding, broke the bones in his legs. Aurang snarled at the soldiers.

They didn't say anything to him.

One of the Krake soldiers projected a holoscreen from his power armor, and Aurang saw the Prime Overseer's face.

"I thought you believed the Humans were not a threat," Aurang said.

"They are not much of one," Prime Overseer Ersevin replied.

"Then why purge all Ovarrow worlds?"

"All things end in time. Ideas spread between worlds, corrupting our experiments. There's no longer a point in continuing with any of them."

"So, you have the answer, then," Aurang said, and Ersevin regarded him. "You don't. You don't know. I thought that was the reason for all of this."

"That's exactly what you were supposed to believe."

Aurang kept trying to push Ersevin off-balance, and instead the opposite was occurring. "I've been enlightened. I'm not one of your Krake drones."

"Are you so sure about that? Perhaps you're a single tool that has always done what I expected it to do."

"But you still don't have the answer to the question," Aurang said. "After hundreds of years of research, pushing the boundaries, we still don't have an answer."

"The concept—or question, as you put it—as to why there are no other Krake worlds is something we will be thinking about long after this conversation ends," Prime Overseer Ersevin said.

"There are only Ovarrow worlds. Even if you succeed in your purge, there will be others. It's almost as if there is a universal constant."

"That's exactly the kind of answer I would expect from someone who has had the psychological conditioning you've had. Everything—every thought or idea or opinion or fact that you've had—was engineered by me."

Aurang looked away. "Impossible."

"You understand who I am. I've been in power for a very long time, and I will continue to be in power for very long time. Things will change, but not me or my role. The fifth column network was a useful tool that now must be cast aside."

"And what of the Humans?" Aurang asked.

"It was easy to manipulate your allies," Ersevin replied. "I simply gave Sadoon what he wanted. Our predictive models need no further experimentation. Therefore, there is no more need for the Ovarrow, or the Humans, for that matter. Wondering why we are alone in the universe is a concept for primitive minds to ponder. This is beneath us."

"You underestimate me."

"No, I don't think I do."

"Then you already know what I've done. You know what I've set in motion," Aurang said.

"At some point, it just doesn't matter what you've done," Ersevin said. "Your influence is fragmented and ineffectual. However, a tool can be reused. You've been reused multiple times."

Aurang accessed his implants. "You underestimate a lot of things," he said and activated the bomb he had placed in the armor on his chest. The explosion killed him instantly, and he had the satisfaction of knowing that the Krake soldiers who had taken him into custody would also be dead. But what gave him the greatest satisfaction was knowing that his death would set things in motion that Prime Overseer Ersevin would never anticipate. Aurang knew this because he'd used the same predictive models the overseers employed. Their arrogance would blind them.

24

CONNOR LOOKED at the arch gateway on the SRD video feed. Thousands of predators had gathered around it, watching it intently. The platform was still active, but the gateway had been shut down. The Gesora and the CDF had managed to move the Gesora refugees several kilometers away. The predators hadn't noticed them.

Connor uploaded a set of coordinates to the arch gateway and activated it. The gateway activation sent waves through the predators that had gathered around it. After a few minutes, they began running through the gateway. He chuckled a little.

"Where did you send them?" Dash asked.

"Someplace they're not going to come back from," Connor replied.

Samson glanced at them. "Where is it?"

"Actually, we don't know what's on the other side," Connor replied. "The probes we've sent through just show darkness and a lack of atmosphere. There aren't any planets. There aren't even any stars. I don't know how long the creatures are going to go for this, or if the Krake will notice what we've done and shut the gateway down."

They watched the video feed for a few moments, each of them shaking their head. A comlink registered itself, and a message came.

"Monin wants an answer," Samson said.

"I'm not about to start fighting the Gesora over this. We can recall the other platform if we need it. Do you have 3rd Platoon's current location?" Connor asked.

"They're making progress. They should be at the waypoint within a few hours," Samson said.

Connor nodded and they headed toward the Gesora, who were walking ahead of them. He'd been more than a little surprised to hear from Lars Mallory and the 3rd Platoon of the SID.

"The Phantoms have a good record," Samson said.

Dash pointedly did not make any comments. He knew who was with that platoon, and Connor understood that the two would never trust each other. Some wounds would never mend. That was just the way it was.

"They have a bit of a reputation," Connor said.

"They're survivors, and that's saying something, considering some of the worlds we've sent them to," Samson said.

Connor arched an eyebrow toward him. "It sounds like you respect them."

"I don't approve of what they did before, but they achieve their objectives, and they follow orders. That's all that matters to me right now."

"Agreed."

Specialist Ruo ran up to them, holding a device in his hand. "General Gates, the control interface has been added to this

module. We also have explosive charges set to disable the arch
gateway after it's used."

Connor took the blocky module from Ruo. "Thank you."

Specialist Ruo saluted Connor and then went back to his
squad.

They made their way up the line to where Monin waited for
them. Connor handed him the control module for the arch
gateway.

"We can control the gateway with this?" Monin asked.

"Yes, and we programmed it with the coordinates of your
home world," Connor replied. "Once the last of your people go
through, you can close the gateway, and that will trigger the self-
destruct."

Monin peered at the module for a moment and then looked
at Connor. "Are you certain you won't reconsider coming
with us?"

"There might not be any other gateways on your planet
anymore. We would be stranded. I understand your reasoning
for wanting to return home, and I do hope you find survivors.
When we're able, we'll come back to check on you."

"You will not return to your home world?" Monin asked.

Connor shook his head. "Not yet. We've received a
communication from some of our soldiers that found their way
here from another planet. We'll rendezvous with them and then
use the other platform to take us to another destination."

"If you return home, you could just come back with more
equipment and soldiers."

"It's not that simple, Monin. If the Krake have started their
invasion, we won't have equipment or soldiers to spare."

"I'll give you some time to clear the area before I activate the
gateway. I hope you succeed. I wanted to do more, but my
people need me," Monin said.

Connor thanked him and rejoined the others. The 7th Ranger Company quickly left the area, heading toward the rendezvous point with the 3rd Platoon. Not knowing the state of the Gesora home world, he didn't know if he was ever going to see Monin again. Had the Krake just destroyed the cities, or had they sought to corrupt the biosphere so the planet was unlivable? Connor understood why Monin wanted to return. He wanted to fight for his home, and he wasn't ready to give up.

An alert appeared on his internal heads-up display. Monin had activated the arch gateway. Connor checked the status of the second gateway and saw that the predators had stopped going through. He shut it down.

A few minutes later, he saw a bright flash illuminate the sky. The Gesora had finished going through the arch gateway, and it had now been destroyed. Connor prayed that Monin would be able to find survivors.

The 7th Ranger Company made its way through rocky terrain, heading toward the waypoint, and Connor settled into a rhythm of navigating the uneven landscape. The combat suit computers helped them adjust for unstable footing. At some point, he glanced at Dash, who was shaking his head while muttering to himself. Dash noticed Connor watching and shrugged.

"I was just wondering if those creatures were going to follow the platform once we recall it," Dash said.

It was a good question, and Connor didn't know the answer. "I'll assume the answer is yes. We can hold them off and get through."

A comlink broadcast registered on Connor's combat suit, and it made him stumble. He hadn't been expecting it, and it hadn't gone just to him. It was a broadcast on all frequencies. It took a few seconds for the Krake translation device to decode it.

"What the hell was that?" Samson asked.

"It's a message," Connor said, unable to believe what he was saying. The broadcast had come from the tower they'd been to earlier.

"Who's it from?" Samson asked.

"It's from Aurang."

25

CONNOR ORDERED A HALT.

"Why would he broadcast a message?" Samson asked.

The message was encoded, and Connor used his ID to authenticate. Aurang must've gotten it from their last comlink session. Connor opened his personal holoscreen, and an image of Aurang's face appeared. It was a recording.

"General Gates, there is a high probability that I am going to be dead soon. I've set some things in motion that will give you a chance to achieve your objectives. I'm sending you the coordinates of a ship, and on it is the location of Quadiri. There are safeguards in place that prevent me from transmitting these coordinates through a broadcast. When this broadcast is received, it is going to generate an alert to the Krake sector chief in your region. They will be able to decode this message. Once that happens, they will investigate the ship and probably destroy it. This message and the ship are all I give you.

"You were right. The fifth column was a tool of Prime Overseer Ersevin. However, he might not predict the information I stored on that ship. That, along with what I suspect you've learned throughout all your exploits into the multiverse, creates many possible outcomes—so many outcomes that it will be impossible for them to predict. You have a chance to do what no one else has ever done. I expect you to question my motives. That much is clear. My loyalty has always been to the Krake. It is for them that I give you this information. You will need to move quickly."

Included with the message was a set of regional coordinates.

"What good is one ship going to be?" Samson asked.

"I don't know, but he says the coordinates for the Krake home world are there."

Holzer cleared his throat. "This could be some kind of trap."

Connor shook his head. "Aurang wouldn't need to do all this to alert the Krake to us being here. This isn't a trap, and we can't wait for the Krake to react before we do something. I don't think the Krake are going to give that ship up without a fight."

"And Aurang just happened to have a ship here on this world? It seems a little too convenient for me," Samson said.

"I don't know why he had a ship here, but if there's a chance we can find the location of the Krake home world, I'm going to take it."

"Maybe we should return to New Earth and come back with support for a mission like this," Samson said.

Holzer's eyes widened, and he nodded vigorously. "Yes, returning to New Earth would be prudent."

Connor looked at Dash. "Confirm our location if we were to open a gateway to home."

Dash used his combat suit computer to show their location on New Earth.

"You see? It's nowhere near any colonial city," Connor said. "It would take too much time for the CDF to get a response team out, and it's time we don't have. You heard what Aurang said. The Krake are invading all worlds, including New Earth. They could be fighting right now while we're here discussing what to do next." His words were sharp.

There was a flutter of motion along the fringes of their ranks. Then he saw 3rd Platoon of the Special Infantry Division running toward them. Two soldiers came over to Connor and the others. Their IDs showed on his internal heads-up display. It was Lieutenant Miller and Lars Mallory.

Connor felt a flash of relief that the 3rd Platoon had joined them, but he had to address his soldiers. Seconds were slipping away, and Samson was questioning whether they should keep going. Connor gritted his teeth and stepped away from the others. He opened up a broadcast comlink.

"CDF soldiers, the broadcast we all just received was a message for me from a member of the Krake fifth column. His name was Aurang. He is likely now dead. He gave me the location of a ship that has the coordinates to the Krake home world. He also confirmed that the Krake are invading all Ovarrow worlds in some kind of massive purge. New Earth is on their list of targets. There is a good chance that New Earth is under attack, and we've already engaged them.

"We are at a crossroads: return home to help the fight, or validate the truth of the enemy intel we've just received. I am going to find that ship. Some of you might want to go home to fight there. There's not a second that goes by that I don't think about my family, but the best way I can protect them is to find the Krake home world. With that knowledge, we can end the war. With that knowledge, we can return to New Earth and mount an offensive against the enemy.

"But if we let this opportunity slip through our fingers, I don't know what's going to happen. The way to defeat the Krake is to take this fight to their homes, just as they brought it to ours and countless others. So, the only thing I want from any of you is volunteers. Come with me. Fight for your homes and families. For anyone who doesn't want to go, I will give you the gate control module and you can go home right now."

Connor closed the broadcast comlink, and there were a few moments of silence. The only sound they heard was the gusting winds across a dark landscape with the faintest twilight in the distance. Then, a light appeared on the helmet of a nearby soldier. Connor looked at him. It was Lars Mallory. More soldiers lit up their helmets, speckled here and there at first, but after a few moments, there was a gleam of solidarity as the soldiers of the CDF made their intentions known.

Connor glanced at Samson, who had also switched his light on. Holzer looked around as if he didn't know what to say. Dash turned his light on as well and then showed Holzer how to do it. The members of the diplomatic envoy mirrored the others. Connor could have ordered everyone to follow him, and they might've done it. In fact, they probably would've done it, but there was nothing more powerful in a situation like this than a person who volunteered. Those were the soldiers who fought the hardest, and those were the men and women he wanted to fight with. And if it was required, he would die with them.

The coordinates of Aurang's ship were several kilometers from their position.

"This isn't a bad place to hide something you don't want anyone else to find. I mean, who else would come here? This is a nightmarish landscape filled with hibernating predators," Dash said.

Connor felt his lips curve a little and then looked at the new arrivals. "Lieutenant Miller, Sergeant Mallory, I'm glad you could make it."

"We wouldn't have missed this, General," Lieutenant Miller said.

Connor looked at Lars.

"General Gates," Lars acknowledged.

Lars glanced at Dash, and the two regarded one another. Then Lars looked away.

"We don't have any time to waste," Connor said.

They would do reconnaissance along the way. SRDs had been sent to the area, and they kicked their Nexstar combat suits into high gear.

Connor already suspected that they hadn't been looking for the Krake home world in the right place, and Aurang had confirmed it. So where could it be? He kept mulling the question over in his mind as they ran to their destination. Aurang seemed convinced that they would've found Quadiri eventually, which meant they'd at least been on the right track.

As they got closer to the location, the SRDs detected incoming Krake ships. They were troop carrier-class vessels that were atmospheric-flight ready, matching the profiles of Krake ships observed on other worlds in previous CDF missions.

The landscape began to change, becoming more even, leading into several canyons. It was a place one could easily get lost in, or hide something in. Now, they had to search. The Krake ships flew overhead, conducting their own search.

Connor opened a private comlink to Samson. "We need to split up and cover more ground. I'll take Miller's and Lafferty's platoons with me to search this area. You take the other side, and we'll meet up in the middle."

"I'd rather watch your back, General."

"I thought you said your guys are the best. We'll be fine."

"I'll see you on the other side," Samson said and closed the comlink.

The CDF soldiers diverged and began moving in opposite directions. Connor also led Holzer and the rest of the diplomatic envoy, as well as their CDF squad.

They went down into the canyons, which were about a half a kilometer in depth, staying close to the walls to give them some cover. Krake troop carriers flew overhead. No doubt, they were searching for them.

The SRDs scouted ahead, scanning for any power signatures, but none were detected. Connor had the drones map the area ahead of them. They were looking for a place to hide a ship. It might have helped if Aurang had told them what kind of ship he'd hidden here, but the Krake rebel must've been in such a rush that he hadn't been able to include that kind of information. Connor doubted that it was a large ship. He just hoped it was operational.

They made their way through the canyons, searching for a hidden landing platform or a hangar that could house a small ship. A loud explosion sent shockwaves that shook the canyon walls. Rock and dirt rained down, and several Krake ships flew overhead.

"General, Major Samson has engaged the Krake," Lieutenant Lafferty said, pausing for a moment. "They've found a shallow cave in an open area that the canyons all lead to."

Connor ordered them to quicken their pace, and their weapons were ready as they headed to the location. As they reached the end of the canyon, they came to an open area more than a kilometer wide. Flashes of light appeared from the other side where Samson and the other 7th Rangers were firing on the Krake that were attempting to land near a shallow cave. Krake soldiers dropped to the ground from the troop carriers flying overhead and began firing on them. They hadn't noticed Connor's group.

Connor ordered them to stay close to the canyon walls as they skirted around to flank the Krake soldiers. Then they fired on the enemy, who was out in the open. Some of the Krake soldiers went down before one of the Krake troop carriers swung around and fired their weapons at them. Connor and the other soldiers scrambled out of the way, but there was nowhere for them to find cover. Several combat suit heavies opened fire on the troop carriers, tearing into them. One flew overhead and crashed into the side of the canyon, tumbling violently to the ground in a large explosion, but the Krake soldiers quickly recovered and several CDF soldiers near Connor went down. Plasma bolts blazed toward him, piercing the Nexstar combat suit armor and burning a hole through the chest of the soldier nearest him.

Connor's group was closer to the cave where Aurang's ship was, and the Krake began pressing the fight to them.

An alert from the SRD showed that there were more troop carriers inbound.

A comlink opened from Samson. "I'm going to open the gate for you. Get to that ship," he said.

Samson's two platoons had more combat suit heavies that were capable of delivering some heavy ordnance. Explosions rocked the area, scattering the Krake soldiers and tearing them apart. Troop carriers flew overhead, cutting large swaths through the CDF soldiers. The battle was brutal and quick.

Connor knew they had to run for it. They would find cover in the cave. Krake troop carriers fell out of the sky as they were shot down, but Connor ordered his two groups to move. They crossed the field, heading toward the cave, which was much bigger than he'd expected. Just inside the cave, the ground sloped downward toward a small freighter-class vessel. It didn't have any weapons that he could see.

"Dash, see if you can get us on board that ship. Specialist Ruo, go with him," Connor said.

Dash and Ruo ran inside the cave.

"We need to hold this position," Connor said.

Lieutenant Lafferty ordered the troops to cover the entrance to the cave and provide covering fire for the soldiers who hadn't reached it.

Krake soldiers were focusing their efforts on the cave. Bright flashes of orange plasma bolts lit up the night and struck the cave walls.

Connor went to the opening of the cave and looked for the other two CDF platoons. He accessed the SRDs' video feeds and saw that more Krake troop carriers were heading toward them.

"Samson, you've got to move, now," Connor said to himself.

Samson had access to the same SRDs and knew what was coming.

Connor watched as the two platoons pushed forward. If they got pinned down here, then more Krake soldiers would arrive and this battle would be over for them. The two platoons didn't cross the middle of the open area. They hugged the canyon walls, using the wreckage of a troop carrier for cover while the remaining Krake soldiers attempted to keep them pinned down.

He received a comlink from Dash.

"Connor, we need you here. The doors won't open without your identification."

Connor muttered a curse. "On my way."

He ran into the cave, approaching an area where there were side doors, and Dash was waving him forward. They had a Krake interface up, and Connor entered his information in a series of prompts. Aurang must have set this up so only Connor could access the ship.

The door slid open with a slight hiss, and the interior lights of the small freighter began to come on.

"You two go inside and see if this thing is flight-ready," Connor said.

"Wait. What? You want us to fly this out of here?" Dash asked.

A bright flash lit up the cave, followed by a big explosion outside as Connor ran toward the entrance. The flaming wrecks of three Krake troop carriers lay in the middle of the open area outside the cave. Connor scanned the area, looking for Samson and the others, and couldn't find them.

A few CDF soldiers were injured, and Lieutenant Miller ordered them taken farther into the cave.

Several squads of CDF soldiers ran around the Krake troop carriers, and Connor spotted Samson among them. Another troop carrier flew overhead and opened fire. Heavy plasma bolts tore through the ground, sending rocks into the air, and the line of fire ripped through the CDF squads. One moment they were running toward them, and the next, there was nothing. Armored bodies were tossed into the air.

Connor jerked forward and cried out, but someone held him back. He tried to pull away, abandoning reason. Screaming in rage, he fired his weapon at the Krake ship.

"No, Connor, no! You can't go out there. They're already dead," Lars said, and repeated himself.

Lars and Lieutenant Miller had grabbed onto Connor, and they dragged him back to the cave. Connor used his implants to search for the biometric readings of Samson and the others. They were all off-line. They were gone. They were just . . . gone.

Connor yelled in rage. He brought up his weapon and fired at the Krake soldiers. More were moving into the area, taking up positions around the wreckage. Several troop carriers were turning about, but he didn't care. His friend was gone.

Connor wanted to run out there and kill all the Krake. He wanted them all to burn. Instead, CDF soldiers dragged him back into the cave, then all the way onto the ship. The remaining soldiers went inside.

The door shut and Connor stared at it for a few moments as remnants of reason pierced through his fog of rage. He heard the high-pitched whine of the ship's engines engage, and then there was a slight shift in the floor as the ship began to move.

Connor raced toward the bridge.

Someone guided him. The bridges of Krake ships weren't at the front but toward the rear. Connor reached the bridge, and there was a large green holoscreen showing a video feed of the outside. The walls of the cave quickly faded from view as the ship blew past the Krake troop carriers that were firing on them.

"Return fire," Connor said.

"We can't," Dash said. He'd taken a position standing near one of the control terminals.

"I said return fire!" Connor shouted.

"I don't know how," Dash said. "I don't think this ship has any weapons."

"He's right, General," Specialist Ruo said. "I can't find any weapons systems on any of the ship's control systems."

Connor swung his gaze toward an open console. Then he remembered what he'd seen of the outside of the ship. They were right. There weren't any weapons systems.

"I'm getting us out of here," Dash said.

The Krake ship increased velocity and soon left the troop carriers behind. Dash flew them into the upper atmosphere where the Krake troop carriers couldn't follow.

26

Sean grimaced. The latest munitions report for the *Vigilant* and the rest of Trident Battle Group wasn't good. They needed to resupply. The Krake invasion force had managed to take out almost half of the CDF space gates, adapting their tactics after losing several ships. The new protector drones and HADES V missile groups were even more effective than Gabriel's predictive models had anticipated. After several clashes with the enemy, both sides were in the process of regrouping.

Sean sat in the commander's chair on the bridge of the *Vigilant* and looked at a video comlink to Engineering where Noah was working.

"So, you think you can improve the performance. That's what you're saying?" Sean asked.

"Sean, you're asking me to gamble our lives on what I *think* I can deliver," Noah replied. "It's not that simple. Increasing the reliability of the Casimir power core has a draw on Gabriel's computing cycles, which you need for the combat warfare suite."

"Well, which one is it?"

"You can either attack or defend. You can't do both at the same time," Noah said and frowned. "Let me rephrase that. If you shift priority to managing the Casimir power core, it affects tactical capabilities, and the firing solutions across the battle group will be diminished."

"We can spread the computing load to the other ships. That ought to free up some resources."

"Only if you don't want them to use the artificial gravity field to protect themselves. It's an *either-or*, Sean, not an *and*."

Sean felt a flash of irritation. He didn't like the options he had, and needed something better. He was running out of protector drones and HADES V missiles, which meant that in order to take out Krake ships, he had to engage them a lot closer than they were right now. But, if he couldn't get more performance from the Casimir power core, they would all die.

"I know this isn't what you want to hear, but it's the best we can do right now," Noah said.

Sean tried not to glare at the holoscreen. It wasn't Noah's fault. "Keep working on it," he said and closed the comlink.

Major Shelton and Oriana had been listening. Sean looked at them and shook his head. "Not the best news."

"Have the Krake been detected anywhere else closer to New Earth?" Oriana asked.

"No, not yet. Home fleet has been deployed, and our defense platforms are moving into position. But it's only a matter of time."

"At least we *have* time," Oriana said.

"No, we don't," Major Shelton said. "As long as the Krake have the initiative, then we don't have any time at all."

Oriana considered this for a moment and then looked at Sean.

"As long as we remain on the defensive, they'll win. Nobody

wins a war with a strategy that's entirely made up of defense," Sean said.

Oriana sighed and looked away. Her eyebrows were knitted together in deep thought.

"The Krake want to draw us into another battle with them. They know they have the advantage of numbers," Major Shelton said.

"I don't want to give them what they want, but there has to be more going on here."

"What do you mean?" Oriana asked.

Sean shook his head. "Why are they still here? Why haven't the Krake headed to New Earth? It has to be their end goal, so what are they still doing here?"

"They could just be a scout force, which means they weren't sure we were here," Major Shelton said.

"Well, now they know," Sean said.

Lieutenant Scott turned from his workstation. "Colonel, they've been focused on our space gates near Sagan, even as more of their ships arrive. For some reason, this area is a top priority for them."

Sean nodded. "The Krake know we have a space force. Since we have ships and a means to defend ourselves, they'd want to sneak into this universe and attempt to take us by surprise. But that doesn't explain why they did it here."

"They should have done it farther out in the star system where there are fewer defenses or the ability to detect them," Major Shelton said.

"That's what we expected them to do. We have defense platforms and detection systems monitoring out there as well. They've been there since the Vemus War. They could still do that and move a fleet in from somewhere else, but we also know they're not too keen on using mobile space gates."

"I bet that has changed. They'd have to adapt," Oriana said.

Sean smiled with one side of his mouth. "I wouldn't bet against you." He rubbed his chin. "New Earth has to be the target, but for some reason, they're focused on the space gates we have here. There has to be a connection there somewhere, and we need to figure that out."

They'd been moving the remaining space gates away from Sagan and farther into the asteroid field, using it for cover. The asteroid field was composed of the remnants of Sagan's third moon that had been destroyed. Sean wanted to engage the enemy, but he needed an objective that helped them defeat the Krake. An idea ignited in his mind and gained momentum. This spawned other thoughts and gathered data that his analytical mind had finally pieced together.

"We need to figure out what universe the Krake are coming from." Sean looked at the tactical plot on the main holoscreen.

"You don't want much, do you, Colonel?" Major Shelton said.

The tactical plot showed that the Krake had consolidated their forces on the colony's two remaining space gates.

"If it were easy, then anybody would do it. So, the question becomes, How do we get them away from their space gates?" Sean asked.

"I don't understand," Oriana said.

"We can't identify what universe the Krake are coming from. The only way to do it is to send somebody through the gateway to access the control module on the other side, then transmit the data back to us."

Oriana's mouth opened a little, and she glanced at Major Shelton.

"It would be a suicide mission," Major Shelton said.

"Let's just say we get the information somehow. Then what?" Oriana asked.

"Then we use our space gates to go to that universe and bring the fight to them," Sean said. "They won't be expecting that. Plus, there has to be something in the vicinity that they're so concerned about protecting. I don't know what it is. Could be nothing, but that's what we need to find out. If we stay out here and wait for the Krake to come to us, then . . ." He let the thought go unfinished. They knew the stakes. "So, we need to get the Krake to come after us and then send an infiltration team to those space gates."

Major Shelton frowned in thought. Then she arched a dark eyebrow. "We can lure them with bait. If they're so worried about our space gates being in close proximity to Sagan, then perhaps we should use that."

Sean smiled. "A ruse."

"You want to pretend to use our space gates to make the Krake attack us," Oriana said.

"Yes, but that will only work for a large chunk of their ships." Sean pressed his lips together and looked at Major Shelton. "Talon-V Stingers might be able to get in there."

"We'd need to punch a hole for them."

"We'll have to divide our forces," Sean said, already working at the fleet division in his mind.

"I realize I'm outside the chain of command here, but shouldn't you alert COMCENT about this?" Oriana asked.

Sean nodded but didn't reply. He looked at the tactical plot, which showed that the Talon-V Stingers and Lancer-class ships were holding position in the outskirts of the asteroid field.

"Colonel," Major Shelton said, "the resupply ships are on their way here from Phoenix Station."

They needed those supplies, but he didn't want to wait that long.

"How many space gates do you think it will take to get the Krake to commit?" Oriana asked.

"All of them. They must have counted all of them. If we use anything less, they'll be suspicious. They need to believe we're launching a major operation through the space gates."

They worked out the details of the plan. Sean would liked to have used the *Vigilant* to punch a hole through the Krake forces, allowing Talon-V Stingers to execute the mission through the Krake space gate, but the Krake would see right through that. The Krake had to see that the CDF's largest warship was defending the space gates, or they'd never commit their forces to it. They'd have to use long-range missiles and the remaining Talon-V squadrons. Priority for them would be to protect the three designated Stingers as they engaged the Krake space gateway.

Over the next hour, they deployed the remaining space gates in formation near the planet. They activated all the space gates at once, which sent a gamma burst, alerting the Krake that the space gates were active. This drew an immediate response from the Krake. They'd committed almost all destroyers and were now quickly making their way toward the colonial space gates. Sean had deployed them on the other side of the planet, which would take them a little bit of time to reach.

When he alerted COMCENT to the mission, he received an update to their subspace communications. There were Krake warships en route to New Earth. The invasion of the colony was about to begin in earnest.

27

NATHAN STOOD at the holotank at the command center in Sierra. He preferred to stand. He'd much rather work on his feet than sit at a desk anyway. A video comlink appeared in front of him.

"There have been intelligence reports from both the Konus and the Mekaal about a new type of predator detected by their scouts," Colonel Randall said. "I've prepared an intelligence briefing, and I'm circulating it to the other bases."

A data window opened next to the video comlink, and it showed an image of a predator Nathan had never seen before. It was the size of a berwolf and had pinkish-gray armored plates, a wide mouth filled with jagged teeth, and a thick talon at the tip of its tail.

"The reports indicate that the predators appeared out of nowhere," Randall continued. "We believe the Krake are using gateways to bring them here. They kill almost anything on sight and are heading to the Ovarrow population centers."

"We have orbital defense platforms in place and can bombard the areas where the gateways are located," Nathan said.

"I've suggested that to both the Mekaal and the Konus, and they've indicated that the gateways are temporary and appear almost at random. They can't predict where they're coming from at any given time. They've engaged the ryklar control signals to bring the ryklars into the area. The two apex predators will engage one another while both militaries fortify their positions."

The ryklars were fierce, deadly predators of New Earth that had been genetically modified to be controlled by the Ovarrow. They had done this to help them prepare against a Krake invasion, but no one had been able to confirm when the practice started. Nathan was beginning to wonder if this was a Krake practice that the Ovarrow had simply copied. Ovarrow history wasn't straightforward to understand, even with the Ovarrow who had come out of stasis. Many of the records had been lost.

"Then it's only a matter of time before we start seeing those creatures by our own cities. If they follow . . ." Nathan stopped and frowned. "They must've been scouting the area. Otherwise, how would they have found the Konus or the Mekaal?"

"There have been sightings of smaller, unknown ships flying in the area. They haven't come near colonial cities as of yet," Randall replied.

"We need to increase our patrol envelope to include the Mekaal city. I also want coverage over the Konus city as well. We need eyes on them. We can use our own combat drones as well. Have there been any reports of Krake soldiers?" Nathan asked.

"Negative, General."

"Very well," Nathan replied.

"I do have some good news," Randall continued. "We've had reports from several rescue teams that have been patrolling the alpha site. They've made contact with some of the away teams and have successfully extracted them. But there's also a significant number that haven't responded. Still no word from General Gates or the Gesora. They sent a stealth recon drone through, and it looks like they were hit pretty hard."

"Understood. And tell them to keep searching the Gesora world. I want confirmation of whether our away teams have survived. Until we have that, I'm not counting General Gates out," Nathan said.

This drew a few inquisitive glances from his commanding officers, but he didn't care. No one was going to question his orders. And he wasn't about to give up on any soldiers who'd been on away missions until their deaths had been confirmed. As of now, they were simply missing.

"Understood, General," Randall replied. "I'll relay your orders to the rescue teams. However, there is evidence that the Krake used large-scale bombardment weapons to destroy Ovarrow cities. There might not be enough remains to identify."

Nathan gripped the edge of the holotank, clutching it as if he wanted to strangle it, but the metallic alloy was unyielding. "I understand the task is difficult, but my orders haven't changed. No one is being abandoned."

"Yes, General," Randall said.

"Colonel Hughes," Nathan said, "what's the status of protector drone production?"

"We sent all remaining prototypes to the home fleet, but there weren't that many of them. We're working on building them, but none of our manufacturing lines are configured for this. We're updating the configurations as fast as we can to get them made, but I'd be remiss if I didn't tell you that we might not be ready in time."

"Understood, Colonel. We're already out of time, so

anything we can do between now and when the Krake show up in force is something better than we had before."

Nathan was getting tired of people managing expectations. He understood exactly what was happening. The protector drones were a prototypical type of weapon that Sean had been testing and had proved effective. Now they needed them yesterday, and they weren't going to get them. He'd tried to keep the edge out of his voice while speaking with Colonel Hughes, but it was still there.

"General Hayes, I have a request to send more ships from the home fleet to assist Colonel Quinn," Colonel Watts said.

Nathan had received Sean's plan to engage the Krake out by planet Sagan.

"Their ammunition stores are low," Watts continued. "Even with the resupply, there were more Krake ships gathering. They need our help."

"I agree, Colonel Watts, but the home fleet is needed to defend New Earth."

"Colonel Quinn doesn't have to fight the Krake alone. His record indicates that he's used to working with limited resources, but in this case, we can assist him."

Nathan inhaled deeply and allowed his gaze to take in the other holoscreens where his commanding officers waited for his reply. "He knows what it is to face the Krake better than anyone in this room. Including me. If he really needed ships from the home fleet, he would've asked for them, but he knows where the priority must be. I don't like it either. He's being resupplied by freighters from Phoenix Station. Colonel Quinn is not going to put himself in a position where his back is against the wall and we lose Trident Battle Group. I've seen his plan, and it's not that kind of fight.

"There have also been reports of Krake ships heading toward

us, but they're not using their best speed. They're waiting. The fact that the Krake are now using space gates to stage this invasion means that we have to be ready to engage them without any warning. This is where we hold the line. We don't know where the Krake are coming from, and we can't afford to start looking for them right now. Trident Battle Group is attempting to answer that question for us. When we know more, we will adapt accordingly."

Nathan knew this was the worst part—the waiting, the anticipation. But he also understood that these were precious minutes he wasn't going to ruin by making rash decisions.

Colonists who couldn't fight went into protective bunkers and secure locations, both inside the cities and away from them. The colony was now as ready as it was going to be to fight the Krake.

There was a speaking request from Major Denton, who was the commanding officer of the CDF base at Sanctuary.

"Yes, Major Denton," Nathan said.

"General Hayes, we should be trying to identify the universe that the Krake are sending these predators from. We have our own arch gateways, and we can be more proactive about this. This idea was presented to me by some of our reserve forces—the combat veterans, General. They know their business. They volunteered to do this, so it won't impact our defensive posture here at the city."

Nathan felt his eyebrows knit in a thoughtful frown. "What are they proposing?"

Major Denton smiled with somewhat of an aggressive look. "Something insane and highly risky, General. They want to find one of the gateways the enemy is using to send the predators through and go to the other side. It's much like what Colonel Quinn is trying to do with the space gate. They want to identify the universe that these things are being staged from and then use our own gateways to attack them."

Nathan's lips curved upward. "Authorization is given. I want some of our own scout forces to join them. Alert the Mekaal and the Konus of what we're doing. I don't want anyone caught in what could be friendly crossfire. Then tell whoever came up with that idea that I owe them a case of bourbon when this is done."

Major Denton smiled. "Of course, General."

The time ticked away as these updates kept coming in, but when the Krake did finally show up, they started with scout ships that were attempting to perform aerial reconnaissance of colonial cities. They were searching in a grid-type pattern, which meant the Krake navy hadn't arrived yet. In each instance that the Krake ships were spotted, CDF response fighters chased them out of the area. In some cases, they were destroyed. In other cases, they disappeared, which meant that there were many more gateways being opened by the Krake than they had originally thought. Then the soldiers came, and the fighting began.

28

Several CDF soldiers cried out in pain, and Connor turned toward them. Combat medics were evaluating the injuries of the wounded soldiers. He heard them recruit others nearby to help. There were several soldiers with severe burns from Krake weapons that penetrated combat suit armor. The combat suit med kits discharged pain blockers, but the medics had to assess the injuries, often using healing packs to treat wounds and stop the bleeding.

He saw Sergeant Mason doing a quick head count and shouting for the 7th to sound off when he said their names. Connor listened to the soldiers respond, as well as the deadly silence of the people who were no longer with them.

"Don't take us too far beyond the thermosphere," Lars said.

"We'll be totally exposed," Dash replied. "The Krake are going to be hunting for us. We've got to get out of here. We need to get as far away as possible."

"You need to listen to me. Throttle back the engines and let the ship settle into a geostationary orbit. That ought to buy us some time."

"I don't take orders from you."

Connor heard the clash of two CDF combat suits coming to blows. He spun and saw that Lars had been pushed back against the wall, and Dash was holding him in place.

"Don't you put your hands on me," Dash snarled.

Lars held his hands up in a placating gesture. "Easy."

"Hey!" Connor shouted. "Enough."

Dash's gaze flitted to Connor, and then he backed away from Lars.

"Lars is right, Dash," Connor said. "The Krake will be able to find us if we keep going the way we are. Settling into an orbit will make it harder for them to detect us. They'll be looking for a ship that is flying away as fast as possible."

Dash sighed and returned to the console. "Throttling down the engines."

"Good. Can you run a diagnostic and get a current status of the ship systems?"

Dash nodded once and said, "Yeah, I can do that. I'll get right on it."

"I'll send someone up here to help you," Connor said.

He left the bridge area and walked down a ramp, with Lars following him. In the corridors, CDF soldiers sat on the ground, some of them wounded. They'd lost a lot of them, his friend among them. He felt numb and emotional all at once as his mind tried to rationalize what had just happened. The more disciplined part of him knew he needed to focus. He spotted Lieutenant Lafferty and walked over to him.

The soldiers nearby were asking questions, mainly about missing comrades, and wondering what had happened to Major Samson.

Lieutenant Lafferty saw Connor and stood up straight. "General, sir."

The discussion went silent.

Connor gritted his teeth and exhaled. "Major Samson died in the attack." Stunned silence hit the 7th like a wrecking ball. Samson was among the best soldiers he'd ever known. The soldiers of the 7th respected him. He'd formed them into one of the best special forces companies in the CDF.

Connor let them have a few seconds to digest the news. "We need to check the ship," he said and looked around. "Specialist Ruo, I want you to head to the bridge. Help Mr. DeWitt check the ship systems."

Specialist Ruo saluted Connor and hastened toward the bridge.

"General, is DeWitt an expert on Krake technology?" Lieutenant Lafferty asked.

"Dash knows his stuff. We need to make a sweep of the ship. Visual inspection only. I don't want anyone touching anything we don't know about," Connor said.

"It doesn't look like it's that big of a ship, so it won't take much time. We'll get it done. Major Samson made sure we knew how to spot Krake tech," Lieutenant Lafferty said.

Sorrow closed Connor's throat, and he nodded. "Understood."

Lieutenant Lafferty walked away, and Lieutenant Miller came over to him. "General, put us to work."

The 3rd Platoon of the SID was comprised mainly of people who'd been banished from the colony. They may have joined the CDF to earn a commuted banishment sentence and be allowed to rejoin the colony, but they had proved to be an effective fighting force.

"Coordinate with Lieutenant Lafferty," Connor said. "We're

going to check the ship. I want to know if we've got weapons. We need to see what's available."

"Yes, General. Atmospheric readings are a bit off. We should check life support systems first," Lieutenant Miller said and glanced at Lars.

"I want Sergeant Mallory to stick with me," Connor said.

Lieutenant Miller nodded and began organizing his soldiers.

Lars looked at him.

"You're my other tech expert as far as the Krake go," Connor said.

"I'm not an expert on the Krake, sir."

"Lars, I know you. You're an expert on the Ovarrow, and you've studied everything you could get your hands on regarding the Krake. You've got good instincts, and I need them right now."

For the next half hour, they made a sweep of the Krake ship. It was some kind of cargo carrier, but it also had the capacity to transfer personnel. One thing that became abundantly clear was that the ship hadn't been used in quite a long time. The life support systems needed the Krake equivalent of oxygen scrubbers to be replaced. They found replacement filters in sealed containers, so they hadn't decayed. After that, they were able to switch away from their individual life support systems. The air still smelled stale, with the tangy after-smell of socks that hadn't been washed, but that would hopefully improve over time.

Connor wondered why Aurang would compile strategic data about the Krake on an old ship, as well as how long the ship had been in that cave. He watched Aurang's message again. The Krake rebel had stressed that there were restrictions on sending the coordinates of Quadiri.

Dash sent him an update about the power core cycling back up to nominal power levels. They didn't know how it worked beyond what they'd studied from other Krake ships and facilities the CDF had been to over the years. This was the first intact Krake vessel they'd ever been on. They didn't find any Krake combat drones on the ship, and nothing else indicated any kind of offensive combat capabilities, but they weren't defenseless. Sergeant Mason found what he thought were mines but had no idea how powerful they were.

The current headcount made Connor go hollow inside. They'd lost over eighty soldiers in almost the blink of an eye. The diplomatic envoy was among the survivors, and he had no doubt that the protective detail assigned to them had been largely responsible. Holzer joined him. Aliza Winfry was medic-certified and helped care for the wounded. Gellner was assisting her.

Connor headed back to the bridge where Dash and Specialist Ruo were working. Lars and Holzer followed him. A few moments after they arrived, Lieutenants Miller and Lafferty joined them as well.

"The ship's hull seems intact. No obvious issues with it and no alerts on ships systems," Lieutenant Lafferty said, and then he added, "I wouldn't want to take it into a battle."

"Understood. We might not have much of a choice," Connor said and looked at Dash. "What have you found?"

"I think Aurang was using the ship as some kind of backup system. There's a lot of data here, more than I would expect to find on any ship."

"Maybe it was part of some contingency plan he had for some reason. He said that the location to Quadiri was here. Were you able to find it?"

"It looks like there's a complete list of space gate coordinates to multiple universes. I've been cross-referencing their list with ours, but I think these are the coordinates to the Krake home universe." Dash put the data up on the holoscreen.

Connor stared at it for a few moments. This was what he'd been after, and now it was right there in front of them. The question now became what they did with it. Should they return home and send their own fleet to the Krake home universe? If the Krake were already invading, then the CDF fleet would be defending New Earth. The Krake military had more ships and more firepower, and leaving New Earth to attack the Krake home world might not be possible.

"That's not all," Dash said. "I think what he has here is direct access to the Krake communications network."

"That doesn't sound right. The Krake can't only have one communication network," Lars said.

Dash shrugged a shoulder. "I think what I'm looking at here is access keys to their communications, and it includes their space gates. If I'm reading this correctly, it gives us command-override privileges. The interface is similar to what we saw on the arch gateway on the planet."

"Are you saying we can control gateways with this ship?" Lieutenant Lafferty asked.

"Yes, I think we can send commands through their automated processes."

Connor nodded. "We knew the Krake were heavily reliant on automation. I think we could use this."

"Hell yeah, sir," Lieutenant Lafferty said. "We could tell all those gateways down here to point back to the Krake home world and let the predators do the rest."

The others nodded in agreement, and Connor frowned in thought. "I don't think it's going to work. Aurang was adamant that we couldn't reach Quadiri from the planet below. I don't think we can reach the Krake home world from any NEC planet including New Earth, which means that the Krake home world must be on a different planet in another universe. That's why the

Ovarrow could never find it, and that's why we haven't been able to find it either. We've been searching in the wrong place."

Holzer cleared his throat. "Excuse me, General Gates, but how can we use this information to stop the invasion?"

Connor pressed his lips together and then looked at Dash. "Can you open a comlink to the Krake communication network?"

Dash navigated the Krake interface, and another holoscreen appeared. It took a few moments for the Krake translator to work. "We have direct access."

"How long before they block it? They must be able to detect it somehow," Lars said.

Connor peered at the holoscreen with multiple thoughts racing in his mind. They had an opportunity here, but Lars had a point. If they were detected, the Krake might block their access. But this opportunity would slip past them if they didn't act. "Aurang wasn't here when he sent that last broadcast. So, the Krake must have some kind of automated communication through their gateways, and they haven't blocked his access yet."

Lars's eyes widened. "We can upload new coordinates to gateways on the planet and the other staging worlds."

"But what does that get us?" Holzer asked.

Connor would've liked to send the predators to the Krake home world somehow—give the Krake a taste of their own medicine—but that wasn't going to work. "We can stop them from invading other worlds. We'll override all the gateways using the coordinates we used before and send them to the dead universe."

The dead universe was a place Sean had stumbled onto when they were first learning how to use the space gates. There was nothing there, not even stars.

"What's to stop the Krake from just changing whatever we

do?" Dash said. "For example, we send this updated configuration out and it updates the arch gateways on the planet, but what's to stop them from just changing it back?"

Lars smiled and stood up straight. "Because you don't just give it a new command. If we can force all these gateways to change their destinations, then we can set up our own automation that will reset the coordinates back to the dead universe every time they try to make a change. By the time they figure it out, we could do enough damage to stall the invasion altogether."

Connor knew Lars was no stranger to how computer systems worked. He'd given Noah a run for his money while hiding what he was doing for the rogue group. Connor looked at Dash and then at Lars. "I need you guys to work on this together."

Dash's gaze narrowed, but it was gone in a second. He nodded and walked over to a nearby console. Lars joined him.

They worked out the details for their configuration update to propagate through normal Krake communication protocols. This would allow it to spread and give it the best chance for maximum penetration, stopping the predators from invading Ovarrow worlds while also decimating their numbers. They were able to send specific instructions to the three staging worlds that were in the ship's database. Connor didn't think the Krake would notice the change until it was reported back by the ships that were also part of the invasion force, which meant the Krake ship commanders would first need to observe the lack of predators and then have it investigated. That would take even more time, and the Ovarrow on those planets being invaded would be able to escape their cities.

"We still need to destroy these locations to stop the Krake from doing this again," Lars said.

"He's right, General," Lieutenant Lafferty said.

"How is this even possible?" Holzer asked. "Their operations cover the entire planet."

Connor nodded. "They do, but I have an idea. First, we'll need to use the space gate in the system. After we use it, I want it to reset to the same dead universe so anyone who follows us won't be able to get to New Earth."

There was a space gate near the planet, but there weren't any Krake warships here—at least none that they had seen. Connor put them on an intercept course with the space gate and then told them about the next part of his plan.

"You're cutting them off and—" Lars began, but some type of alert appeared on the holoscreen.

It was a comlink request.

"Should I acknowledge it?" Dash asked.

"No, stay on course," Connor said.

He looked at the upload status for the arch gateways. It was already done, but they couldn't track how fast the update would propagate through the Krake communication systems. He frowned in thought.

"General?" Lieutenant Lafferty asked.

"Nothing."

Lafferty turned his attention to the holoscreen that Specialist Ruo was working on. Connor felt isolated. He knew the people around him, but there were only a select few that he'd confided in. He kept looking for Samson, who would often make a pointed comment that provided either a logical counterargument to or an affirmation of what Connor's intentions were. But he was gone. It felt as if a space nearby that was normally filled with Samson's presence was empty. There were others Connor conferred with, people he trusted, but in this case, he was surrounded by junior officers and a few civilians.

"Noah would call this a leap of faith," Lars said quietly so only Connor could hear him.

Connor looked at him, and Lars met his gaze. Lars was only a few years over thirty but had the gaze of a much older man. He'd seen and done too much, some of which he wasn't proud of but believed had been necessary. Connor recognized the look because he'd seen it whenever he stared at himself in the mirror.

"Yeah," Connor replied just as quietly.

The old Krake ship flew toward the space gate, and the Krake comlink request went unanswered. Connor wasn't surprised that there were no other ships in the area. He doubted many came to this universe. The Krake had designed the gate with minimal oversight in mind. They must have spread their military quite thin to fulfill their objective of purging Ovarrow worlds. Even knowing that, he still didn't know what they were going to find once they went through the space gate. This ship didn't have weapons or any offensive capabilities, aside from dumping a few hundred mines. It was a salvage ship, which bothered the others. Connor thought of it as some sort of camouflage. What had Aurang learned that made him give this away? The fifth column leader must have had a plan. He must have been betrayed, but Connor doubted he'd ever learn the truth.

Dash had figured out how to cross-reference the known universe coordinates with those listed in the database. New Earth was among those listed as active. The Krake were invading New Earth. Dash knew and so did Lars, but the others didn't. The Krake were conducting invasions from these staging worlds where millions of those predators were. But now he had a way to halt the Krake invasion, and nothing was going to stop him from doing it.

29

THE OLD KRAKE ship approached the space gate, closing the distance at an unhurried pace.

"Access the control interface and transmit coordinates," Connor said.

"Uploading coordinates and override, sir," Specialist Ruo said.

Connor watched the holoscreen and waited for the space gate control interface to acknowledge their commands. After what felt like a long, stretched-out moment, the data on the holoscreen changed.

"The space gate is active," Dash said.

"Take us through it," Connor said.

There was no outside video feed, so they were reliant on the ship's sensors to indicate their proximity to the space gate. He knew there would be a gamma burst as they went through the gateway, but that was unavoidable.

"We're through," Dash said.

Connor waited while an automated check-in sequence on

the Krake ship broadcast its presence and waited for an acknowledgment. This was the part of the plan that no one liked, including Connor. If things went wrong, they'd have to go back through the gateway as fast as possible. But they had to let the automatic check-in occur because it would be impossible for him to know of any Krake communication connections in the star system without it. What was a friendly handshake between friends, or in this case, between two Krake communication systems? They didn't have time to come up with a more delicate camouflage. In essence, they were hiding in plain sight. It was a tried-and-proven tactic from his old NA Alliance military days, but it was definitely more nerve-racking now.

"Okay, we're getting acknowledgments," Specialist Ruo said.

They were now in one of the other two universes the Krake were staging invasions from. Connor had no idea if there were different creatures on the planet, and they weren't going to get close enough to find out.

"Upload the packages, Specialist," Connor said.

This time, not only were they including an update that would be transmitted through the Krake regular check-in intervals, but it also searched for a previous update they'd sent from another universe.

"Package has been sent," Specialist Ruo said and kept his gaze on his console. "Receiving an update from the Krake base on the planet. No more communications or acknowledgments, sir."

"Got it!" Dash said. "It worked. There it is."

On Dash's holoscreen was a carefully crafted image made of symbols that would be meaningless to the Krake. It was a group of triangular symbols, with the longest being in the middle.

Connor smiled. "I almost wish they could understand the message we're sending."

The soldiers around him chuckled as they watched the image of what used to be known as the one-finger salute.

"All right, open a gateway to the next set of coordinates," Connor said.

There was a third staging world that they weren't going to because they didn't need to. The automatic updates would already have sent the gateway configuration update to the third staging world by the time they executed the next part of Connor's plan.

"Shut down the automatic communication check-in on the ship," Connor said.

"Automatic check-ins have been disabled, sir," Specialist Ruo said.

They went through the gateway and emerged near another NEC. The planet was the color of mustard and covered with impact craters, as well as deep fissures or chasms near the equatorial region.

"Where's the mining operation?" Holzer asked.

"It's supposed to be near the planet," Connor said. "We'll fly around to the other side and find it that way. The planet matches the description from the mission report."

Connor wanted to keep their presence in this universe a secret as long as possible. Unlike the staging universes, this place was more than likely to have Krake warships protecting it. Sean had executed operations here, and the Krake were aware that the CDF knew this location. However, considering the magnitude of the mining operation, it was unlikely that the Krake would cease all operations here. Why would they? The Krake didn't think the colonists were a threat to them.

It took them just over thirty minutes to orbit the planet, and during that time, Dash had figured out how to get the external video feeds to work. The ship's computer system took data from sensor feeds and built an image that could be displayed on a holoscreen. Showing on the sensors now was a colossal structure that dwarfed anything the colonists had ever built.

The Krake had built an enormous, multi-leveled, circular structure where asteroids were flown in from the outer system. The asteroids were guided to processing stations—thousands of them. A spider-like network of shafts fed one of four massive stations. Rocky streams were ejected toward the planet in an ongoing bombardment. Glowing metal in long rectangular strips quickly cooled as they exited. To see the strips at this distance only reinforced how massive they were. There must've been a significant source of metal in this star system. It was no wonder the Krake had built the massive mining installation here.

They flew away from the lifeless planet, and Connor peered at the holoscreen in awe of what the Krake had built.

"That's odd," Holzer said, breaking the silent reverie. "Once they process all this material, they send the refined metal back out into space while the rest goes to the planet."

"They wouldn't waste it," Connor said.

"I think the report said there were ships that took the material back to wherever it is that they go," Dash said.

Connor had shared the mission report with the others when he'd told them about his plan. "All those materials are on a trajectory somewhere. There has to be another installation out there."

Dash snapped his fingers. "What if there's another space gate out there? Why would you use ships to transport them when you could just put them on a trajectory to go through another space gate?"

Connor nodded. It made sense. "I don't suppose any of you know what the range of the sensors are?" He waited a few moments. "Neither do I. But this is worth checking out before we do anything."

They flew away from the planet, careful to stay clear of the giant metallic ingots coming out of the mineral processing plant. There were thousands of metric tons of rich metals being guided away from the planet.

Connor pressed his lips together for a few moments. Then his eyes widened and his pulse began to race. "Not just another space gate. What if they're sending it to another planet?" He walked closer to the holoscreen, his mouth hanging open as he traced his fingers along the trajectory the ingots were following. "Holy shit! I know where this is going. I can't believe this." He looked away from the others.

"Connor, can you tell us what you're thinking so the rest of his can share in this eureka moment you're having?" Dash asked.

"It's Quadiri, the Krake home world."

"But that's a different set of coordinates. Their home world isn't supposed to be in this universe," Dash replied.

"We were so close. We were so damn close before. Sean had nearly found the damn thing." Connor brought up his personal holoscreen. He had Sean's mission briefing on it, which included a scan of the star system. He used his suit computer to quickly calculate the planetary positions in the star system, and it was a match. "There's another planet out there, and that's where all this material is going. It's heading to the fourth planet. We thought the Krake home world was here," he said, gesturing toward the NEC. "It's not. The Krake come from another planet. Back home, we named it Sagan!"

The others looked at the holoscreen and then back to Connor.

"Holy shit!" Lars said. "No wonder the Ovarrow couldn't find it."

"They had no idea. They had absolutely no idea. There's another space gate out there by the fourth planet, and I guarantee that they take all this material and send it back to the Krake home world to use."

He watched the others as they glanced between the multiple holoscreens.

"That means our plan isn't going to work," Dash said.

He was right. There would definitely be Krake warships in the system. They were in a universe that had a connection to the Krake home world, and it wouldn't be unprotected. Now all he needed to do was to think of a new way to make his plan work, preferably without getting them all killed. He squeezed his eyes shut, and an image of the sapphire eyes of his wife and daughter pierced his chest. They were standing in the sunshine, surrounded by pale birch trees amid a smattering of green foliage. He saw movement behind them. Charging toward his wife and daughter were the armored predators from the staging world.

He opened his eyes and he clenched his teeth. "I'm going to need a few minutes."

"General, a couple of Krake ships just appeared on the sensors," Specialist Ruo said.

Connor's gaze darted to the tactical plot. The ships had just traversed through the space gate near the planet. They weren't on an intercept course with them, at least not yet, but it couldn't be a coincidence that two Krake warships just happened to come here.

"Dash, get back on that console and put us on an intercept course with those ingots. Best speed," Connor said.

Dash hastened toward one of the consoles.

Connor looked at Lieutenant Lafferty. "Do we have any comms drones left with subspace ability?"

Lieutenant Lafferty brought up his wrist computer and his personal holoscreen. His eyes scanned the data. "Yes, General, but we only have one of them."

"We have another one, sir," Lars said. Lieutenant Miller looked at Lars, his eyebrows raised. "I got one from the supply depot before we left the alpha site."

"I thought our request was denied," Lieutenant Miller said.

"It was."

Connor smiled. "I'm glad it's here. We're going to need it. Lieutenant Lafferty, get the comms drone to the airlock and ready to launch." Lafferty stepped away from them and began relaying Connor's orders. "Specialist Ruo, upload the space gate override package to the comms drone. I want it to be ready to send. I also want secondary protocols that will send an update in two hours."

Specialist Ruo looked confused.

"It's the same configuration package that we set up for this space gate, except I only want it to be initiated via the comms drone or when the timer expires. Nothing else has changed," Connor said.

"Understood, General," Specialist Ruo replied. Lars walked over to Ruo and started helping.

Connor peered at the tactical plot on the holoscreen.

Lieutenant Lafferty joined him. "The comms drone is ready, General."

Connor nodded.

"The package is ready and has been uploaded to the comms drone, General," Lars said.

Connor looked at Lafferty. "Tell them to launch the comms drone."

Lafferty relayed the orders and nodded to Connor. "It's done."

"Good," Connor said. "Dash, we need to get closer to those ingots than that."

"How close do you want me to get?"

"I'd like to be able to lean out of the airlock and touch it," Connor replied.

Dash's gaze flicked back to the flight controls. The tactical plot showed that their ship was nearly on top of the ingots, which it classified as a large-mass object. A few moments later, the two icons merged as if they were one.

"I matched velocity with the ingots," Dash said.

"Excuse me, General," Holzer said, and Connor looked at him. "Will the Krake warships be able to detect the comms drone?"

"No, it's on standby. It will maintain its position here to remain in close proximity to the space gate."

Connor had Dash fly the ship to the opposite side of the ingots so they'd be shielded from the Krake warships. The enemy ships maintained their position near the space gate for a few minutes and then flew toward the mining complex.

Connor watched the tactical plot and waited. After a few minutes, he said, "Punch it."

Dash increased the ship's engines to maximum. With the burst of speed, they flew past the long line of ingots that stretched all the way to the fourth planet in this star system. The Krake warships did not appear in their sensors.

For the next hour, they traveled like this.

"The scope of this is amazing," Holzer said.

"Why would they even build all this in the first place?" Lieutenant Lafferty asked.

"The Krake are pragmatic almost to a fault," Connor said.

"So they're doing this because they have to. What are they planning to do with all this material?" Holzer asked.

"They could've exhausted their resources in their own star system," Connor replied.

"They could've mined resources on . . ." Holzer began and paused. "I was going to say an NEC, but I guess that doesn't work anymore. If the Krake home planet isn't on any Ovarrow world, then they still have the issue of transporting materials back to their own world."

"Like I said, the Krake are pragmatic."

"General, we need to ease off the engines. Power fluctuations are being reported," Specialist Ruo said.

They lessened the strain on the ship's engines just as their sensors showed another processing plant ahead of them. It appeared as if it was redirecting the ingots, putting them on a trajectory near the fourth planet.

"Should I initiate the automatic comms check-in so we can see what else the Krake have here?" Dash asked.

That had been the original plan, but Connor was reluctant to do that. "No, see if we can contact that processing station."

A few moments later, Dash had a data communication link to the station, which redirected the ingots to more than a dozen space gates. The station also slowed the ingots' velocity as it redirected them.

"General, Krake warships are behind us," Specialist Ruo said.

Connor looked at the tactical plot and saw that an update now showed the presence of two Krake warships. They must've followed them, staying just out of scanner reach.

"Specialist Ruo, give me comlink control," Connor said.

Specialist Ruo's eyebrows drew together for a second, and then a comlink became active on Connor's combat suit computer. "Can you get the processing center to maintain the speed of the ingots or increase them?" Connor asked.

After the ingots flew through a processing center that

redirected them and helped reduce their speed, they continued to fly through a series of smaller processing centers that looked like mobile space docks. These further slowed the ingots.

Specialist Ruo nodded once. "I think I can do that. When do you want it done?"

"As soon as you can," Connor said, looking at his personal holoscreen.

The space gate control interface controlled not only the destination of the space gate but also its location. The space gates were in close proximity to the fourth planet—less than two hundred thousand kilometers. Connor did a quick calculation.

Holzer came to stand by his side. "What are you going to do?"

"I'm going to send a delivery to the Krake home world," Connor said.

Holzer's eyes widened and he glanced at the holoscreen. Connor finished his configurations and sent the update to the space gates. Once the space gates processed the update, they would alter their trajectories slightly so they could still be in line with the incoming ingots, but it would change their velocity as they flew through. Connor checked the current active gateways and saw that they were already pointing to the Krake home galaxy.

"General, Krake warships are closing in," Specialist Ruo said.

"Understood. What's the status of the processing centers?"

"Executed now," Specialist Ruo replied.

Connor hastened over to Dash's workstation and looked over at Lars. "Time to see if those mines can do anything."

For the past hour, they'd been assembling the mines near the airlock. Lars ran off the bridge and opened a comlink to his team.

"General, they launched combat drones," Specialist Ruo said.

Connor looked at Dash. "Stay close to the ingots. They'll give us cover, but we need to push the engines. Take us to the nearest space gate."

Dash's eyes widened and he looked uncertain. "I don't know if I can do this."

"You're doing fine. I'm right here with you. Just do what I tell you to do. That's all you have to worry about."

"But Connor, this is combat. I'm not a combat pilot."

"That's good because this isn't a warship," Connor said. "If I put anyone else in the chair, they'd try to fly the ship like a warship, and that's not going to work. You have to trust me."

Dash exhaled sharply and then shoved his hands back into the holographic flight control interface. The ship's speed increased amid alerts coming from the engine control systems. They didn't have a choice.

"General, we're ready to release the mines," Lars said.

"Wait for my order," Connor said.

Dash used the maneuvering thrusters to alter their course so they wouldn't fly through the processing center. The Krake combat drones closed in on them.

"Release the mines," Connor said.

The mines scattered out of the airlock and past the Krake combat drones. The mines weren't explosive. Their earlier analysis of one of them had indicated a powerful magnetic field.

Connor watched the holoscreen. The Krake combat drones flew through the mines and showed no signs of slowing down. The two Krake warships closed in.

After flying past the processing center, Dash brought them close to the ingots again. Flying to the other side for cover, they sped forward.

Lars returned to the bridge and engaged a personal holoscreen, making it larger. It showed a video feed from a stealth recon drone. Connor saw the Krake combat drones being pulled toward the metallic ingots. The combat drones attempted to course correct, which pulled the ingots out of alignment. Instead of a long shaft traveling through the processing centers, they were coming in horizontally. The combat drones continued their tug-of-war, pulling the ingots out of alignment and narrowly avoiding the processing center. But that put the ingots on an intercept course with the Krake warships, which immediately attempted evasive maneuvers. The Krake warship armor was highly resistant to energy-based weapons, which was why the CDF preferred to use mag-cannons—because of their capability of penetrating the armor. They would normally follow this up with HADES V missiles to destroy the ship. Although the Krake warships outmassed the metallic ingots, there was no avoiding a collision with dense, massive objects, and they tore through the armored plating.

Their own ship crashed into the ingot nearest them, and Dash was unable to get away in time. The ship listed to the side so suddenly that Connor was nearly pulled off-balance. They were spinning almost out of control, but Dash was able to keep their trajectory on target as they flew through the space gate.

Once they were through the gate, Connor saw a bright blue planet teeming with life. There were space infrastructures all around, and Dash quickly altered their course to avoid colliding with the damaged space stations.

"Now, Specialist!" Connor shouted.

Large metallic ingots nearly a thousand meters in length punched through the Krake infrastructure on the other side of the gateway. Connor had altered the angle of their entry, and there were dozens of them heading toward the planet. The highly refined material was moving so fast that nothing could stop them from bombarding the Krake home world.

"Initiated automatic comms check-in. Gateway configuration update has been deployed," Specialist Ruo said.

The automatic comms check-in alerted them to the locations of the space gates in this universe. It also uploaded an update that would redirect the space gates to the dead universe. This update would spread to the arch gateways that the Krake used on the planet. There would be no escape for them.

"General, one of the Krake warships made it through the gateway," Specialist Ruo said.

Connor swung his gaze toward the holoscreen. More Krake warships were detected. He had no idea how they were going to get out of this.

———

PRIME OVERSEER ERSEVIN left the council chambers on the surface of Quadiri. Something had gone terribly wrong. There were gateway malfunctions being reported from all over the planet. Their entire Krake military operation had suddenly become cut off, and soldiers were escorting him to an escape vehicle. He hastened onto a shuttle, and the pilot engaged the engines. They flew out of the government building, heading away from the city. Ersevin glanced up at the sky and saw massive, glowing shafts penetrating the atmosphere—too many to count. Each time they hit the ground, there was a huge explosion on impact. He didn't need to calculate those impacts to understand that the planetary crust was being penetrated all over the world, which would trigger a chain reaction of destructive forces.

"Pilot, take us to the emergency gateway location. Beta site initiated," Ersevin said.

The pilot flew them toward another part of the city, where a personal arch gateway waited for him. When the reports of gateway malfunctions had begun to come in through intelligence channels, Ersevin had ordered this one to be brought off-line. Whatever was afflicting the other gateways would not hinder him here.

The shuttle hovered over the landing pad and then sank down onto the skids. Ersevin hastened out and ran toward the gateway, forwarding his credentials with the beta site coordinates. The other overseers waited for him. He ordered one of the soldiers to go through the gateway. The Krake soldier, without hesitation, hurried to the gateway and plunged through. They waited, but he did not return. The affliction that was affecting their gateways was also happening here.

One of the overseers asked what they did now.

Prime Overseer Ersevin glanced up. What had once been a clear sky was now filled with explosions, fire, and the darkest cloud he'd ever seen. The impacts from the bombardment pierced the planetary crust and were triggering volcanic eruptions throughout the entire planet. There was nowhere for them to go. Ersevin sat on the ground, knowing that he was moments from death—and not just his death but the death of all Krake.

30

IT WAS on days like these that Sean understood why there was a commander's chair on the bridge of a CDF warship. The entire crew had been in their own suits that were capable of individual life support, which gave them a fighting chance to survive if they lost atmosphere in the ship.

Space warfare was normally a long, arduous, logistical movement of ships and defense platforms in order to control that final engagement with the enemy, but the actual exchange of weaponsfire could be very quick and very destructive. For that reason, this phase usually didn't go on for extended periods of time, but no matter what he did, the Krake just kept coming. The recent update from the Talon-V strike teams that had attempted to infiltrate the Krake gateways showed their off-line status on the dispassionate amber holoscreen in front of him. The entire team had been lost. They couldn't get a team close enough to the Krake gateway to determine which universe they came from. Krake warships pursued the CDF space gates using highly aggressive tactics that bordered on fanatical. Whoever was commanding the ships didn't care what the cost was to take the gates. They'd focused their attack drones on destroying them, even at the cost of leaving their ships open to attack from Trident Battle Group.

"Colonel, the Krake ships are no longer maintaining their positions around their own gateways," Lieutenant Scott said.

Sean's eyes darted to the tactical plot on the main holoscreen. It showed the Krake destroyers moving away. "Ops, are you able to detect any gamma bursts from the area?"

"Negative, Colonel. I'm showing a reduced gamma radiation detection, as if the gateways are no longer there," Lieutenant Hoffman said.

The last CDF space gate had just been destroyed, and the active scans showed that the remaining Krake warships were altering course, heading away from Sagan.

"Colonel, their current trajectory is taking them toward New Earth," Lieutenant Hoffman said.

Why would the Krake close their own gateways? Why would they cut off their own supply line? Even without the protector drones, the CDF had destroyed multiple Krake ships.

"Helm, put us on an intercept course with the Krake fleet now. Comms, alert the rest of Trident Battle Group that we're following the Krake warships," Sean said.

His orders were confirmed.

"It doesn't make any sense, sir," Major Shelton said. "Why would they close the gateways and then head to New Earth? There's already a fleet of Krake ships attacking there anyway."

"I'm not sure. Ops, is the subspace communication array back up?"

"Yes, Colonel," Lieutenant Hoffman replied.

"Comms, open a comlink to Colonel Hughes at Lunar Base."

"I have Lunar Base actual, Colonel," Specialist Sansky said.

Sean informed Colonel Hughes of their current status, including the peculiarities they'd observed.

"You're not going to believe this," Colonel Hughes said. "We're seeing the same thing here. The Krake were maintaining at least three gateways that we knew of as they established a foothold, and then suddenly they were gone. All indications are that they're dissipating as if they'd been closed on the other side. This even occurred as Krake ships were coming through them."

"How are the remaining Krake responding?" Sean asked.

"Their tactics have become more aggressive, as if they've been cut off from whatever strategic command they were operating under. It's given Colonel Watts a chance to regroup the home fleet, and she's engaging them, along with the defense platforms."

Sean couldn't help but think that there was something else going on. Something was happening from whatever universe the Krake were coming from. "We're about to engage the Krake again, but can you push this up to COMCENT? Maybe there's something else going on."

"Will do, Colonel Quinn."

The subspace communication link to the lunar base was severed.

"Colonel, several ships from the battle group are not able to keep up. They've sustained damage to their engines," Lieutenant Hoffman said.

"Understood," Sean replied.

They had exhausted their supply of HADES V missiles. The only way Sean was going to be able to stop the remaining Krake warships was by getting close. He glanced at the empty seat of the auxiliary workstation nearby. Oriana had gone down to Engineering to help Noah with the Casimir power core. They were going to need it.

The Krake ships had taken some damage. They weren't flying

as fast as they could have. Their stock of combat drones must have also been low, but Sean had no idea how many drones their ships carried.

Sean shook his head and looked at Major Shelton. "They're cut off. I don't know how, but they are. And now they're running to rendezvous with the rest of their fleet. Otherwise, they would've just stayed. They destroyed the space gates, but why wouldn't they keep fighting?"

"They could just be realigning their space gates. They could be moving them somewhere else," Major Shelton said.

"Helm, kick her in the ass. I want maximum speed," Sean said and then looked at Shelton. "They can't move space gates faster than those ships can fly. Something's wrong."

"I hope you're right. I just wish we could've seen where they were coming from."

They'd lured the Krake away from their gateways but failed to get any of the Talon-V squadrons to them. They'd been going to make another push to the Krake gateways, but then they were gone.

Sean opened a comlink to Engineering, where Noah and Oriana were. Noah answered.

"We're going to need the artificial gravity field for longer than before."

"How much longer?" Noah asked.

"Colonel," Lieutenant Scott said, "Krake attack drones detected."

"A lot longer," Sean said.

"Understood."

The comlink severed.

A secondary window appeared on the main holoscreen that showed the Casimir power core's status, along with the artificial gravity field status.

"Tactical, confirm control of the artificial gravity field," Sean said.

"I have control, Colonel," Lieutenant Scott replied.

The ships of Trident Battle Group brought up their best defense against Krake attack drones. Without long-range missiles, they were reliant on mag-cannons.

"Tactical, I need a firing solution based on our current trajectory."

"Yes, Colonel, firing solution is ready."

Sean had no doubt that his tactical officer had several firing solutions ready at all times.

Mag-cannons used highly dense, cone-shaped slugs designed to penetrate the hull of a ship. They could pierce the armor of Krake warships and, with enough velocity, could also destroy attack drones.

The *Vigilant*'s point defense systems were online. As the Krake attack drones closed in on the ship, Lieutenant Scott engaged the artificial gravity field. The Krake attack drones slid over the gravity field and were redirected away while also causing them to lose velocity. There were bright flashes as some of the attack drones collided with each other and were destroyed. The downside to having this protection was that when the CDF fired their own weapons, their trajectory was affected unless the combat AI could get the timing right. It became a balancing act where Gabriel, the *Vigilant*'s AI, would control the efficacy of the gravity field and time it with the pace of fire from their mag-cannons. There was no way any tactical officer could do this manually. Only the ship's AI could take in the amount of sensory data and get the timing nearly perfect while also preventing the Krake attack drones from reaching the ship.

Trident Battle Group, weary but determined, closed in on the Krake warships. Space filled up with fire from their forward mag-cannons, with the *Vigilant* leading the charge. Multiple volleys sped toward the Krake ships, crossing the distance at staggering speeds. The rearmost Krake ships bore the brunt of the attack and took the most damage. They listed to the side and began to rotate out of formation with the other ships.

Krake attack drones circled around just beyond the gravity field, trying in vain to pierce the field.

Sean gritted his teeth in a somewhat hidden snarl. Each ship he destroyed would be one fewer that reached New Earth, one fewer that the CDF home fleet had to engage in defending their homes. There would be no retreat and no more of the clever tactics that had brought them this far. The Krake must be stopped here and now, and Sean was determined to make sure that it happened. He glanced around the bridge and saw the same determination mirrored in everyone else. It was going to be the Krake or them.

The artificial gravity field fluttered and went off-line. The Casimir power core had failed. Point defense cannons immediately went online and fired into the Krake attack drones.

It was as if the Krake attack drones sensed that the artificial gravity field was gone because they flew in a spiraling formation, surrounding the ship and pushing closer. Impact alarms blared on the bridge as the Krake attack drones pierced the *Vigilant*'s hull near the aft section.

Sean replied to the updates from his tactical officer, as well as his operations officer, as more attack drones breached the point defense system. The *Vigilant* and the remaining ships of Trident Battle Group kept firing on the Krake warships. They kept firing their weapons even as their own ships were heavily damaged. More Krake ships lost lateral control and tumbled out of formation, which provided more pronounced targets for the CDF weapons.

Trident Battle Group maintained a flight formation that balanced both attack and defense. Point-defense-systems coverage could assist other nearby ships, since the Krake attack drones tended to focus on a few ships at a time.

Sean knew the last of the Krake warships had been destroyed when the attack drones suddenly ceased to operate.

The main holoscreen on the *Vigilant* was nearly filled with a long list of damage reports. Almost the entire stern of the ship had been gutted by Krake attack drones that sought to destroy it, but the Krake didn't know where the *Vigilant*'s vital systems were located. Bulkhead doors had sealed to prevent the decompression of large sections of the ship. Sean scanned the damage reports and shot to his feet. His stomach sank as he instinctively drew in a quick breath. The Casimir power core had been obliterated by the Krake attack drones. There was so much damage in the surrounding area that rescue crews were still trying to reach it.

Oh my God! Sean swallowed convulsively. Oriana had been there, and so had Noah.

He tried to open a comlink to Oriana, but there was no response. Her comlink was off-line. Biometric scans were off-line because there was so much damage to the ship. He tried to contact Noah and also got no response. A quivering fear seized hold of his chest and slithered down his spine. They couldn't be dead. Not dead. Not her. Not him.

"Colonel," Specialist Sansky said, "we're receiving multiple requests for rescue from . . ."

His comms specialist went through a list of ships that had been heavily damaged. Some had had to abandon ship. Escape pods needed to be retrieved, but everyone on the bridge sounded so far away as his mind refused to focus on anything around him. He looked at the doors to the bridge, wanting to run to

Engineering to see it for himself. There had to be some kind of mistake. Oriana . . .

He heard his name being called by someone, sounding like a distant echo. He had to focus. He exhaled a long breath and looked around the bridge. His officers were waiting for his orders. Purpose and duty strengthened his spine. He wouldn't let them down. He couldn't shove aside his personal grief, and he couldn't ignore it. It was with him like an open wound in his chest that he couldn't get away from. He steeled himself to face what was in front of him because if he let his mind wander, he might not be useful to anyone. Then, he began giving orders to coordinate search and rescue.

31

RESUPPLY ships arrived from Phoenix Station, and Sean ordered that the *Dutchman* and the *Burroughs* be resupplied first. They still had intact missile tubes capable of using the HADES Vs. After they were resupplied, he had them track down the remains of the Krake ships and destroy them.

Major Shelton stood by his side and looked at him. "Sean, I'm so sorry. I know you and Oriana were close."

Sorrow threatened to close up his throat, but he walled off his emotions as best he could. "We lost a lot of good people, Vanessa."

She gave him a single nod, and they both went back to work. There were stranded crewmembers near the damaged parts of the ships, and rescue crews were working as quickly as possible to free them.

A comlink registered on Sean's personal line. It was from his friend, Chad Boseman. Sean opened a comlink that was showing a video feed coming from Chad's combat suit. He, along with other Spec Ops soldiers, was assisting with search and rescue and were in a decompressed part of the ship. They had just cut through deck plating that had bent and sealed off a section of the ship.

"Colonel, I thought you'd want to see this," Boseman said. "Open it up."

Sean felt his mouth hanging open as the deck plating was pulled back by the CDF soldiers in combat suits. Inside were seven people in their environment suits. His gaze darted to the names that appeared on their chests.

O. Evans.

N. Barker.

A joyous laugh bubbled up from his throat. "Boseman, I owe you for the rest of my life for this."

Chad laughed. "Don't make promises you can't keep, sir. Just doing my job. I thought you'd want to hear this firsthand. Their suits have been damaged, which is why you couldn't reach them via a comlink. We'll get them inside and into the sick bay so they can be checked by the doc."

The comlink closed, and Sean felt a huge weight lift from his shoulders. Major Shelton looked at him with eyebrows raised.

"They're alive."

She smiled widely. "I've got this, Colonel."

Sean hastened from the bridge and headed to the medical bay at midships. He'd only gone down two corridors from the bridge when Major Shelton called him back.

"A Krake ship has appeared on our sensors, Colonel."

Sean swore. He wanted to go to the medical bay, but he needed to be on the bridge. "On my way."

He ran back to the bridge.

"The *Babylon* detected the ship. It's closer to Sagan," Major Shelton said.

"Comms, get me *Babylon* actual."

A few seconds later, Captain Richard Pitts of the CDF destroyer *Babylon* appeared on Sean's personal holoscreen.

"Colonel, it's a Krake ship, but it's not a warship."

"I don't want to take any chances, Captain. Destroy it."

"Yes, Colonel," Captain Pitts replied.

The comlink closed. Would more Krake ships arrive?

"Colonel, I've just received a subspace communications link," Specialist Sansky said. "It's not a ship-to-ship-type comlink but from a CDF comms drone."

Sean frowned. "Connect it to my screen."

Sean watched his holoscreen as he waited for Specialist Sansky to make the connection. Then, the last person he ever expected to see appeared on the screen.

"Colonel Quinn, please don't blow us up."

"Connor!" Sean said, momentarily abandoning all military decorum. Then he narrowed his gaze. "Confirm that it's you."

Connor grinned. "I taught you how to shoot a rifle, Cadet Bling."

Sean laughed and shook his head, then sent a message to Captain Pitts not to destroy the Krake ship.

"What's your status, General?"

"We've got a lot of wounded and one hell of a story to tell you." Connor looked as if he was going to say more but stopped.

"They're still fighting on New Earth. It's pretty bad," Sean said, then proceeded to give Connor an update.

As he spoke, he knew he wasn't giving him the information he really wanted. Sean had no idea whether Lenora and his daughter were still alive. He wished he could answer that question, but he couldn't.

SIX HOURS LATER, Connor stood in the main hangar bay of the *Vigilant*. They'd off-loaded the wounded first to a designated area in the bay, which had become a temporary hospital. It was there that the CDF soldiers were assessed, and the most critical cases were taken to the medical bay. Connor had seen to it that everyone who'd been with him was taken care of. Across the hangar bay, he saw something that tugged at the fringes of his memory. Sean, Noah, and Lars stood speaking together. Dash was a short distance away, but Connor watched the trio. In one moment, he was standing on the hangar bay of the *Vigilant*, seeing three men whom he'd watched grow to adulthood, and in the next moment, he had been snatched back to a much younger version of the trio standing on a hangar bay aboard the *Ark*. Sean, Noah, and Lars had escorted him from the *Ark* to New Earth for the first time. For a few seconds, he felt like he was living in two timelines, and the edges of his lips curved upward just a little bit. They were all family to him.

He glanced at Dash and supposed that he was their youngest brother. Each of the men carried their own burdens, but there was a strong bond between them, something that could get them through the tough times. Even though the bonds once forged between friends could decay over time, they could sometimes be renewed.

Although Connor couldn't pinpoint it, he felt that Lars stood a bit apart from the others. It was something in the way he stood and the look in his eyes. It wasn't anything dark, but there was something maybe deep within Lars that just made him appear out of place now. Connor had seen a change in him, and he suspected Lars was still changing.

Connor joined them.

"I informed COMCENT that you're alive, and they want to meet," Sean said.

"What a surprise," Noah said. "I was going to ask you where you've been while we were doing all the heavy lifting, but Lars and Dash tell us that you've been doing quite a lot of heavy lifting of your own."

"You could say that, but it's no more than what you've accomplished here. I'm just glad you all made it through," Connor replied, then looked at Lars. "Sergeant Mallory, I'd like you to inform the 3rd Platoon that you've been given a temporary reprieve of restricted contact with the colony. Go find your families and let them know you're still alive."

Lars smiled and nodded. "Yes, General," he said and walked away from them.

"What's going to happen to them?" Noah asked.

"I don't know," Connor said. "They all have years left to serve in the CDF before a decision is made about whether they can rejoin the colony."

Noah glanced at Sean for a moment. "I don't want to jump the gun here, but if this war is over and the Krake have been defeated, maybe that'll have an effect on some things."

"It's not up to me, Noah. I will say that, in any courtroom you walk into, the facts still remain. But we'll see what happens."

"We should go, sir," Sean said.

"Go on," Noah said. "Dash and I are going to exchange notes. Plus, I want to have a look at that ship." He jutted his chin toward the Krake ship behind them.

Connor and Sean headed to the conference room near the bridge. Connor knew there were going to be a lot of questions for him in particular. He had a few of his own.

A comlink message notification chimed from his wrist computer, and he checked it.

::*Lenora and family are safe. Sanctuary held up well during the attack.*:: Gen. N. Hayes.

"Thank you, Nathan," Connor said, quietly sighing.

Then he walked into the conference room.

32

THERE WAS NOWHERE on New Earth that had escaped the Krake invasion. Perhaps among the hardest hit cities were those of the Konus. Over the last several weeks, Connor had learned that the Krake first entered their world in the region near the Konus city. The Konus had increased patrols in their territory and reported the suspicious activity days before Connor had left New Earth. The Krake had staged reconnaissance missions and were able to identify the other colonial cities on New Earth, including the Mekaal. Even though the Krake navy had been defeated, it'd taken weeks to finally stop the Krake soldiers and the thousands of predators that had been stranded on New Earth.

The Ovarrow had utilized their control of the ryklars to help in the defense of their cities. Connor had seen recorded video from SRDs, which showed the two apex predators throwing themselves at one another. The Ovarrow didn't have to maintain the command signal that controlled the ryklars for them to seek out the Krake predators. They only more or less needed a nudge in the right direction, and then the two would fight. However, there were enough Krake predators that they had penetrated the defenses of the Konus city. Krake scouts must've coordinated with the staging worlds because the Krake predators even appeared at colonial cities behind the defensive measures that were in place. They were meant to cause chaos, but it didn't work in the colonial cities because the colony was too well prepared.

When they'd had to rebuild their cities after the Vemus War, they'd built them with an eye toward defense. The civilian population still remembered the Vemus War and had been quick to act when the Krake invasion finally began. Colonial militias assisted the CDF in defense of their homes. Sanctuary was the colonial city with the least amount of impact, which Connor attributed to the smaller population that was mostly made up of former military and research scientists. It was a frontier city. There were reports of Krake predators in Sanctuary, but not at the level of some of the other cities. Connor figured that by the time Sanctuary had appeared on the Krake's radar, his rogue gateway configuration update had become more widespread, which stifled the invasion.

Orbital defense platforms had been able to assist the colonists in fighting the Krake invaders. They were capable of precision shooting with mag-cannons in orbit, as well as deploying more heavy weapons where the Krake were concentrated outside the cities, which included the predators. The Krake soldiers were no stranger to battle, and upon realizing that they'd been cut off from their supply lines, they sought to withdraw from the attack and hide. So for weeks, the CDF, Mekaal, and Konus soldiers had been sweeping the region to wipe out the remnants of the Krake military. The CDF assisted with reconnaissance by deploying SRDs, as well as their other arsenal of weapons, to help spot Krake soldiers and their predators.

Ryklar populations had severely diminished over the years, and these battles had decreased their numbers even further. Connor didn't know what the future was for the ryklars. They were highly intelligent and had the beginnings of a primitive culture. He had a few ideas of his own where the ryklars were concerned, one of which was to relocate them to another planet that was similar to New Earth but didn't have the Ovarrow there any longer because of the Krake. Then nature could take its course, and the ryklars' future would be their own.

Colonial lives had been lost. Connor wasn't sure what the current number of deceased was, but he knew it was a lot less than what it could have been. But that was a cold comfort to the families who had lost loved ones. Recovery from this would take a while.

He hadn't been back at Sanctuary very long before he had to travel to Sierra, so he brought his family with him. During the attack, Lenora had been at the bunker near the Ovarrow dig site, which had become an encampment for the CDF reserves. During the first few nights upon his return, he and Lenora had long conversations into the night. He told her everything. Years ago, he might not have, preferring to lock things away or shield her from some of the horrible things he'd seen. Lenora listened to him recount what happened after he left New Earth. She cried with him when he told her about Samson, but there was a growing weight that had settled on his shoulders, and she couldn't share it with him.

Connor would never change what he'd done to the Krake, but there were moral implications to genocide. He had single-handedly destroyed life on not only one planet but three others as well, including the Krake home world. The Krake deserved it. They had visited untold horrors on the Ovarrow in multiple universes and showed no signs of stopping, so he didn't feel

guilty per se. He hadn't watched the end of the Krake civilization
on Quadiri. He'd only had a glimpse of it from the scanners of
that old Krake ship. The CDF had sent reconnaissance drones to
the Krake home universe, and the planet had become a broiling
oven. The number of impacts from the kilometer-long refined
metals hitting the planet at staggering speeds had been enough to
take out large regions of the planet. Earthquakes had followed,
and Quadiri was getting a massive reset. Colonial scientists
estimated that it would take thousands of years for the cycle to
run its course.

Connor sat alone in a conference room at the CDF base at
Sierra. He had half a cup of coffee sitting in front of him, and he
simply stared at it.

Nathan walked in, looking like he'd aged almost ten years
since Connor left, and sat next to him.

"So where do we go from here?" Connor asked.

Nathan poured himself a cup of coffee from the carafe and
added heavy cream. "The Security Council has been sent your
full report."

"I'm not worried about them. They wouldn't be here feeling
conflicted if I hadn't done what I did."

"Don't punish yourself, Connor. I don't have to tell you that
it was the Krake or us. There was never going to be a middle
ground with them."

Connor looked at Nathan. "I don't feel anything, and
sometimes that worries me. Sometimes I think I should feel a
little bit of remorse, but I don't. Does that make me a monster?"

"No, you're not a monster. You're just trying to rationalize
everything that's happened over the past few weeks. We'll all
work it out. I like to think that if I'd been in your shoes, I
would've done the same thing—if I could've figured it out the
way you did."

"You would've figured it out," Connor said and took a sip of his coffee, draining what was left in his mug.

Nathan leaned forward, rested his elbows on the table with his hands steepled in front of his face, and looked at Connor. "You saved this colony again. You, the 7th Ranger Company, and 3rd Platoon of the Special Infantry Division. We might've held them off here for a while, but this was going to be it for us. You were the one who cut the head off the monster."

"No, I didn't. Aurang gave me what I needed to do this. If he hadn't, then . . ." Connor shook his head.

"You convinced Aurang that the overseers were using him," Nathan said and smiled. "What do you think was the last thing those bastards thought right before they were about to die?"

Connor felt his lips lift a little, and he arched one eyebrow. "You know, if anyone else suspected that you were this ruthless, they might be more worried about you than they are about me."

"It would shatter my nice-guy image, I know, but it's just us here."

Connor chuckled. "I bet they thought that somehow they'd miscalculated."

"You have a knack for understatements. I don't know if I'll ever understand why the Krake did the things they did."

"Have you seen the reconnaissance data from their home star system?"

Nathan nodded.

"There was another planet there, an NEC. We haven't taken a closer look, but the preliminary reports suggest that it has a poisoned atmosphere. We've seen the Krake do this to other planets. This means that a long time ago, there were Ovarrow that had evolved in the Krake home universe."

"And these two civilizations fought a war. The Ovarrow lost, and the Krake developed technology to travel between universes," Nathan said, then finished his coffee.

"Except that everywhere they went they only found Ovarrow planets teeming with life. Every other universe they explored did not have Krake," Connor said.

Nathan sighed and shook his head. "So, you think this knowledge had a profound impact on Krake society?"

"Aurang said as much in his message. Initially, the Krake might have sought to understand why a version of their species was not in any of the other universes, but eventually their objective changed. You saw what they did to the Ovarrow. They might've been perfecting their predictive technology and running all kinds of tests on the Ovarrow, but I think they were also punishing the Ovarrow. Over and over again."

Nathan's eyebrows knitted in a thoughtful frown. "Why? Why would they do this?"

"Because the Ovarrow existed and the Krake didn't."

Nathan looked away while he considered it for a few long moments. He chewed on his bottom lip and then looked at Connor. "This is crazy, but what's so crazy about it is that it makes sense to me. I almost wish it didn't."

Connor flattened the edge of his napkin as he folded it over.

"We've gotten reports in from Monin," Nathan said. "He's searching for survivors and organizing them so they can rebuild. Colonel Watts took a few ships from the home fleet and destroyed the Krake invasion ships that were still in the area. The protector drones are quite effective against the Krake attack drones."

The protector drones had proved themselves, especially in the operations that had taken place after the invasion. The Krake were trapped in whatever universe they happened to be in. Using the data recovered from Aurang's ship, the CDF had been able to conduct offensive operations using their own space gates to decimate the remains of the Krake navy. Perhaps for the first time in Krake history, their naval forces were outmatched.

Connor looked at Nathan. "I know you're my superior officer, but I'm never leaving New Earth again."

Nathan chuckled, which bubbled up into a full-on laugh. "Not superior, Connor. Merely a higher-ranking one," he said and smiled.

"I'm serious, Nathan. I don't care who's asking. I am not leaving ever again. Someone else can go. Anyone else."

"Understood, Connor. I read you loud and clear." Nathan rubbed the bottom of his beard for a moment. "We've been sending reconnaissance drones to check out that massive mining installation the Krake built."

"Is it still there?"

"Yes, it is. What made you think to move the space gate so that when it ejected the unwanted material, you could angle it toward the NEC?"

"I had help," Connor said.

"You gave the orders. This was your plan."

"It wasn't enough to reconfigure all the gateways on the planet to point to the dead universe. I wanted to make sure they could never be used again."

"I'm pretty sure you accomplished that," Nathan said. "The condensed material coming out of that mining installation is nearly a kilometer in size, and it hit the planet at speeds approaching sixty thousand kilometers per hour."

"We'd talked before about orbital bombardment as a way to stop the Krake. That's why we were building our own space gates. We just didn't know the Krake home world was where Sagan was."

"I didn't see that coming, but it makes me think about the war the Ovarrow fought before they triggered the Ice Age."

Connor frowned for half a second. "What do you mean?"

"Well, they were trying to figure out how the gateways worked, or at least that's what we thought. But they also stumbled upon sending material at an accelerated rate through space. That's the theory, that they had somehow linked gateways across space. But if you think about where they were linked here in this universe, it paints an interesting picture. Something was bombarding Sagan with chunks of ice that came from the lake near New Haven. But what if there was a group of Ovarrow here who'd figured out where the Krake home world was? They didn't have ships, but they were trying to find a way to bombard the Krake home world."

Connor's face reflected his surprise as he considered it for a full minute. "But the Mekaal had no idea."

Nathan shrugged. "There were multiple factions of Ovarrow at the end. Who knew what one group knew about versus some of the other groups? The knowledge could've been lost."

Connor sighed heavily. "If they could've figured that out, they'd have been much closer to defeating the Krake than we thought."

"We often look at the Ovarrow and see a species that developed a little bit less technologically than what we've accomplished, but sometimes I think we underestimate them. It's something we're going to have to keep in mind for the future."

Connor nodded. "Well, neither of us is going anywhere, so we're going to have to learn to live together."

"I hope so, my friend. I really hope we can."

33

A SOMBER SILENCE settled over the crowd of colonists in Sierra. Connor sat among the VIPs behind the podium and listened to Governor Mullins speak. Dana Wolf, the former governor of the colony, caught his eye with a knowing glance. She was an older woman who had aged significantly as a result of the virus that had nearly killed her. Her recovery had been long, but she was making steady progress toward regaining strength. He should have known she would be here for this commencement to honor the fallen. Across the colony, in each city, colonists gathered to honor those who had died and to honor the Colonial Defense Force.

Dana sat near the edge of the stands, and for a moment, they shared a look. She mouthed the words "Thank you."

Mullins must have shared the intelligence reports with her. Dana was the type of person who knew how to work with people. She built bridges among competing viewpoints—a skill that Connor admired.

Connor nodded once and then turned back to the podium.

Governor Mullins said, "Please join me in observing a moment of silence for all the people who have made the ultimate sacrifice, and for those who are injured and suffering because of this war. Join me to honor the men and women of the CDF."

Connor rose to his feet. It was an odd feeling to stand among thousands of people who were completely and utterly silent. He heard the rustling of a gentle breeze and thought about absent friends he'd never see again.

Samson had intended to leave New Earth with the second colony. He'd never accepted this place as his home, and yet he'd fought to protect it. After Samson had chosen to leave, Connor had had many conversations with his friend, and he now understood more of what Samson had been saying. Leaving New Earth was his way of moving on and getting his own second chance. Connor had always felt responsible for what had happened to the old Ghost Platoon. Waking up on a colony world far from home had impacted all of them, but Samson could never accept it. New Earth would never be his home. Connor understood that now, but his friend was dead. He'd never get to travel to the colony world he'd volunteered to protect. Connor no longer railed against the unfairness of it. There was a cost to war. Samson and other CDF soldiers had died for a purpose. They'd stood for something. And yet, Connor wished that his friend had gotten to join the colonists who were leaving.

The ceremony ended, and he headed back to the CDF base. He'd be returning home to Sanctuary soon, but there were a few things he had to take care of first.

Connor found Lars near a landing pad on the CDF base. The whine of the Hellcat's engines diminished as the engines were shut down.

Lars looked at him and saluted. "General Gates."

"Sergeant Mallory. How was New Haven?"

"It was tough. My father came to see me on base."

"Tough? What do you mean?" Connor asked.

Lars swallowed and regarded him for a moment. "I'm leaving, sir."

"Where are you going?"

"Major Samson submitted a recommendation on my behalf for the *Ark II* program. I'm going to the second colony."

Connor did a double take and his eyes widened.

"I think it's for the best."

"Lars," Connor said slowly, "are you sure you want to leave? You have a family here. Eventually, you'll be allowed to rejoin the colony."

Lars nodded. "I know," he said and exhaled with a sigh. "But I don't know if I *can* come back. Not after everything that's happened."

"And you think traveling to a world three light-years away is the answer?"

Lars shrugged a little. "I don't know. I *really* don't know. But it's a second chance, you know?"

"How did your father react when you told him?"

"He didn't like it. He doesn't want me to go."

"I bet. I don't want you to go either," Connor said.

"Thank you for that, sir."

"Well, I mean it. I don't know if this is the best decision for you to make. You might feel differently in a few months."

Lars's smile was sad and filled with remorse. "My father said the same thing, but then he said it was my choice."

Connor didn't want Lars to leave but couldn't think of anything to say to get him to stay. He was reminded that one day when his own children were grown, they might leave him also.

"It's not just me," Lars said. "There are a lot of people in 3rd Platoon who feel the same way. I'm trying to persuade Dr. Ashworth to allow them to come."

Connor sighed. "This is your decision, Lars, and I respect it. You've got to walk your own path."

"Thank you, sir."

Connor nodded once.

"There's a lot I'm going to miss about this place—my father, the friends I've made," he said and regarded Connor for a moment. "Mentors I've had. But I think there's a lot I have to offer to help in establishing a new colony."

"You've got the experience," Connor said. Lars had been among the early risers when the *Ark* first landed at New Earth. "I don't know if you'll escape *that* easily, though."

Lars raised his eyebrows.

"Do you think Noah is going to be okay with this?"

The same small smile, tinged with sadness, appeared. "No, he's not going to like it."

"You're damn right he's not, but not only that. I wouldn't put it past him to finish proving that crazy theory of his just so he can fly a ship to the second colony."

Lars frowned. "The star system is three light-years away. It's about a ten-year journey to get there."

Connor shrugged. "I don't know all the specifics of his theory, but he thinks it might be possible to travel faster than the speed of light."

Lars snorted. "Just make sure he doesn't die in the process."

Traveling across vast distances in space was a dangerous undertaking. They might make a ship that went faster than the *Ark II* was going to travel, but they still had to navigate the distances and avoid obstacles. It wasn't going to be easy, but five thousand colonists had volunteered to go, reminding Connor never to underestimate people's willingness to explore and push the boundaries.

34

Sean stood in the living room of the apartment he'd shared with Oriana on Lunar Base. There was a long couch by the wall and a wooden table in front. There were scuff marks on one side from where he rested his feet when he sat in one of the chairs nearby. Oriana preferred the couch. He looked at the wallscreen that showed a live video feed of the pale lunar surface. A few shuttles flew by in the distance.

His focus changed to include the square shipping containers stacked near the door. One of them hadn't been properly sealed, so he walked over to it, opened the container, shuffled the contents inside so they fit better, and resealed it.

He decided to make one last sweep of the apartment. It wasn't overly large, just a few rooms. He walked toward the kitchen and spotted a coffee mug on the counter. It must have been left there. Neither he nor Oriana had returned here in the six weeks since they'd left. The pale mug drew his eye, and he felt an ache in his chest.

"All right, I've gone through the bedroom. The shipping containers are ready—Sean, what's wrong?" Oriana asked.

She hadn't escaped the Krake attack completely unscathed and now walked with a slight limp. She'd sustained multiple broken ribs, a broken right arm, and a broken hip where she'd borne the brunt of the impact when the Krake attack drones punched through the armored hull of the *Vigilant*. Considering the decompression and catastrophic damage to the area where she and Noah had been working, it was a wonder that anyone survived.

She walked over to him and winced. Sometimes when she moved too fast, she experienced pain, but the doctors assured them that she would make a full recovery.

Oriana peered into the kitchen and frowned. "Oh, is that mine?" she said and grabbed the mug to put it in the washer. "Sorry about that. I know you hate that."

"It's okay."

Her eyes twinkled. "Stop telling lies."

"Fine, you're a slob."

Her eyes widened. "There's the brutal honesty we all know and love."

He shook his head and smiled. Then the smile drained away. "I thought you had died. I almost lost you."

Oriana rubbed his shoulder. "You didn't."

He loved her eyes—their shape and the way her dark lashes curved upward. Her high cheekbones. The fullness of her lips. The way her lips felt when they kissed.

"I'm still here," she said.

"I know." He glanced where the mug had been. There was a small ring on the counter marking the place. "But you almost weren't. Then I come in here, and I'm surrounded by all these reminders of you. I keep thinking, What if I had to come here after you'd really died?"

"I think about the same thing. I worry that something bad is going to happen to you all the time. How would I deal with the things we've accumulated? All the reminders. Do I keep them? Do I give them away? I don't know. It's not something I'm willing to plan for."

"You'd give away my stuff?" he asked in mock severity.

"You didn't expect me to cart it around, did you?"

They smiled.

Sean sighed. "I don't think I would've stayed here if something had happened to you. I would've volunteered to go on the *Ark II* with the second colony."

Oriana arched an eyebrow, unconvinced. "Really."

"Yeah, I'd be so heartbroken that I couldn't stay here," he said, only half-jokingly. He'd thought about it.

She looked at him for a moment. "No, you wouldn't."

Sean chuckled.

"Neither would I, for that matter."

She was probably right.

"I don't think Kara is ever going to allow Noah to leave her side again," Oriana said.

Kara had been planet-side when the Krake had attacked. Sean had heard Noah reassure his wife that he had no plans to ever leave her again.

"Kids," Sean said in mock exasperation. "A little bit of danger and they get all clingy."

"You're one to talk. Weren't you just in here, overwhelmed with emotion because a coffee mug reminded you of me?"

She had him there. He'd really backed himself into a corner with that. "Okay, fine, I admit it. My life would suck without you. There, I said it."

Her full lips curved upward. "Colonel Quinn, you woo me with your eloquence. I don't know if my heart can take it."

Sean hugged her and stopped short of lifting her into the air. She was still hurt, and he didn't want to add to her pain. She smiled, her eyes gleaming.

"So, about the not-leaving-each-other's-side thing," he said.

Oriana frowned a little. "I thought you hadn't been reassigned yet."

There'd been a reshuffling of the ranks, and command of Trident Battle Group had passed to Colonel Watts, who'd previously been in command of the CDF home fleet. Watts was currently leading raids into other universes known as the Krake core worlds. Sean had written the tactical book on fleet engagements with the Krake, and it was time for others to utilize it and expand on those tactics.

"I haven't, but I think I'll have some say in the matter."

Oriana nodded. "We made some improvements to the Casimir power core, but there's still a lot of work to be done. We're going to study it further on the remains of the Krake ships we have, so maybe you could request a posting at Phoenix Station?"

Sean smiled with one side of his mouth. "You just happened to think about this right now?"

"Don't be silly."

"Or was it that older physicist? The one who was chasing you."

Oriana shook her head, amused. "Sometimes, Sean, you really are—"

"You don't have to do that. I know."

Oriana rolled her eyes and began to step away from him.

"Just wait," he said. "I have something I need to ask you."

"All right, what is it?"

He felt the heat rise in his chest and wondered if it had reached his face. "It's important."

Oriana smoothed her features and regarded him. He didn't know how she did it, but sometimes when she looked at him, he just felt it, as if some unseen force surrounded him.

Then he asked her.

35

WHEN CONNOR finally returned to New Earth, his daughter hardly left his side. She was clingy in the days that followed, and he indulged her without fail. Lauren wanted reassurance that he wasn't going to leave her again. She wouldn't go to sleep unless he was in her room, so he did what any father would do—he stayed with her until she went to sleep. After about a week, Lauren began to return to normal, and he marveled at the resilience of children. He wondered what she understood about what had happened. The best way to explain the invasion to the colonial youth was being discussed in many places, but Connor would have preferred that Lauren and the other children forget about it until they were old enough to understand. She needed time to just be a child. He had no problems with advising adults of the dangers they had to be concerned with, but scaring children was something else entirely. Diaz joked that he liked to give grown men and women nightmares.

When he'd returned to Sanctuary, he'd had the pilot make

several sweeps of the surrounding area. Connor saw the weapons'
impact from the orbital defense platforms. He also saw how the
Krake soldiers had approached Sanctuary, and the piles of
predators that had been slain. Disposal efforts were still ongoing
in some colonial cities. None of the cities were walled-off
fortresses, but they did have defensive measures in place. He
hoped that one day that wouldn't be necessary. He couldn't
imagine any city back on Old Earth having hidden mag-cannons
within the buildings, spaced out to form a protective grid. Each
colonial city had CDF bases with a ready force that was capable
of almost immediate response should the need present itself.

Connor remembered Tobias Quinn, the first governor of the
colony and the head of the *Ark* program. Tobias hadn't wanted
the first human interstellar colony to be a militaristic society, but
he'd come to recognize the need for protection beyond that of an
ordinary police force. Tobias had been a good man who had died
defending the colony during the Vemus Wars. It was important
to remember the sacrifices of the people who'd given their lives in
the protection of others.

The *Ark II* was scheduled to leave New Earth soon, and there
were commencement ceremonies being celebrated in every
colonial city. It was a marked accomplishment in the history of
the colony when they had not only survived on a new world but
established themselves enough to send out a second ship to
colonize another world.

Diaz was hosting an outdoor party at the Salty Soldier to
celebrate the launch. Several holoscreens showed the *Ark II*
docked at the lunar shipyards. It was early evening, and the air
was losing a bit of the warmth from the day. New Earth's rings
shone prominently to the south.

Connor walked with Lenora. Lauren spotted some of the

other kids and went running off to catch them. She didn't get more than a short distance before Noah scooped her up and brought her back toward Connor and Lenora.

"I think you lost something," Noah said.

Lauren looked at Noah. "Put me down please," she said in a calm, even tone.

Noah's eyes widened, and he smiled. "How can I resist such a little lady? But first, I need you to answer a question for me."

"What is it?"

"I heard a rumor that you've found the perfect name for your baby brother. Is that true?"

Lauren's eyes widened, and she smiled brightly. Connor glanced at Lenora, and she nodded encouragingly toward their daughter.

"Yes, his name is going to be Ethan," Lauren said matter-of-factly. She looked at Connor. "Mommy told me that Ethan was grandpa's name. I like that name."

The way Lauren looked at him made his throat swell with pride. His father, a military man, had died when Connor was a teenager. "It's a good name. I like it too."

Noah lowered Lauren to the ground. She ran over to Connor and hugged him, then ran off again.

Connor sighed, watching her go. He looked at Lenora. "Are you sure about this?"

Lenora smiled. "Of course. I've always loved your father's name."

Connor looked at Noah. "Speaking of children."

"Oh, no. Not for us." Noah glanced at Kara. "Not yet, right?"

Kara grinned a little. "The night is young, and the stars are shining."

They laughed.

Diaz walked toward them and kissed Lenora and Kara on the cheek. "I just heard about Sean."

"It's about time," Noah said.

Connor frowned. "What about Sean?"

"He popped the question."

Diaz grinned. "The kids are all grown up."

Connor nodded. Noah had told him that Oriana was injured during the Krake invasion. They were lucky to be alive. Connor looked at Lenora, and she shared a knowing glance with him. Sometimes coming face-to-face with your own mortality had a way of putting things into perspective, and deciding what was important became very clear. He glanced at Lenora again and smiled. Diaz had a round of drinks brought over to them, and they raised their glasses.

Noah came over to Connor's side. "What happens now?"

"We'll have a few more drinks and watch the *Ark II* leave."

Noah shook his head. "That's not what I meant. I'm talking about the Krake," he said quietly.

"We'll need to monitor for them. We've got several ongoing missions setting things up to do just that."

"They can't all be gone."

"Probably not, but their home world is in ruins," Connor said. "Their infrastructure has been destroyed, and they have nowhere near the strength they had."

"I understand all that, but I just wonder if they have their own backup site somewhere."

"I don't know. They could, but at the same time, they might not. They'd never anticipated what happened."

Noah nodded but still looked unconvinced.

"The Krake tried to control everything, and I mean that in every way possible," Connor said. "We can't be like that. We'll keep an eye out for them if they try to rebuild, but more importantly, we'll have allies who are going to do the same thing."

"I guess it'll just take some getting used to. We spent so much time worrying about the Krake, I guess I don't know how not to do it anymore. That'll get easier in time, but it's going to take years."

Connor nodded. He thought Noah was right. It would be a long time before he stopped worrying about the Krake altogether.

"They're gone. Let's enjoy it," Diaz said.

They watched the holoscreen, which showed a video feed of the *Ark II*. Five thousand colonists were in stasis aboard the massive ship. There were auto factories and equipment storage aboard that would give the colonists an excellent start for establishing the new colony. And with subspace communication, they'd be able to monitor the *Ark II*'s entire ten-year voyage.

"I wonder what they'll encounter in the new colony," Diaz said.

Connor arched an eyebrow toward him. "Regret not going?"

Diaz shook his head vigorously. "No way. Once was enough for me."

"I hope Lars does all right there," Noah said.

"Me too. I think he will," Connor replied.

"I'm surprised he went," Diaz said. "After everything, he volunteered to leave."

Connor shrugged. "Sometimes a second chance can make all the difference, and not all of us get to choose," he said, thinking of Samson and Lars.

Lenora wrapped one of her arms around him and gave him a sideways hug. He was glad not to have missed this.

The docking clamps holding the *Ark II* released, and

humanity's second interstellar colony ship began its voyage into the deep dark.

AUTHOR NOTE

Thank you so much for reading. *Invasion* is the 11th book in the First Colony series. I've been writing in this series almost exclusively for more than three years. New Earth has been home to my imagination for a long time. Helping me to stay motivated to write these stories has been the enthusiasm of the readers who've reached out to me and the people who took the time to review my books. I hope you enjoyed this latest book in the First Colony series. Almost inevitably, I get the question about whether this will be the last book in the First Colony series. No, it won't. I think there are more stories to tell in this series and more characters to explore. *Invasion* marks the end of a major series arc, but it's not the end of the series. I have a few ideas both for the First Colony series and perhaps some spin-off series. One of which will be centered around what happened to Old Earth. Another has to do with the second colony. I'm not lacking ideas for stories I'd like to write, but I am at a crossroads. For the better part of three years, I've only worked on the First Colony series and have only recently branched out to write something new. If you haven't checked out the Federation Chronicles, you should. It's a fun series, and I'll be writing two more books in it in 2021. The crossroads I'm at is balancing my writing schedule, so I'm writing stories that you would like to read. I know I won't be able to please everyone. The more series I write, the more this might become a problem because I'm not working on a series that you'd rather I be writing. If you fall into that category, then please be patient. I will get to it and give those stories the attention they deserve. I take a lot of pride in my work because I think the quality of the story matters, as well as your experience in reading it.

Thanks again for reading my books. Please consider leaving a review for Invasion

The series continues with the 12th book.

First Colony - IMPULSE

If you're looking for another series to read consider reading the Federation Chronicles. Learn more by visiting:

https://kenlozito.com/federation-chronicles/

I do have a Facebook group called **Ken Lozito's SF readers**. If you're on Facebook and you'd like to stop by, please search for it on Facebook.

Not everyone is on Facebook. I get it, but I also have a blog if you'd like to stop by there. My blog is more of a monthly check-in as to the status of what I'm working on. Please stop by and say hello, I'd love to hear from you.

Visit www.kenlozito.com

ABOUT THE AUTHOR

I've written multiple science fiction and fantasy series. Books have been my way to escape everyday life since I was a teenager to my current ripe old(?) age. What started out as a love of stories has turned into a full-blown passion for writing them.

Overall, I'm just a fan of really good stories regardless of genre. I love the heroic tales, redemption stories, the last stand, or just a good old fashion adventure. Those are the types of stories I like to write. Stories with rich and interesting characters and then I put them into dangerous and sometimes morally gray situations.

My ultimate intent for writing stories is to provide fun escapism for readers. I write stories that I would like to read, and I hope you enjoy them as well.

If you have questions or comments about any of my works I would love to hear from you, even if it's only to drop by to say hello at KenLozito.com

Thanks again for reading *First Colony - Invasion*

Don't be shy about emails, I love getting them, and try to respond to everyone.

ALSO BY KEN LOZITO

First Colony Series

Genesis

Nemesis

Legacy

Sanctuary

Discovery

Emergence

Vigilance

Fracture

Harbinger

Insurgent

Ascension Series

Star Shroud

Star Divide

Star Alliance

Infinity's Edge

Rising Force

Ascension

Safanarion Order Series

Road to Shandara

Echoes of a Gloried Past

Amidst the Rising Shadows

Heir of Shandara

Broken Crown Series

Haven of Shadows

If you would like to be notified when my next book is released visit KENLOZITO.COM